D0342493

DEPTH OF LIES

OTHER TITLES BY E. C. DISKIN

Broken Grace
The Green Line

DEPTH OF LIES

E. C. DISKIN

This is a work of fiction. Names, characters, organizations, places, events, and incidents are either products of the author's imagination or are used fictitiously. Any resemblance to actual persons, living or dead, or actual events is purely coincidental.

Text copyright © 2017 by E. C. Diskin
All rights reserved.

No part of this book may be reproduced, or stored in a retrieval system, or transmitted in any form or by any means, electronic, mechanical, photocopying, recording, or otherwise, without express written permission of the publisher.

Published by Thomas & Mercer, Seattle

www.apub.com

Amazon, the Amazon logo, and Thomas & Mercer are trademarks of Amazon.com, Inc., or its affiliates.

ISBN-13: 9781542045735
ISBN-10: 1542045738

Cover design by Damon Freeman

Printed in the United States of America

In loving memory of a dear friend, taken too soon.
Your spirit still makes me smile.

CHAPTER 1

April 1
8:07 p.m.

SHEA'S MIND SWIRLED THROUGH UNCONSCIOUSNESS.

A woman's voice rang in her head like a lullaby. *You'll feel better tomorrow.*

But she was wrong.

A man's face, so close to hers, his taste, his scent, the eyes that turned dark, hands that wouldn't let go, fingers that dug into her arms.

What happened, what could have happened, pinballed through her brain, exploding into all the mistakes. The lies and half-truths. The damage done. She should have told Ryan.

The air felt cold, exposing her, chilling her. It carried her through dark woods until slowly, gently, she relaxed into a warm pool, a hot spring, its floor like quicksand, pulling her down . . . first to the shoulders, then the chin, cheeks, eyes, hair. Her whole body submerged.

She hesitated. Something inside wanted to hold on, but there was power in the force that held her under. She looked up at the moon above the water, the circle of light shrinking, dimming. Then it was gone. She was in too deep. Everything went black. She took a breath. Liquid filled her lungs, her life ending just as it began: alone and naked in a pool of water.

CHAPTER 2

April 8

KAT TOOK A DEEP BREATH and removed her sunglasses as the taxi turned off the expressway onto the tree-lined streets of Maple Park. They passed Union Park, where uniformed little girls blissfully swung bats at a plastic tee and ran bases while parents sat in folding chairs along the sidelines with their coffees. None of those families realized how quickly it would all be over.

Kat took another deep breath, let her head fall back onto the seat rest, and blew the air up at the roof. It felt like she couldn't get enough air in her lungs. She replaced her sunglasses to mask the redness of her eyes and returned her focus to the budding maples and blooming magnolias.

As the taxi neared Saint Andrew's, it looked like the turnout for Easter. The church lot was full, and parked cars lined the streets in every direction.

Kat stepped inside just moments before the service began. Her shoes clacked loudly against the marble entry and echoed off the travertine walls, drawing attention from fellow mourners seated near the back. She took a program from the basket on the nearby table, stepped into the carpeted nave, and quietly found a seat, avoiding the eyes around her.

The minister stepped to the pulpit and recited a prayer while Kat gazed down at the program's inside cover: a familiar but cropped photograph of Shea, looking tan and happy in a strapless sundress, an orange hibiscus flower in her wavy blonde hair. It was from last summer's luau-themed farewell for Shea's youngest child, Leigh, as she headed off to Michigan State. In the photo, Shea had a big, open-mouthed, mid-laugh grin. The fuller picture, which sat in a frame on Kat's mantel at home, included Kat and several other women from the neighborhood, numerous margarita glasses, and the glow of café lighting strung in the trees behind them.

When the service ended, she followed the crowd outside. "Kit Kat!" It was Victoria, Tori to her friends, striding toward her, arms outstretched from under a black cape, eyes hidden behind Jackie O–style glasses, her dark hair pulled back slick. Tori removed her glasses just before their embrace. They held on, both speechless.

When Tori finally pulled back, she held Kat by the shoulders and smiled, her chestnut eyes similarly red and weary. "Look at your hair!" Tori said gleefully.

Tori's gift was her ability to lighten a mood, like complimenting a hideous haircut or making someone feel better about gaining twenty pounds: "I think you look younger," she'd once said after Kat spent a month stuffing her face with Oreos while mourning her dad's death. "A fuller face means less wrinkles. Why do you think I get fillers?"

Kat touched what remained of her hair. "Let's not talk about it." Kat's new life had included chopping her not-long, not-short "mom do," as she'd always referred to it, in favor of an allegedly high-fashion pixie cut—her attempt to blend in with the chic European women with whom she now spent so much time.

Tori forcefully turned Kat's shoulders, quickly scanning all angles. "It's fantastic," she said. "Like Sharon Stone. Hot mama."

Kat smirked and rolled her eyes. "Doubtful." The hairdresser had said the same thing, but when Kat looked at her wispy blonde-and-white strands, she was reminded of her son's hair, back when he was twelve.

"Where's Mack?" Tori asked, glancing back toward her husband, Herman, who was talking to several of their friends.

"He couldn't get away." A lie. "He said to say hello to you all, though." Another lie.

Lina stepped over to welcome Kat home with a long embrace. Kat felt another friend slipping away. Lina's once muscular frame felt frail, and when her hair brushed against Kat's face, she felt a synthetic imitation of her beautiful thick, dark hair. "Mi amor," Lina said in that gorgeous, raspy voice that suggested a lifetime of cigarettes, despite her clean living.

"Hola, mi amiga," Kat replied.

Lina loved speaking Spanish with Kat. Lina's Cuban parents had refused to speak English at home, a fact the women had bonded over when they'd first met, both being children of recent immigrants. For Kat, the home language had been Finnish, but she'd gone on to master the Romance languages in college with dreams of world travel.

"How long are you in town?" Tori finally asked as the three women relaxed into a small circle of conversation.

"I've got about a week. I have meetings in the Chicago office on Thursday and Friday, so I'm staying at the hotel downtown. I was hoping to visit with you all while I'm here."

"Absolutely," Lina said. "I can't believe you didn't tell us you were coming."

"It just kind of happened," Kat said. "I saw the post about the service on Facebook yesterday. I had to come."

"Shoot. I'm sorry, Kat. I said I'd call you back with service details, didn't I?" Tori said. "I guess I'm just a little dazed."

"I understand." She wasn't surprised. Other than Tori's call four days ago about Shea's death, she hadn't heard from these women in the three months since she'd moved away. It felt like she'd slipped out

4

of the group as quickly and easily as she'd slipped in all those years ago. She knew it was juvenile to expect more, that no one chatted on the phone anymore, that life went on, that people were busy, but without Shea, who'd essentially provided these friends, Kat wondered if she'd ever see them again after this.

"I don't understand what happened," Kat said. "I thought she was happy." She didn't mention the fact that she might have known why it had happened if only she'd answered Shea's call. That unanswered call had consumed her thoughts since hearing the news.

"We'll talk, but not here," Tori said, her eyes darting around to the other mourners nearby. "Listen, you've got to come with us. We're leaving this afternoon for Catawba. Just like old times."

"The lake house?"

"Shea would want us to do something," Lina said.

"And where else, right?" Tori added. "We're going to do what we used to do: eat too much, drink too much, tell stories and laugh till it hurts. You must come."

Tori's lake house was on one of the channels off Lake Erie, and when they visited in late summer, a thirty-minute boat trip to the four-hundred-acre South Bass Island—otherwise known as Put-in-Bay—was always on the agenda, given its reputation as Key West of the Midwest. It attracted more than two million visitors each season, drawn to the fishing, historic landmarks and homes, quaint shops, restaurants, bars, and wild nightlife.

And Shea had died on that island. One week ago today. "I'm in," Kat said. The guilt might swallow her whole if she didn't find some answers. Going there might be the only way to get them.

"Excellent," Tori said. "You'll be with me and Lina. We'll swing into the city on the way out of town and grab your things. Dee is going in Evelyn's car later. Georgia can't make it, but we've got four, now five with you." She put an arm around Kat's shoulders. "It'll be great."

E. C. DISKIN

"I should find Ryan," Kat said, stepping out of Tori's arm, looking around. People were leaving, and she surveyed the crowd, spotting Shea's husband, Ryan, and the kids a half block down the sidewalk, heading home. Ryan's left arm was draped around Stephen's shoulders, even though the twenty-year-old was taller than his father at this point. Ryan's other free hand held Leigh's. She'd become a replica of her mother in the last couple of years—the same hair, posture, those sun freckles, ice-blue eyes, even the innate sensuality in her gait. It was impossible not to blink, hoping that Shea was fine, headed home right now, walking hand in hand with her husband. Kat wanted to catch up to them and hug them all, but it didn't seem like the right time.

She turned back to Tori. "How could this happen?"

"We'll talk," she said, entwining their arms and guiding Kat down the steps to the sidewalk. "Come on. My car's over here."

CHAPTER 3

WITH THE SUNROOF OPEN, the cool air wafted through Tori's car as they pulled on to the highway. The radio was set to a Top 40 station, and Tori was singing along and tapping her hands on the wheel. Kat didn't recognize the song; she didn't spend a lot of time in cars these days.

Lina, sitting up front, finally started searching for a new station. "You're torturing me." Lina had played drums in an all-girl band in high school and often remarked that real music died in 1979.

"Fine," Tori said, "just nothing depressing, please. I don't think I can handle any more tears today."

Lina found the Eagles playing "Hotel California" on a classic rock station. She and Tori sang along. Kat grinned, relishing the sounds of friends and music that reminded her of college, but as she closed her eyes to soak it in, she saw Shea's face and the smile she'd never see again. And when the song took a dark turn and Don Henley began singing about how someone could check out of that hotel but never leave, she thought of Shea, checking in to some hotel on Put-in-Bay and never walking out again. Suddenly, the air felt cold and the music too loud.

Tori must have had the same thought. She abruptly turned off the radio without a word, letting the car fill with silence. Kat looked at her phone to see if Mack had tried to reach her, but he hadn't. She wrote him a quick text. Done with service, heading to Catawba with Tori, Lina, and gang. Call you later. She reviewed the note and added a couple of heart emojis to the end before hitting "Send." If she acted as if nothing were wrong between them, perhaps she could will it to be true.

Tori asked how everyone's kids were doing. For decades, their group had bonded over sleep deprivation, potty training, bullies, grades, sports, and teen drama. But now all their kids except Tori's youngest, a junior in high school, were off at college. Lina and Kat offered single-sentence updates, and Tori regaled them with stories of her middle daughter, Viv, now a freshman at University of Illinois, who'd recently confided in Tori about the guy who'd dumped her after a passionate, slightly intoxicated hookup, a recent pregnancy scare, and a friend's near-fatal alcohol poisoning. There seemed to be no topics untouched.

Kat couldn't help but feel grateful that her son, Peter, now a junior at Tulane, limited his updates to the broad brushstrokes of "going out," "parties," and "you, know, the usual." The only detailed information she could extract related to classes, internships, and money.

Kat suddenly feared being the one to bring up Shea too soon. Maybe Tori and Lina knew more than she did, facts that would devastate any hope of an enjoyable drive to the lake. "So, Lina," Kat asked, leaning forward from her middle seat in the back, "how are you feeling?"

Lina turned. "Well, I'm sure you've noticed I'm as bald as a newborn, but today's a good day, and I wouldn't miss this weekend for anything."

Typical. Lina was never one to complain, simply advising her friends via text last fall, Girls, the big C is back. Bastard. But I'm a fighter. No worries. Onward and upward. Well, hopefully no time soon. The women had to pry details and press her to accept their help, so no one knew exactly how bad it was.

"What about you, Kat?" Lina asked. "How's the new job?"

"Good. Busy." There were many other adjectives that might fit: *stressful, all consuming, overwhelming, marriage crushing*, but she didn't want to go there. No one wanted to hear her complain. These women had long ago dubbed Kat's life jet-setting, glamorous, and exciting. When she had to miss happy hours or dinners, it was almost always prefaced with "Sorry. In Hong Kong," or "In Bali," or "In Spain . . ." Since she'd moved to Houston, her new position involved overseeing new hotel openings around the world. It was a dream job for the girl who'd wanted a life of travel and adventure, though, like everything else, nothing was as good as it looked from the outside. "I've got some trips to Europe coming up, but of course I miss Maple Park. I miss you all."

"Well, it sounds fantastic to me," Lina said. "My bucket list included several European cities." Kat noticed the past tense but chose to ignore it.

Tori glanced back at her, eyes wide. "Do they ever have celebrities at your openings?" The prospect of a celebrity spotting drew Tori's attention like shouting "squirrel" to a dog. She could tell you about breakups, affairs, pregnancies, and drug arrests in Hollywood with more authority than *E! News*.

"Not usually," Kat said, "but there are some good perks. I think by the end of the year Mack and I could take a trip around the world with all my miles. I just don't know when we'll have time."

"Sounds like a great reason to retire." Tori gripped the steering wheel and looked off to her left before glancing at Kat in the rearview mirror. "Life is too short."

That had certainly been true for Shea. She had come to Chicago from Florida more than thirty years earlier for college, a first stop in her grand plan to see the world, but life got in the way and she'd never left. They'd taken family trips, of course, but she'd never been out of the country. Kat and Shea used to talk about taking a couples' trip, an adventure to Australia, once the kids were grown and off the payroll.

"I think retirement is still beyond the horizon," Kat said. The word *retire* was not in her vocabulary. She and Mack had both chosen careers for the work more than the pay. And just when her job finally offered a nice salary, Mack's situation had tanked.

Tori couldn't possibly understand. She'd been blessed with some sort of trust fund, a life without financial worries, Shea had once confided. Fortunately, other than her expensive wardrobe and extravagant vacations, most of the time it was easy to forget that Tori came from some stuffed-toy empire.

"How's Texas?" Lina asked.

"Still assessing," Kat said with a smile. It had only been a few months. She held out some hope that the fighting and tension were temporary. Her phone buzzed in her hand. Mack had answered her text: Have fun, two harmless words, coated in passive aggression.

"What's the new house like?" Tori asked.

Kat put the phone away. "Different. It has potential. We're on an acre, and it was built in 1990."

Tori and Lina both chuckled. That was definitely different. Maple Park had city-size lots, except for a few of the old estates, like Tori's place, built for the town's earliest and most influential settlers. Nearly all the homes had been built between 1890 and 1930. The community bonded through a love of historic architecture, shared issues that came with living inside antiques, and the ability to see, while standing at the kitchen sink, inside their neighbors' homes.

But Kat's new house was also different because it didn't feel like home yet. Boxes hadn't been unpacked, rooms sat empty, and Kat had yet to share more than a wave with neighbors as she passed in her car. Everyone was friendly, but no one needed new friends. And, of course, Kat had never been too good at making the first move.

Shea had practically been Kat's personal cruise director when she and Mack moved in next door all those years ago.

"How is Mack? Does he like it there?" Tori asked.

"He's . . . adjusting."

"And he can do the work virtually? Isn't it great that he was able to do that?" Lina added.

"Yeah," Kat said. There was nothing great about it. His IT job disappeared when the company restructured, and he'd been asked to stay on as consultant for half the pay, which was why there'd been no real discussion about whether or not she'd accept her promotion. Mack didn't want anyone to know those details until he'd figured out his next move. And she didn't want anyone to know they were drifting apart. "What about Herman?" she asked.

"My man leaves for China on Monday morning, so I'm a single mom all week. But he's good." Tori had once said that her husband's name had nearly been a deal breaker when they met, but after she started calling him "my man," and he started referring to himself as "her man" while pointing at Tori, she embraced it. He was a good decade older, an intellectual who spent 80 percent of his work life traveling and most of his free time alone, reading about world history. It was hard not to wonder where the spark between them came from, given Tori's preference for parties and outlandish reality TV shows.

"Have you made any girlfriends yet?" Tori continued. "There must be a Shea in every town."

"I'm sure there is one, but we're at different stages. They're babies—and I don't just mean the children," Kat joked.

It was the perfect opportunity to mention Shea's call, but Kat's guilt was like a gag. She hadn't even told Mack about it. Every time Kat thought about how she'd ignored that call, tossing the phone aside as if Shea were a nuisance, her heart ached. She had died the next day. Alone in a bathtub. Far from home. Leaving a husband and kids and an entire community baffled and heartbroken. She'd obviously needed her friend. She'd reached out to Kat, and Kat had tossed her aside.

"Do either of you understand this at all?" Kat asked, leaning forward. "Why Shea came all the way out to Put-in-Bay alone? Why she'd get that drunk? It just doesn't make sense."

Lina looked at Tori, who took a deep breath before she answered. "I know she and Ryan were having issues."

"What kind of issues?" Kat had heard the occasional argument over the years; it couldn't be helped with homes just ten feet apart. But as far as Kat knew, their marriage was solid.

"He's been out of work for quite a while. He didn't tell anyone, not even Shea. She only found out because some letter came to the house about an exit interview. He'd been leaving in the morning for weeks, like it was any other day. And even after she found out, he wouldn't talk about it. It was weird." Tori turned back to Kat. "Well, that, and remember our last girls' trip out here at Thanksgiving?"

"I couldn't go, remember?" Tori, Shea, Lina, and a few others had decided to do an impromptu getaway, a "battery charge" before the turkey-day duties. Kat would have loved to recharge her batteries, but work had conflicted. Her side of the fence always felt more harried. But Shea and Tori were great at coming up with reasons for GNOs—girls' nights out—or all-girl getaways. They would fly off to Miami or Vegas for the weekend almost twice a year. Kat sometimes felt like a visitor at the cool kids' table, simply because she was around less, because she had to work. Though, when it was just Kat and Shea, it was different. Shea was one of those people who could make you feel like you were the most important person in the room.

"Well," Tori continued, "she told a few of us in confidence that she was going to leave Ryan."

Kat couldn't believe it. Shea had been her closest friend. They'd lived next door to each other for two decades, and there was almost no one, other than Mack, Kat thought she knew better. She couldn't believe Shea had been that unhappy and never said a word to her.

Had Kat been too oblivious, too wrapped up in her own life to notice Shea was going through something? Had Shea tried to tell her? She recalled the dozens of conversations between Thanksgiving and Kat's departure in January. Nothing had seemed off.

She thought of their good-bye three months earlier, looking back as she and Mack rolled away in their overstuffed minivan, while Shea and Ryan stood on the sidewalk, bundled in their coats. Ryan had pulled Shea close, kissing the top of her head. "They seemed fine."

"He was cheating," Lina said.

"No." It came out as a whisper, too unbelievable to be true. Ryan was a flirt, particularly when he'd had a few drinks, and a notorious close talker, like everything he wanted to tell you was a secret, but he looked at Shea like he'd continued to marvel, every day, at his good fortune in somehow landing a woman far out of his league. He'd said as much a thousand different ways.

"Well, that's what she said back in November, but she didn't share any details," Tori added.

"She found an *undergarment* in his drawer after that luau party," Lina said carefully, like she was trying to avoid getting specific.

"I never heard about that," Tori said.

"In August? She was sure it wasn't hers or Leigh's?" Kat asked.

"Correct," Lina continued. "But she didn't tell me more. She was kind of a mess that weekend, throwing back shots like water. I'm sorry. I shouldn't say that. It's just that, at first, I didn't know about the Ryan thing and she was flirting pretty intensely with this man at the bar on the island."

"You all went to the island?" Kat asked. "I didn't even realize you could boat over that late in November."

13

"Oh, sure," Tori said. "The ferries usually run till the end of the month, though the water was really rough that weekend. We'd already dry-docked the boat for the season."

"The ferry was like a roller coaster," Lina said.

"Not good after an afternoon of drinking." Tori pointed toward her throat and stuck out her tongue.

"Anyway," Lina continued, "Shea was chatting up this gorgeous guy who was like ten years younger than any of us, and they left the bar together, holding hands."

Tori chuckled. "She had a right. I mean, if Ryan was cheating, then he deserved it."

"Oh my God!" Kat exclaimed. "Is that why she went back to the island last week? Could she have been having an affair?"

"I don't think so," Lina said. "It was just flirting. He was with a big group, we were in a big group, it was nothing . . . it's not like she went home with him. Right, Tori?"

Tori didn't respond.

"What?" Kat asked.

Tori's gaze was fixed on the road ahead. "Actually, I know for a fact that she didn't go back to see that man from the bar."

"How do you know?" Kat asked.

"He's dead."

"What?" chimed both women.

"I was up here about two weeks ago, getting the house ready for spring, and there was an article in the local paper advising boaters to be careful as the season began. It included photos of several people who died on the lake last year. I recognized one of the pictures. I brought it back to Maple Park and showed Shea."

"And?"

"She pretended that she didn't remember if it was him, but I could see it on her face. The crazy part was, he disappeared the night we met him. His body was never found, but his boat washed up on one of the little islands about a week later. The lake began to freeze by early December, so it wasn't easy to do a search and recover."

"Did you tell anyone?" Kat asked.

"What do you mean?" Tori asked.

"Well, that has to be relevant. Maybe that's why she went to the island."

"Maybe she felt guilty," Lina said.

"About what?" Kat asked.

"If she was drinking with him and his drunkenness caused his death, maybe she felt some sort of misplaced responsibility."

"I don't think we'll ever know," Tori said. "But no, I didn't tell Ryan that Shea kissed a stranger on one of our girls' weekends and that the guy died. What good would that do now?"

Kat sat back, looking out the window at the open plains along the road. Her image of Shea had always been of the carefree, laid-back life of the party. Always in the yard or at the window, smiling, offering a glass of wine or a good story to Kat on those nights when Kat would return home frazzled, exhausted, or overwhelmed from a long day. Shea was the one to lift everyone up. And yet everything about her death suggested she was someone who'd been in a lot of pain.

"We need some gas," Tori said as she slowed to pull off at the exit ramp. "We're just a few miles out now. Let's fill up, hit the grocery, and grab some snacks and bevvies. I don't know about you two, but all this talk makes me ready for happy hour."

Kat couldn't agree more.

CHAPTER 4

Four months earlier
November 24

SHEA SAT AT ONE END of the table, her kids on one side, her parents on the other, and focused on the centerpiece of flowers she'd arranged, the silver she'd shined, the china, the rolls baked from scratch, the turkey, looking picture-perfect.

"To my wife," Ryan said, his wineglass raised. "Somehow, she manages to pull this off every year with very little help from me, and I just want to say, to my darling wife, that on this day of thanks, I am most thankful for you."

Her parents and the kids raised their glasses, gazing toward Shea with love and admiration. She wanted to crawl under the table or run out the back door. Instead, she wiped the tears pooling in her eyes, thanked Ryan, and told everyone to dig in.

Shea looked over at her father, holding a serving dish while her mother took some vegetables, and then at her mother, who did the same for him. That was what a marriage was supposed to look like.

She looked at Ryan, at his smug grin while he began to tell a joke. He was laughing, as if nothing was wrong and they were some Norman Rockwell painting. But there was someone else. He'd probably called *her* earlier today, to thank *her* for whatever the hell she did for him. He'd probably made plans to be with *her* after the holiday. And no one else at the table even knew that the allegedly high-powered, successful executive had been out of work for four months.

Everything was a lie. It was as if the walls of the room were pushing inward, the oxygen was being forced out.

And now she had more than Ryan's infidelity to face. She'd caused her own damage. It was as if she'd taken on the challenge to one-up him in the effort to throw their life away. She'd spent all her energy focused on the holiday in the three days since her return, but every night, as she lay in their dark room, with the sound of Ryan's obliviously peaceful breathing beside her, she was assaulted with a freight train of images from the island. Blake's face, that kiss, the boat, his hands . . . She couldn't believe that in one night, she could do such damage. She'd made the same mistakes in college more than once, getting drunk, finding herself in compromising situations, but at fifty-two years old, how could a mother, a wife, an otherwise smart woman be so stupid?

She'd been so angry with Ryan, at the giant mess he'd made of their marriage, and she'd just wanted to get numb. Every drink felt like a magic cleanser that could wipe it all away, at least for the weekend.

While her friends blissfully ate their pizza at Rudolph's, chatted about their kids, and joked about trivial beefs with their husbands, Shea could think of nothing but the conversation they'd all had the previous night about how sometimes men cheated because they took their wives for granted. Evelyn, the only divorcée among them, had joked that women needed to show men how easily they could be replaced. She'd argued, like a good debater, that men were easy, and if women found good-looking, younger models, the way men so often did, and showed their husbands how easy it had been to get that man's attention, perhaps they'd shape up. Everyone had laughed and joked about attempted seductions of such men. "Come on," Evelyn had joked, "we all know how men love a cougar!"

It was clear now that all that was just banter, meant more for entertainment than anything, but in that tequila-soaked moment, as Shea sat in the bar, she had been inspired. With each shot, her determination to even the score had grown. And when everyone started chatting with a group of men who'd merged into their table, Shea let her gaze land on young, gorgeous Blake, who was looking at her like she was something to behold. When was the last time Ryan looked at her like that? When had he even touched her last?

She practically undressed Blake with her eyes as he moved over to sit beside her at the table. He showered her with compliments and Shea felt a surge of adrenaline when his hand first grazed against hers under the table. When he followed her toward the restroom and gently pushed her against the wall, examining her like some beautiful specimen, she melted. When he kissed her, the mix of alcohol and guilt was surprisingly enticing. Why couldn't she have ended it there? Just enjoyed the attention. Why'd she have to leave with him?

"Mom, Mom," Leigh said, finally snapping her fingers in front of Shea's face. "You're a million miles away."

Shea looked over at her daughter, those big blue eyes, those freckles, a face so like her own, but so young and innocent. She forced a smile and apologized. "Sorry, honey. Just strolling down memory lane a little. I was thinking about our first Thanksgiving in this house."

CHAPTER 5

April 8

DESPITE THE FIVE-HOUR DRIVE FROM Maple Park, once they were close, it was easy to remember why Tori and Herman had built a home on Catawba. There was a rural quality, a peace and serenity to the barren landscape and ponds that led up to their house. A couple of kids with fishing poles were sitting on the railing of a narrow old bridge, giant lily pads covered most of the water below, and dozens of geese waddled along the side of the narrow road.

They turned onto the long gravel driveway and meandered past an acre of trees before arriving at the house. Tori and Herman both came from large families who were scattered around the Midwest, so, despite having only three children, their five-bedroom house could easily sleep fifteen. With cedar-shake siding, dormer windows, and a large widow's walk perched on top of the roof, it reminded Kat of Nantucket. The channel and mouth to Lake Erie could be seen from atop that walk. But most impressive was the view out the back. The large deck spanned the full width of the house, with a pergola and sunken hot tub on one side, a fire pit on the other, and a large seating area in the center. Several steps down, an antique brick path meandered through ornamental grasses to the dock at the water's edge. Tori had filled the quarter acre of land between the deck and the water with nothing but native grasses. The simplicity of looking out toward the water, past a few hundred-year-old oak trees and a vast expanse of tall, feathery stalks blowing in the breeze, was hypnotic.

Inside, the living room ceiling was at least fifteen feet high, with windows to match, and other than a few large paintings, the decor was mostly white, black, and natural woods. Every time Kat visited, she went to those windows first, took a deep, cleansing breath, and marveled at the view.

Tori began setting out the first round of appetizers on the back deck, and Kat set up the fire pit. Lina synced her phone to the speakers and streamed some Beatles before heading to a bedroom to change. When she returned from her room, her face had been scrubbed free of makeup, and her wig had been replaced by a bright-orange silk scarf that complimented her olive skin. Her face really needed no adorning, with expressive dark eyes, long lashes, and skin that seemed to belie her age. Lina touched her scarf. "Those wigs make my head so hot!"

Kat smiled. "It's beautiful."

"I miss my hair."

Kat reached back to feel the wispy remains at the nape of her own neck. "Yeah, so do I," she said with a smile.

Kat and Tori changed out of church attire, too, and they settled on the deck. Within the hour, Evelyn and Dee had arrived and the chaotic melody of women at play was at full volume. With drinks in hand, they sat on the deck around a coffee table of cheese, dips, and snacks, marveling at the soft blues and grays fading into peach and pink along the horizon.

Tori pulled out her smartphone. "Come on, ladies, picture time!"

Everyone grumbled, preferring to keep their sweatpants, bare faces, and puffy eyes off social media.

"Hey," Tori argued. "No one posted more pictures online than Shea. We're going to post a pic of us as we celebrate her."

She had a point. Thanks to Shea's constant social media use—posting photos from dinners, parties, baseball games, and the gym and even the occasional quip about a TV show—Kat had felt connected to her, even though they hadn't had a single conversation since January. The women leaned in, raised their glasses, and smiled for the camera.

Tori settled onto the love seat and tapped her long, perfectly manicured nail against her glass, commanding attention. All conversations paused.

"Ladies," she began. "None of us understand why this happened to such a wonderful, beautiful person, but I'm grateful that you were all able to join me this weekend, to help celebrate our dear friend." She paused to regroup, and Lina patted her knee. Tori squeezed her hand and continued. "It's okay. I'm okay. Well, no, I'm not. None of us are. But my point is that I know Shea wouldn't want us to sit around crying all weekend. Of course, she'd be thrilled to have a weekend centered around her . . ."

Kat laughed a little louder than the others. Shea's love of the spotlight was as foreign and horrifying to Kat as it was enviable. The first time Kat watched Shea climb on top of a table to get the attention of a roomful of people, she'd assumed Shea was drunk but soon realized alcohol was an unnecessary lubricant to her swagger. Shea was the go-to volunteer—be it at the kids' schools, fund-raisers, or block parties—to stand atop the nearest furniture or finger whistle until a crowd was tamed, usually offering a silly pose or brief dance while she had everyone's attention.

"She would want us to share funny stories about all of our misadventures, play our silly games, and promise to cherish each other and our families and . . ." Tori couldn't finish.

Evelyn dabbed her eye and raised her glass. "To Shea."

"To Shea," the others echoed.

"Hey, did I ever tell you guys about my first Shea spotting?" Dee said. "I hated her."

Everyone laughed, wiping back tears.

"No, really," Dee continued, grabbing a handful of nuts, pulling her legs up into her chair, and crossing them like a kid at story time. "I was at the baby pool over at Covington Park. I was super pregnant with Eddie, hot and miserable, probably up a full sixty."

"No way," Tori said, shaking her head. "Not possible."

Dee was barely over five feet tall, and she was one of those women who used food as mere fuel for survival. She could sit in front of a bowl of M&M's for two hours and never notice it.

"Oh, believe me," Dee said. "It's possible. You'll just never see proof because I waddled away whenever a camera got near me. Anyway, I hadn't had highlights in like six months, so I had two inches of dark roots and was too exhausted to even deal with this." She grabbed a wad of her thick, straight auburn hair. Dee had often joked about her naturally frizzy hair that had caused buckets of tears and heartache as a child, until that day in college when she'd discovered the flat iron—a magic wand that had changed her life. "And I'm sitting under the umbrella, watching Cee Cee play in the water, feeling like a big ol' tub of goo, and I noticed Shea at the other end of the pool. I immediately hated her."

"Why?" Tori asked, her tears evaporating with each giggle.

"Because she was pregnant and huge, but she was wearing this wide-brimmed hat, dark sunglasses, and bright-orange lipstick. She had on her tiny little bikini top with her enormous belly, tan and proud, shoulders back, and a sequined sarong around her hips. She looked like some frickin' Bain de Soleil ad."

Everyone laughed at the accuracy of Dee's depiction.

"I'm telling you," Dee finished with a grin, "it really pissed me off."

"She was meant to live on an island," Kat said. Shea's sun-streaked, dirty-blonde hair was usually wavy—that beach look others paid a fortune for—and she never clouded her freckles with makeup. Her signature enhancement: bright lipstick on her full lips and a little mascara. Summers were spent in sundresses or scarves with exotic prints. It was like some wind machine was offstage when she walked into a room.

"That's what I loved," Tori added. "Women pick themselves apart and try to cover every imperfection, but Shea embraced it all. She walked into every room like she owned it. Though she did joke once about carrying her pregnancies in her ass. I think she said there was another baby stuck in there."

Dee nearly spit up her drink. "Yeah, she was an ass girl long before the Kardashians."

"And that laugh," Lina added. "It was like Santa Claus swallowed Woody Woodpecker, with those rapid-fire *ho-ho-ho*s." She attempted an impersonation, which led to a competition over who could do it best.

"What about you, Kit Kat?" Dee asked. "Do you remember the day you first met Shea?"

"Oh yes," Kat said, sitting back and pulling her legs up to her chest. "Stephen was strapped to her chest in one of those harnesses. We were moving in. I was ready to pop with Peter."

Tori stood. "Just a sec." She was heading inside for a refill and offered to waitress for the others. Everyone's focus shifted, providing a natural end to Kat's story. She took a sip of wine, enjoying the private memory. These friends would never have believed it, anyway. Everyone dismissed Kat as being some sort of superwoman, as if she had no problems juggling career, travel, child, house, and husband. Kat preferred their image, so she usually kept the truth to herself. Shea was the only one who ever witnessed the cracks in her facade.

It had been after one of the movers had dropped a box filled with Kat's wedding china. Kat had shrieked and waddled away from the sidewalk, unable to look at the damage. She'd collapsed on the porch in a puddle of tears, overwhelmed, exhausted, and short of breath—though she knew Peter was at fault for the air shortage. Shea appeared, Stephen sleeping on her chest, a scarf in her hair, shuffling toward Kat in flip-flops like some carefree granola mom. Kat had wiped her eyes, mortified to meet her new neighbor in such a state. But Shea smiled and said, "I love crying, too. We're going to be best friends."

Kat liked her immediately.

"I'm Shea—this is Stephen," she said, patting the baby's head, "and please don't be embarrassed. You're soaking in hormones."

"I'm Katherine. Kat. Hi."

"Let me guess—you're due in less than a month."

"Twenty days and counting."

"Perfect. Our kids will grow up together! Welcome to the neighborhood."

"Thanks."

"Husband?" Shea asked, looking toward the open front door while the movers carried in more boxes.

"Business trip."

"Men," she smirked. "Oh my, look at those cankles!" she added with a chuckle.

Kat looked down at her swollen ankles, like two small tree trunks.

"Why do you think I'm wearing these flip-flops?" Shea said. "This little guy is three weeks now, and I still can't fit in my shoes. Let's get your feet up."

"Can't. They put all the furniture in the truck first. There's nowhere to sit yet," Kat said as the movers moved passed her again.

"Come on," Shea said, offering a hand to help Kat stand. Kat took it. Shea was commanding like that. The kind of person you just follow with blind trust that she could lead you to something good. Shea led Kat down the sidewalk and past the movers, who were stacking more boxes onto a dolly, only slightly more carefully.

"Hey, guys," Shea said, "be extra careful and I'll have a little something special for you when you're done." Both men stopped and smiled, watching as Shea passed. Even with a newborn strapped to her chest, she was sexy.

Kat followed Shea into her house. "Sit," Shea said, leading Kat to the living room sofa. Kat complied. "Feet up," she said, handing Kat the remote control. "You're going to relax for an hour. I got this."

"No," Kat said. "Thanks, but . . ."

"Listen, this one is quiet and sleeping if I keep moving. I was literally walking out to go round and round the block when I heard your scream. I will happily manage those men and be sure everything gets inside the house. It's my specialty."

"What, moving?" Kat asked, while relaxing back into the sofa. Shea had already walked out of the room.

"No, silly," she yelled from another room. "Men!" She reappeared with a six-pack of beer, raising it in the air. "Motivation," she said as she walked to the front door.

The living room windows were open, and the sheers moved with the breeze. Shea was saying something to the movers Kat couldn't make out, but whatever it was, it led to laughter. Kat smiled and quickly fell asleep. When she woke and waddled back outside, the truck was almost empty and her house had become a home.

Kat finished her wine and went inside for a refill while Lina and Tori shared their own first encounters with Shea two decades earlier.

When she returned, the women were laughing about the first time Shea brought a full happy hour spread of wine, cheese, and crackers, as well as a folding table, to one of the kids' T-ball games. She could turn anything into a party.

"So, Evelyn," Dee said, "You're the newbie to our little circle. How'd you get so close to Shea?"

"Wasn't she your Realtor?" Kat asked.

"She was," Evelyn said. "Oh jeez, I still can't believe this is real." She wiped her eye. "I told her about my divorce, about the new job, being in a new town, and she insisted that I join her for wine one afternoon. I guess the rest is history."

"That sounds about right," Tori said. "When Shea and Ryan moved to Maple Park, she actually slipped invitations under the doors of all their new neighbors and invited them over for happy hour."

"I could never do that," Kat said. Evelyn agreed.

"Why?" Tori asked.

"What if no one came? What if only two came and you stood there staring at each other? What if the neighbors were weirdos or psychos? What if people came and never left? The whole concept blows my mind. I guess I just fear the unknown."

"Oh, Kit Kat," Tori said. "As Taylor Swift would say, 'Shake It Off.'"

Kat chuckled. "I should probably try her strategy in Texas."

"I'm surprised you'd need to. Southern hospitality and all that," Dee said.

"Yeah, well . . ." Kat said, finishing her glass, "you'd be surprised."

Dee leaned forward for a chardonnay refill. "Well, I just think Evelyn is lucky Shea was so confident and outgoing. I don't know if I would have befriended such a hot divorcée, inviting her into my life like that."

Kat rolled her eyes. Dee's tone negated the compliment. The first time Dee told Kat she "wasn't a fan" had been about thirty minutes after Evelyn had been introduced to Dee's husband, Charlie.

Evelyn had made Kat a little insecure when they first met, too, but it wasn't because of Mack. Just a day after telling Shea she was thinking about accepting the promotion that would require a move to Texas, Kat arrived home from work and heard Shea in the backyard, hosting a happy hour. Shea called Kat over to the fence and introduced her to Evelyn, showing her off like some beautiful, younger replacement. She even boasted about Evelyn's job as a computer consultant. It was the first time Shea didn't insist Kat come over and join them. Everything about that moment felt like high school.

"I've often thought about how lucky I was to meet her," Evelyn replied. "It was like she adopted me."

"Yeah," Dee said. "Shea was always taking in strays."

"I guess that's me," Evelyn said, letting the insult roll away.

Kat had probably been like a stray, too. She wasn't single when she met Shea, but she had definitely been in a dark place at the time, and Shea had saved her.

Kat asked Evelyn about her new job, determined to undo Dee's open hostility. "It's good, busy," Evelyn said. It was the same answer Kat had given Tori and Lina in the car. Maybe Shea had been drawn to Evelyn because she reminded her of Kat.

Having moved to Chicago a year earlier for work, Evelyn was starting over somewhere new, just like Kat. To see her easy insertion into social life in Maple Park gave Kat hope for Texas.

"Okay," Dee said, shifting in her chair. "I don't want to get too maudlin here, but our friend just killed herself. We need to talk about it."

"We don't know that," Kat protested. She put her empty glass on the table. "It could have been an accident."

"But they found an empty Vicodin bottle in her room," Evelyn said gently.

"Still, we don't know how much was in her system, right?"

"True," Tori said, drawing out the word. "It takes some time to get the tox screen back."

Lina was wrapping the ends of her scarf around her finger the way she used to wrap her long, thick hair. "Did any of you know she was taking Vicodin?"

"I know she got some a year ago for her shoulder," Dee said.

But Evelyn shook her head. "I don't think it was about shoulder pain."

They fell silent for a moment.

"I've seen television specials about stay-at-home, suburban soccer moms who become addicted to pills," Tori said. "Starts out innocent enough, but some of them lose everything, end up heroin addicts."

"Jesus, Tori," Lina said. "I'd rather not see her name get smeared with wild rumors of drug addiction."

Tori's expression turned wounded. "I'm not spreading rumors. I'm just saying what I've learned. Jeez."

"She wouldn't do that to her kids," Kat said. "I just don't believe it. I mean, obviously, something was going on, but . . . no. You guys, no." She couldn't stop shaking her head.

"People who do this aren't thinking straight," Tori said.

Kat couldn't stop the tears. She knew better than anyone how dark thoughts could go round and round, like a track, and every return to those thoughts carved the track deeper, like falling into a gutter, making it impossible to think of anything else. Her own pre-delivery tears had been nothing compared to the postpartum that followed. Shea had rarely left her alone during those first weeks of maternity leave, popping in each day to suggest a walk, reminding Kat that she was there to put the *commune* in community. She was a master of squeezing a smile out of Kat's tears. But the darkness of those days had been serious enough to keep Kat from having any more children.

If Shea had become depressed, she would have talked to Kat.

But then she remembered: Shea had tried. The night before she died. The memory felt like a brick in the pit of her stomach. Shea had reached out to Kat, only to be ignored. She'd been crying out for help . . . Kat shook her head. No. Her death had to be an accident. It had to be anything but intentional. "Is that what the police suspect?" she asked.

"The police and the coroner could only confirm that she was alone," Tori said. "No sign of foul play."

"So, that's it?" Kat needed more. Like why Shea drove five hours alone when she hated driving alone, why she didn't tell a soul where she was headed, and what was going on to make her drink so much.

With all remnants of sun replaced by darkness and the temperature dropping, they moved to the fire pit and watched the flames dance as sparks rose to the sky. Dee brought out more wine and refilled their glasses. It was obvious she was trying to lighten things up, but Kat couldn't stop staring at the fire, thinking about how she'd failed the friend who'd been there for her too many times to count.

"Hey," Lina said, leaning forward and slapping Kat's knee, as if to pull her from her trance. "Shea was at my chemo treatment two weeks ago, just to sit with me," she said. "I know she was there to keep my spirits up, but she seemed fine. And when I asked how things were with Ryan, she said, 'Great,' emphatically, like that was a big change. I got the sense they were on the mend."

"I thought they were doing better, too," Tori said. "I asked about it at Georgia's Christmas party. Shea and Ryan were flirting with each other and joking around. She said she'd been wrong about him—and that they were working on it. It wasn't the time to dig, so I let it go."

Kat smiled. "See? That's good. We don't know." She nodded, determined to keep the idea of suicide off the table.

"Hey, Lina," Dee said, "side note, next time you have a treatment, just say the word. I'll go with you."

"Me, too," Tori said.

Lina swatted away their somber expressions. "Don't worry about me. I'm still kickin'. And although I can't have more than one drink"—she raised her glass—"I do have some pretty sweet medical Mary Jane with me, so, play your cards right and maybe I'll share."

The idea of smoking Lina's marijuana prompted stories about who had tried it, when, and with what results, fostering much-needed levity while everyone snacked on the goat cheese spread and artichoke dip.

"Dee," Kat said. "What does Ryan think?"

"How would I know?" she asked before chugging the remains of the wine in her glass. "I haven't talked to Ryan in ages."

"I just figured he might have told Charlie something," Kat clarified. "Aren't they pretty tight?"

"Doubt it." Dee stood up. "Who needs more wine?" she asked the others, walking back into the house without waiting for a response.

Tori turned to Kat, ignoring Dee's strange behavior. "Herman talked to Ryan a little. Shea told him she was going to her sister's place in Michigan, something about her niece being in a play," Tori said.

"So Ryan doesn't know why she went to Put-in-Bay?" Lina asked.

"Nope," Tori answered.

Evelyn twirled her glass in her hands. "She had been looking at real estate on the island, but Ryan didn't know about it."

Lina's brows rose. "What did he make of that?"

Evelyn hesitated, and Dee, having returned with a fresh bottle and full glass, said, "Maybe Shea was cheating," before plopping into her chair.

Kat stared at her. "Are you serious?"

Dee just shrugged.

"You guys. She wouldn't do that. Maybe she was going to surprise Ryan with some getaway house she found."

"But Ryan was out of work," Tori said. "Why would she be browsing getaway houses?"

"I just don't want us to assume the worst," Kat said.

"Please," Dee said. "Shea was reckless. Don't you remember that she was the one who taught us the YOLO bit?"

Kat motioned toward the large tree perched by the dock behind Tori's house. "I don't think shouting 'YOLO' while trying to coax us into swinging from that rope into the lake is the same as having an affair."

"YOLO?" Evelyn asked.

"You only live once," Tori said.

"She was an optimist," Kat said.

"She thought nothing bad could ever happen to her," Dee said.

"This coming from the woman who does backflips off the back of my boat every year?" Tori asked.

"Yes, but I can do it."

"Well, that's one of the things I loved about her," Kat said.

Dee scoffed. "I loved her, too, but let's not act like she was a saint. I know for a fact that she was with another man this winter and essentially blew up someone's marriage."

No one spoke. Kat felt like she'd been slapped across the face. She wanted to defend Shea against such an outrageous accusation. Shea was a flirt and sometimes wild, but she was devoted to Ryan. She and Kat had joked to each other for years about their husbands, complaining about minor things—toothpaste caps and dirty clothes and dishes in the sink—but they'd also joked about their sex lives, laughing about the dry spells, the attempts to be alone when kids were in the house, their desire for more date nights. They were solid. And Shea respected marriage. She always wanted to emulate her own parents' marriage. She wouldn't do that. Dee was describing a different woman. None of it made sense.

Dee shook her head, looking remorseful. "I'm sorry, but it's true. And don't ask me to elaborate. I'm not going to say."

CHAPTER 6

November 26

ON SATURDAY NIGHT, SHEA AND Ryan were back to living in silence. The kids were out visiting high school friends home for the holiday, and Shea was curled up under a blanket in the living room, absently watching some made-for-TV movie about a married couple in trouble with secrets and lies. An adulterer, determined to get rid of a wife. *Maybe Ryan should do that*, she joked to herself. *At least he'd get the life insurance.* Her life had become a cliché.

She'd continued to avoid him with busywork: cleaning up from the holiday, doing the kids' laundry, scouring the MLS listings for her two clients. It was too hard to think about what would happen if he finally admitted what was going on and she shared her own secrets. She wasn't ready to face having everything they'd built over twenty-seven years of marriage crumble to the ground.

She looked out the window toward Kat's place. The windows were dark. They'd headed south for the holiday weekend, first to New Orleans to take Peter out for Thanksgiving, and then west to Houston, to look for a new home. Everything was changing. The kids were gone. Kat was leaving. Dee's kids were gone. Tori would probably take off once her youngest got done with school. They had that lake house. Nothing was holding anyone here.

She looked around the room, the walls she'd painted, first pale green when they'd moved in, then beige a few years later. She'd painted every wall in this house at least twice. She'd made every window treatment. The kids' heights were marked on that doorjamb upstairs. Her universe was here, inside these walls, in this town, but the kids had left, Kat was next, and now her marriage was ending.

Ryan walked in with two glasses of wine and asked to join her. As he stood there, looking insecure, asking permission for companionship, she moved the blanket, making some room.

"Something is bothering you," he said, taking a seat beside her and grabbing the remote. Shea watched him hit the "Mute" button.

She took a long sip of the wine and placed it on the table beside her, leaving her fingers around the stem, holding on for dear life.

"You're cheating again," she said, her words aimed at the glass. She didn't want to cry, but she felt a drop escape and quickly wiped her face.

Ryan scoffed. "What? I told you—"

"Stop lying to me. You dismissed that bra in your drawer with no explanation, and, like an idiot, I chose to believe you. I wanted to believe you. I told myself that Leigh must have had a friend here and somehow it got in our laundry and ended up in your drawer. It's ridiculous, even to say it now."

What was more ridiculous was that she chose to believe him at all. It had been three years since he'd been unfaithful, but it felt like they were right back there again. Unmistakable evidence that he'd been with someone else.

"Baby, I swear to God, I don't know where that bra came from. I didn't do anything."

"I should have known this would happen again."

Ryan put down the wine, irritated. "What does that mean?"

She didn't say anything, and for a moment, neither did he. They'd worked through it a long time ago. They'd seen a counselor. She hadn't wanted their family to fall apart. She'd believed he'd never do it again. He'd sworn it had been nothing. Entirely physical. A terrible lack of judgment and a betrayal. He'd said everything she needed to hear.

Shea finally looked at his face, to see the truth in his eyes. "Don't lie to me, Ryan. I can't take any more lies. I saw your e-mail to some woman last week. Sandy?"

His indignation turned to confusion, and then she saw the spark of recognition. He knew what she was talking about. He looked away from her, took a sip of wine, slowly, as if he needed to figure out the best way to spin it, and finally nodded. He put the glass on the table before turning to her. She was struck by a sudden desire to slap him across the face.

"It's not an affair."

"Bullshit," Shea said, tossing the blanket aside. She needed to be able to storm off quickly.

"I swear. I've never even met her." And then he started talking. It was virtual infidelity. He was embarrassed. Some sort of stress relief, he said. It seemed innocent when it all began early in the fall. Some buddy had sent him links to porn sites, and he'd clicked, curious. It was nothing. But then it had spiraled forward.

Shea didn't speak, but Ryan talked nonstop, apologized, and took her hand in his. "I really never meant to hurt you. I convinced myself that it was not really a problem because I never touched anyone. I told you I'd never do that to you again, and I swear, Shea, on our kids' lives, I haven't."

Shea put down the wine and finally met his eyes. She'd always thought Ryan had a tell, an inability to make eye contact if he was spinning a story. And he'd looked into her eyes, practically without blinking, as he explained, with obvious embarrassment, what he'd done.

"So, this is why you never touch me anymore?" she asked.

"Actually, I thought you weren't interested."

"It's not that." It wasn't that she wasn't interested in him. It was just the last thing on her mind. And he rarely instigated, so she'd convinced herself it didn't matter. They cuddled and held hands and kissed good-night. She'd thought that meant everything was great, until she'd found that e-mail on his computer.

"There's no one but you," he said. "I swear."

Shea took a breath. She could feel the tension releasing from her shoulders. The knot that had settled in her stomach ten days earlier began to loosen. She leaned in, head on his chest, disturbed but not destroyed. There was no love affair to fear. There wasn't another woman with whom he dreamed of spending his life. No one had stolen his heart. It was just a woman on a screen.

She took a deep breath as he wrapped his arm around her, pulling her closer. Suddenly, her thoughts turned, as if she'd escaped a burning building, alive and bruised, only to remember that she might have left the gas on and everything could still explode. Ryan had not even kissed another woman, but she had done something terrible . . . A new fear gripped her.

"Here's what I'm thinking," Ryan said. He put her glass back in her hand, pulling her focus from panic back to wine. "We're in a rut, that's all. But the kids are out of the house, and it's just you and me again. We'll be fine," he continued.

She needed that to be true. She loved him, despite their mistakes. She leaned on his shoulder, and he maneuvered his arm around her, holding her close and resting his head against hers.

"If you're stressed, I want to help. Maybe I should look for a new job, too," Shea offered. "Selling a few homes a year doesn't help much."

"You do just fine. And you love it. That's worth something. That job was never about the money."

That was true. Shea had never assumed she'd make much, but she had to do something. There were no more noses to wipe or lunches to make, and then the kids started driving. And she lived in a town of beautiful, historic homes. It was fun.

"Besides, it's only been a few years." Ryan shook his head. "Give yourself some time. We're going to be okay."

"How can you say that?" she asked, finally sitting up and turning toward him. They had to face what was happening. Their savings had to be running dry. How absurd that she didn't know, that she couldn't even go to a computer and pull up their accounts and check. Her face grew hot, and Ryan turned away. He always found it insulting to talk finance. When they'd first married and he'd suggested she quit working to be home with the kids, she'd asked about whether they could afford it, and he'd laughed. "I got this," he'd said. "Don't ever worry about that."

She loved the idea, having spent most of her childhood dreaming of being a mother more than anything else. She'd majored in history, minored in philosophy, never enticed by any one career path, and the idea of walking kids to school, being there for all the scrapes and triumphs, held more appeal than any other job. She had shared with him her student-loan debts and credit card balances and salary, which, as a twenty-five-year-old administrative assistant at a nonprofit, was laughable. In fact, Ryan did laugh and said, "Well, we know who will oversee the money." And he did. He was the accountant. It was his job, both at work and at home, and every bill had always been paid on time. He filed the tax returns and handled investments. She hated all that stuff and he'd never given her a reason to worry, even now. But she didn't understand how everything could continue as usual without his job.

"Can't we talk about this? You never even told me what happened. I know it must have been hard, after all those years with the same company."

He put his hand on hers and shook his head. He obviously didn't want to discuss it. "It happened, it's over, I'm fine. We're going to be fine. I promise."

She opened her mouth to press, but he stopped her.

"What if we just focus on rekindling some of that spark? I know I'm no spring chicken, but I can learn some new tricks." He grinned, raising both eyebrows. "And if you're hoping to release my stress . . ."

Shea smirked. It was that humor that had attracted her to him in the first place. There was a time that every kiss brought butterflies. A time when they never slept in the same bed without being naked, back before kids and homework and house crises and fights over laundry and bickering about the kids—stresses that built with every passing year. He was right—with the kids out of the house, maybe they could get their own fresh start, right here.

Ryan excused himself and returned with the wine bottle, pouring a bit more in both glasses. They turned off the television and reminisced about some of their early escapades—the time they'd received a note from a neighbor to keep it down, the time they'd been kicked out of a taxi for making out "too aggressively," the time Shea's roommate had walked in on them. They laughed and kissed, and Ryan suddenly scooped her up, trying to cradle her in his arms. But he grunted, and she screamed. If he tried to carry her up the stairs, there was a good chance a tragic tumble and ER visit could be next for both of them. Instead, she took his hand, and they brought their glasses upstairs.

A little voice in her head chided her for being easy. She knew there was more to discuss. She hadn't gotten a straight answer about their financial situation. But the job loss had obviously been a blow to his ego, and maybe what he needed was her trust. Faith that he could still take care of them.

And it wasn't as if the bra was a smoking gun. It could have been . . . well, she wasn't sure. But he swore he didn't know . . . he'd looked her in the eyes. He'd sworn on their kids' lives.

"Bubbles?" Ryan called from the bathroom, and she nodded.

While he found the candles, she filled the big tub bought more than a decade earlier. It hadn't been used in years.

CHAPTER 7

April 9

KAT AND THE OTHERS GRABBED jackets, sunglasses, and some blankets for the boat ride to Put-in-Bay. It was only about fifty degrees by noon, but the cloudless sky offered bright sunshine that glistened on the calm water and warmed their faces while Tori navigated slowly through the channel. She throttled up as they approached Lake Erie, and, within minutes, the choppy waters, bouncing, and constant vibration made Kat sleepy. Their evening by the fire had continued well past midnight. Talk had turned away from Shea after Dee's explosive allegation of infidelity, and they'd focused instead on outdoing one another with tales of outlandish college mistakes and worst-date-ever stories.

"So, what's the game this time?" Dee yelled to Tori over the roar of the diesel engine.

"We'll have to come up with one together," Tori shouted. "I forgot to look online!" Tori always had some silly game planned for their getaways. During Kat's last trip to the lake a few years earlier, Tori had organized a relay race in which everyone had a balloon attached to the seat of her pants. While the first woman held the back of a chair, the next woman on her team had to come up behind her and pop the balloon with her pelvis, which, as it turned out, was easier if the first woman bent over the chair. They'd all howled, nearly wetting their pants, at the absurdly suggestive and disturbing maneuvers used to pop one another's balloons.

Tori nudged Kat with her hip. "Did you hear what Dee did during our last trip?" She turned her head and spoke up so everyone could hear the story. "We all drew dares from a jar and had to complete them while we were at the bar. Dee's dare was to convincingly fall down in a large crowd of people.

"You wouldn't necessarily assume that would be funny," Tori said. "But it turns out Dee could be a stuntwoman. She was so good at the pratfall that we all just about died laughing."

"I would have been afraid of hurting myself," Kat said, grinning. "I swear I've twisted my ankle just getting out of bed!"

"Yeah," Dee yelled, standing up. "But I'm spry," she added with a wild kick, her regular imitation of Molly Shannon's fifty-year-old *Saturday Night Live* character.

She joined them under the canopy. "My hip was covered in bruises the next day, but you all enjoyed it so much—and to see the look on people's faces when they saw me fall—I couldn't help myself!"

"What was your dare?" Kat asked Tori.

"I had to walk up to a table of strangers and do a cheer from high school."

"What was Shea's?"

She laughed. "Shea went a little rogue. Keep in mind, she was drinking a lot. But she climbed on top of the bar . . ."

"Oh no."

"You remember what Drew Barrymore did when she climbed on top of David Letterman's desk, as a kind of birthday gift?"

"What are you talking about?"

Lina and Evelyn, both laughing, looked at each other, and Lina counted to three. They both pantomimed a quick breast flash.

"Are you kidding me? Oh my God!" Kat said, laughing, shaking her head. "She was beyond bold."

"Well," Tori joked, "it wasn't like she had that much to show. Not like Dee or Evelyn over there." They both laughed.

"Remember, we all had to use fake names, too," Lina yelled from the bench behind them.

"Oh yeah," Tori added. "If you slipped and called someone the wrong name, you had to cough up twenty bucks. The last one standing got the money."

"So, who won?" Kat asked.

"Shea, of course. She made up all the names, though, so I don't think that was fair! They were all stripper names—like Amber and Trixie."

"I was Lolita," Evelyn yelled.

Kat grinned at the thought of Shea coming up with that one. Evelyn was the essence of conservative sophistication, with that silky, straight blonde hair, pearls, collared shirts—a walking Talbot's catalog, and the antithesis of a Lolita.

After they docked the boat and walked to Rudolph's, Tori ordered a couple of pizzas at the food counter while Dee grabbed a pitcher of beer at the bar. Kat wasn't a huge beer drinker, but it was tradition: always this bar, always pizza and beer, and maybe a few Bloody Marys. Had Shea come here, too? Maybe she had sat at the bar, drinking in a place she knew so well, on an island that had provided years of happy memories, but where no one knew her.

The room was filled with spring visitors, most of them watching the baseball games on the large flat-screens hanging from every wall. They'd been there about an hour when Tori, returning from the bathroom, said, "You guys, look!" and pointed toward the back of the bar.

Everyone followed her finger toward a group of men.

"Those are the guys we were hanging out with in November."

"I remember that one," Lina said, pointing toward the heaviest guy in the group. "Dave. He was funny." He had a big belly but skinny legs, almost like a Mr. Incredible doll.

"So it was their friend Blake that died that night," Tori said.

"Died?" Evelyn and Dee asked.

Tori began telling them what she'd already told Kat in the car, and Kat stared at the men. Maybe they knew how Blake died. Maybe it was relevant to understanding why Shea had come back here. One of them stood and took his pitcher to the bar, and Kat jumped off her stool and joined him.

"Hi," she said.

"Hello," the man said with a smile. "I'm Michael. And you are?"

"Kat. Katherine." She suddenly realized that she appeared to be a bold, confident woman approaching a man in a bar, none of which was true. "This is a little weird, but I came here with a group of friends"—she gestured toward their table near the front—"and they recognized your group of friends from last November. I guess they all hung out together for a while."

"Okay," he said. "I wasn't here in November, but I know several of my buddies come all the time. I guess that's possible."

The bartender appeared, and Michael ordered a refill.

"I know this is a strange thing to ask," Kat continued, "but one of my friends saw an article about a man who died on Lake Erie the night they were here. She thought it looked like one of the men they'd met."

Michael's expression turned somber. "Yeah, that was our buddy Blake." He pointed toward his table.

"I hope this isn't rude to ask, but we were wondering what happened to your friend that night. The article had no explanation."

"Actually, none of us know for sure. Blake was known to pull the occasional Houdini, so when they couldn't find him that night, they went down to the dock and his boat was gone."

"So he just left your friends?"

"Well, they figured he'd hooked up with a woman, but they were pissed because the water was too rough and they'd already decided to leave the boat behind and take the ferry home, just to be safe. His wife called the house around noon, because he'd promised to be back for their son's soccer game and she couldn't get ahold of him. That's when the search began."

Kat didn't visibly react to the married-with-children part. It wasn't relevant, though it was disturbing how casually he said it, as if cheating on one's wife was no big deal.

He told her how it had taken several days before the authorities found Blake's boat capsized on one of the small islands near Canada, and that the police had been a bit dismissive, because, after interviewing his friends, it was obvious that excessive alcohol had been involved.

The bartender arrived with the refilled pitcher, and Michael threw down some cash. "Well, Kat, it was nice—"

"I'm so sorry," she said. "I don't mean to hold you. It's just that we just lost a friend, too, Shea, and her death makes no sense. From what I understand, she and your friend met that night and hit it off. So—"

"Wait—Shea? What did she look like?"

"Like five seven, wavy blonde hair to the shoulders, big eyes, freckles, kind of exotic-looking."

"Beautiful, right? Like forty-five?"

"Yeah." Fifty-two, actually, but she wasn't surprised he'd say that. "When did she die?"

"Just last week. She was here," Kat said. "No one knows why, but she came to the island without telling anyone and was found at a B and B. She drowned in the bathtub."

"Wait, oh my God," he said. "We saw her. She came to Blake's memorial."

Kat felt her heart stop for a beat. "When? What? I thought your friend died last November."

"It was a missing-person case for a long time. His family refused to believe he was gone. But after all those months, they were finally ready to face the reality, and they held a service at a lighthouse on the island he had always loved as a child. We all saw her. Dave pointed her out to me and said she was the woman from that night."

"Hold on, can you come see my friends? Actually, let me just get them." Kat shuffled away and ran up to her table.

"You guys," she said excitedly, "he saw Shea here before she died! She was here for Blake's memorial. Come on." Kat led them over to the men's table.

Tori made quick introductions, and most of them recognized one another from the fall. "Didn't you all have other names last time?" Dave asked. Kat sensed irritation.

"It was just a silly game we played," Tori said.

Michael explained. "Their friend Shea, the one we met at the memorial—she's dead."

"She's *dead*?" Dave asked.

"Did you talk to her?" Kat asked.

"Yeah. We were startled to see her. I mean, she was the last person to see Blake, as far as we knew. We didn't know if they'd gone out on the boat together, if she had died, too, nothing. No one knew her real name, but police confirmed that no one else had been reported missing that night. We couldn't track her down, having no idea where you all came from. And then she just showed up at the memorial."

"So what did she say?" Tori asked.

Dave shook his head. "Not much. I wanted to know what happened that night. No one had ever been able to question her."

"I thought it was strange that she was there," one of the other men said. "I mean, how would she even know Blake died if she was from out of town and had nothing to do with it?"

"She only knew about it because I saw his picture in the local paper a couple of weeks ago," Tori said protectively. "I'm sure she found it upsetting, but she was only with your friend for a little while. We all headed home together that night."

"I saw them leave the bar together," Dave said.

"But she didn't go out on a boat with him," Tori said. "We would have known."

"That's right," Lina added. "Shea came back to the bar not long after she left with your friend. I remember she said he went off to get a bite to eat. Then we got on the ten o'clock ferry."

"So, wait," Kat said, focusing on Dave. "What did Shea say at the memorial? Was she alone?"

"Yeah," Dave said. "I grilled her a little bit, and she seemed genuinely upset by Blake's death. She said she had no idea what happened and that she was sorry, that she just wanted to pay her respects."

"It's so strange," Dee said. "We were all together only a few hours. No offense, but she hardly knew your friend."

"That's what I thought," Dave said. "I asked her if all her friends were here, too—meaning you all—but she said it was just one friend this time. Then she excused herself to the bathroom. I guess she snuck out, because we didn't see her again."

"She killed herself," Michael said.

"No, she didn't!" Kat said vehemently. "I didn't say that. It was an accident."

Michael raised his palms. "Sorry, I just assumed. You said she drowned in a tub."

"Well, it does seem like she knew something," one of the other guys said. "That is a strange coincidence."

"You didn't see her again?" Kat asked.

Dave shook his head. "We left about an hour later and caught the six-thirty ferry. No one was in the mood to do much."

It seemed like there wasn't any more to be said. The women made their excuses, left the men's table, and Lina said she was getting a bit tired. They grabbed their bags and started walking through the park toward the pier and Tori's boat.

Kat's jacket was zipped up, but she wrapped her arms around herself to fight the chill. "So, that's why she came to the island," she said, as much to herself as anyone else.

Tori was walking beside her. "The article I showed her about all those lake deaths didn't mention anything about a memorial."

Lina, just a few steps in front of them, turned back. "She must have found it online."

"But why go?" Kat asked. "Dee was right. They hardly knew each other."

Dee was walking along Tori's other side. "She did leave the bar with Blake for a little while. What if he asked her to go on the boat or something and she said no because he was too drunk, or maybe she knew that he went out on the boat and didn't say anything? Maybe she felt guilty, like she could have stopped him."

"Why didn't she say anything?" Tori asked no one in particular.

Evelyn piped in from behind. "Well, I'm sure it's not easy to tell your husband that you want to go to a memorial for a man you slept with a few months earlier."

Kat turned back and stopped. "Who said anything about sleeping together? I thought it was a harmless flirtation."

Evelyn stopped, too, scanning everyone's faces.

"Did she tell you what happened that night?" Tori asked. Evelyn looked off toward the docks but didn't answer.

"Evelyn, please," Kat said. "Don't you wonder what she might have been thinking? Why in the world she came here for the memorial of a man she'd met one time? I appreciate wanting to keep a friend's confidences, but she's gone."

"I saw them," Evelyn said. "That's all. They were by the bathroom in the bar. They were getting a little hot and heavy, if you know what I mean. And then they ran off together. I guess I just assumed. It wasn't my place to judge. She was having a rough time."

Kat turned away. Who was Evelyn to tell her that Shea was having a rough time, like Kat was just some acquaintance? Kat had known Shea for twenty years.

But why did it feel as if everyone knew more about what was going on with Shea than she did? Why did it suddenly feel like she'd lost Shea months before she moved away? She could hear the juvenile jealousy in her own thoughts. This was not a contest about who knew Shea best.

"Well, I guess we have our answer, right? She must have felt responsible. I mean, considering what happened after she went . . ." Lina didn't finish the thought, and Kat couldn't listen anymore.

The women resumed walking through the park toward the water. They crossed the long pier and boarded Tori's boat, each of them sinking into the swirl of questions that circled like the birds above the water. Tori began working the ropes. The rest of them sat in silence along the cushioned benches as water lapped the sidewalls.

Kat stared back at the park, the strip of bars and restaurants, trying to understand. "She told those men that she was here with a friend," she said to anyone who was listening.

"Maybe she just didn't want them to know she was alone," Dee said. "That Dave is pretty big. I can imagine if he seemed like he was accusing her of something, she might have been flustered."

Evelyn reached over to pull one of the blankets onto her lap. "I guess we'll never know. At least now we know why she would be so upset. Why she didn't tell anyone she was coming. Maybe she had some crisis of conscience about what happened that night."

Shea died here, Kat thought, staring at the giant park and quaint shops. Alone on this island. But why would she have been so upset by Blake's death? If only she'd known what Shea was going through. Maybe she could have helped. Maybe none of this would have happened.

The gentle rocking began to feel more like a washing machine. Kat was feeling breathless again. She inhaled deeply but couldn't get enough air. Heat rushed to her face, saliva pooling in her mouth. She was going to be sick. She stood and climbed onto the pier. She couldn't endure the rocking waves of the lake, not yet. "Don't go without me, okay?" she said, walking away. "I'm. . . going to get a soda."

"You okay?" Lina called out.

Kat didn't turn back, feeling choked by questions in her head, but offered a thumbs-up as she moved down the pier toward the park and shops.

Within a moment, an arm was around her shoulders. "I like soda," Tori said. "Can I come?"

Kat nodded, tears forming in her eyes. "I just don't understand why she came to his memorial. If she had something to do with Blake's death, wouldn't she be afraid to come back here and show her face?"

"It is a little weird," Tori agreed. "If she did something or knew something, I can't imagine why she would come here unless she wanted to tell the authorities."

Kat wiped her face as they pulled the door handle for the chocolate shop. Chimes rang as the door opened. The strong smells of melted chocolate and caramel were an effective mood booster, and the nausea from the boat immediately subsided.

"Soda, huh?" Tori teased.

"Soda and chocolate," Kat admitted. "Shea and I came in here together last time I was here. We declared it a new reason to love these trips to the island."

She and Tori ordered a brick of fudge and some other ridiculously indulgent treats to share with their friends and grabbed a couple of Diet Cokes.

"Best medicine for the blues," Tori joked as they exited the store. They strolled arm in arm along the shops of the main boulevard for a few minutes before reaching the corner.

Tori turned back toward the docks, but Kat pulled away.

"What is it?"

"Not yet."

"O-kay," Tori said, confused.

"She died here. We can't just leave."

"What do you want to do?"

"Where did it happen?"

"It was a B and B. Something with an *H*. Ryan asked me if I had any idea why she would have gone there. Like Hum . . ."

"Humphrey House," Kat said, a spark of recognition.

"Yes! How'd you know?"

"Come on." She led Tori toward a residential side street. "Shea and I strolled up this street the last time we got chocolate." The old homes, mostly of Victorian style, were stacked side by side on small lots along the street. The oak trees lining the road provided total shade from the sun, and suddenly, they felt the chill. "Look," Kat said, pointing toward a blue-and-green-sided Victorian with crisp white trim and a big front porch. A white-painted sign was staked in the small lawn out front: **HUMPHREY HOUSE BED & BREAKFAST**. Shea had pointed it out to Kat, sharing the fantasy of having a little summer place like it someday. A place where the kids would want to visit and bring the grandkids.

"Let's go," Kat said.

CHAPTER 8

December 3

SHEA AND RYAN STROLLED INTO the restaurant holding hands, looking for Dee and Charlie. It was hard to believe how much had changed in just one week. Shea felt like she was dating again, somehow able to block out everything that had gone wrong, focusing only on the fact that naked time was back, several times this week already, along with some much-needed laughter.

The double date was part of their plan to get out more. She had wanted to ask Kat and Mack, but Ryan had reached out to Charlie, and there was no way she'd complain when he'd taken the initiative. Ryan had pointed out that if the group got bigger, it would turn into a women's night at one end of the table. This felt more like a date. He was probably right. It was impossible not to end up laughing in the corner when all the girlfriends got together.

Besides, Dee was hilarious and sure to entertain Shea for hours. She just preferred Charlie in smaller doses and large-group settings. Ryan thought Charlie was fun—always up for card games or golf, always a good time—and he was a good audience, laughing at every one of Ryan's jokes like a laugh track. But Shea found Charlie a little too much. He looked at every woman as if he were starving and she was his next meal.

The restaurant, new to Maple Park, was crowded, the service horrendous. The waitress made up for it by bringing two rounds of martinis to the table with her excuses about the kitchen staff still working out the kinks. The foursome was completely intoxicated by the time their food arrived, so of course none of them was even hungry.

When the waitress finally brought the bill nearly three hours later, Charlie stopped her before she could walk away and, in his typical charm, with his action-hero good looks, said, "Marilyn"—having established earlier in the evening that he'd be addressing her like an old friend—"I believe we might need a little Sambuca, just to be sure that we don't forget an appropriate tip. Don't you agree?" Marilyn smiled and returned with more drinks, on the house, of course. Charlie was a master salesman.

When the foursome finally spilled onto the cold sidewalk, they laughed at the wind and thirty-degree air attempting to slap them sober. No chance. "Hey, the lights are up," Shea said. The lampposts along Main Street were now wrapped in evergreen garland and Christmas lights, shining bright like the evening was still young.

Shea and Ryan had finally gotten better in the last few years about ending things early to avoid the hangovers and exhaustion that had multiplied exponentially with age, but Ryan wrapped his arm around her waist. "Let's jump in an Uber and go dancing."

"What?" Shea asked, laughing. Ryan hated dancing. But she loved dancing, he knew that, and he'd said it was time to revive the spark. How could she say no?

Dee and Charlie never went home early, always having another party to attend, a band to see, or a new club to try, so they didn't hesitate.

"I know just the place," Charlie offered. Within twenty minutes, they were standing on the sidewalk of some street in Wicker Park while Charlie offered a password and secret knock at an unmarked steel door. Charlie was a piece of work. He'd apparently been there with clients. Moments later, they were inside a huge club, music thumping, hundreds of people grinding all over the dance floor.

After several more cocktails and an hour of dancing, the foursome finally found a place to sit: a big, semicircular velvet booth in a darkened corner. They relaxed into the deep, cushioned seat while the bass continued beating inside Shea's head. She'd probably feel the vibrations for days to come, but it felt great to break out of their routine and to surprise herself.

Dee leaned over and yelled in her ear, "It's good to see that you and Ryan are doing better."

Shea nodded and smiled at Ryan. He was leaning back with his hands stretched along the tops of the booth, like this was his second home, sweat soaked from the aerobic workout and bouncing his head to the beat of the blaring music. Shea was sorry she'd told her friends about her suspicions before Thanksgiving. Ryan was good friends with their husbands as well, and everyone knew husbands and wives shared secrets. It made her cringe to think of them all wondering what Shea had learned, what Ryan had said, what really happened. It was no one's business. She should have kept her mouth shut.

Shea leaned in. "How's Gina?" Dee's youngest, now at college, was never far from Dee's mind. She was plagued by life-threatening allergies that had sent them to the ER a dozen times over the years. Shea knew that watching her leave for college had been tough.

Dee started to answer, but Charlie leaned across the table toward them, joking that they looked like they were about to kiss. Their faces were only inches apart.

"Great idea!" Ryan shouted over the music blasting from a speaker overhead.

"I'll second that!" Charlie proclaimed with a wide smile, smacking Ryan on the arm. "I dare you," he said to Dee.

She laughed, looked at Shea, and raised her drink to her mouth before shouting, "Hey, you wouldn't be my first!"

"What?" Shea asked.

Dee practically spit out her drink, giggling. "Charlie loves it when I do this. It doesn't mean anything, but he's like a fourteen-year-old boy."

Charlie leaned in. "It's true, I am," he said with a wink.

Ryan looked positively giddy at the thought.

Shea couldn't believe it, and yet she said, "Okay," like she was fourteen again, being offered her first sip of beer. She closed her eyes as Dee came toward her. She pretended it was Ryan when Dee kissed her. Everyone laughed as soon as they pulled apart. Dee broke out in that Katy Perry song, "I Kissed a Girl," and Shea shook her head, feeling silly and childish, but wild, too, and thrilled to see her husband having a great time, to be rekindling something that had been missing for several years.

Charlie suddenly turned to Ryan and said, "Your turn!"

"What?" Ryan asked, suddenly inching away from Charlie. They all laughed at the implication. "Not with me, asshole! You get to kiss my wife."

Shea hardly knew what to say. How could she object when she'd just done the same thing? Did that make her a hypocrite? Some little part of her drunken mind thought it only seemed right, so when Ryan looked at her, she shrugged and said, "She's a good kisser."

Dee was seated between Shea and Ryan, so it was like she was a kissing doll, turning one way, then the other. Watching Ryan lean in, Shea shouted over the music, "Keep your mouth closed!" He laughed and innocently planted a closed-mouth kiss on Dee. It was weird, but not upsetting.

"Okay, my turn," Charlie shouted, hopping out of the booth and jumping back in next to Shea. Ryan didn't object, and neither did Dee.

Shea hardly knew what to say. Was this what Ryan meant by breaking out of their rut? Charlie's lips parted during the kiss, going for a full make-out, and Shea pushed him off, laughing. "Okay, okay. That's enough, mister."

"Come on," Charlie whispered in her ear. "I heard about you in Put-in-Bay. I'm jealous."

Shea pulled back and looked at him. He raised an eyebrow like they shared a secret. She looked at Ryan, who was oblivious to the comment.

Dee yelled over the speakers blasting above them. "Charlie thinks it isn't fair that we go off on our girls' weekends and have so much fun without him."

Before Shea could even process what Charlie might know, what Dee even knew about that night, Ryan asked Shea for one more dance. Everyone stood and headed to the dance floor, but she'd had enough. "Let's go," she begged, pulling him away from the crowd. Dee and Charlie waved good night, content to go at least another hour.

Heading home in the Uber, Ryan could hardly keep his hands off Shea. When they got home, they were too exhausted for much else, but they lay in each other's arms in their big, empty house, and Ryan said, "I've wanted to do that for a long time."

Shea wasn't sure if he meant he'd wanted to watch Shea kiss someone else, or if he'd wanted to kiss another woman, or Dee, in particular, but she hesitated to seek clarification. She wanted to indulge his fantasies, to take risks, and do whatever she could to keep their next twenty years together fun and exciting, but inside her a darkness rolled in, like a storm was coming.

CHAPTER 9

April 9

STANDING ON THE LARGE FRONT porch of the Humphrey House, Kat pulled open the wide, squeaky screen door to expose the glass-paneled oak entry door. The door was unlocked, and she pushed her way inside, first through the interior entry, its floor covered in mosaic tile, then through the second glass-paneled door, to the large foyer where a dark-stained, ornately carved stairway hugged the wall toward the second floor. A large doorway on her right framed out the view of an old Victorian fireplace against the far wall. "Hello?" Kat called out.

"In here!"

Kat and Tori followed the voice into the parlor. An older woman, perhaps seventy, with thick, short white hair, wearing what looked like a man's flannel shirt and jeans, sat on a love seat, reading a newspaper. The large bay window behind her provided the perfect reading light. Kat and Tori confirmed that she was Mary, the innkeeper, and they introduced themselves as Shea's closest friends, still in shock over her passing. The woman folded her paper and perched her readers atop her head.

"Oh, girls, sure, come and sit with me."

Kat and Tori sat in the two antique chairs facing the woman.

"I'm sure this must be difficult for you," Mary said. "Unfortunately, at my age, I know all too well the pain of losing close friends. It's really no easier than losing family, is it?"

Kat agreed. "We just stopped at that great chocolate shop, a little sugar therapy," she said, opening the bag and pushing it across the coffee table toward Mary.

Mary put up her hand. "Oh, thanks, but no. My sugar days are over. Diabetes."

"I'm sorry," Tori said.

Mary brushed her hand at the air. "No big deal. Ladies, I wish I knew something that would help you, but I'm afraid I don't. I tell you, though, in all my years of running this place, and even with all the crazy behavior I've seen, both from my guests and on the streets, I've never faced anything so tragic."

Tori took a piece of fudge. "So, she came on Saturday, and she was alone the whole time?"

"She checked in alone. She said she was expecting a friend to join her."

"Who was she talking about?" Tori asked Kat.

Kat ignored Tori's question, feeling a spark of hope. Shea had planned to come here with a friend. That didn't sound like suicide. "Did she say anything about who was joining her? Did you assume it was a man or a woman?"

Mary smiled sympathetically. "Girls, I know this must be hard. I so wish I knew something. But no, I didn't give it any thought, to be honest."

"How did she seem to you?" Kat pressed. "Could you sense if she was in a good mood, or preoccupied, or upset about anything?"

"Well . . . no. I didn't know her, of course, but she seemed fine. She was pleasant. She complimented me on the house."

"Did she tell you why she was here?" Tori asked.

"She said she wanted to explore the island and that she was look-ing at some real estate. I suggested she take my golf cart. I have a couple for the guests to use. Next thing I knew, it was a few hours later and she was being helped up the porch steps by my other guest. I guess he saw her outside. She was fairly intoxicated, so I helped her get settled into the room."

"What about her friend?"

"I asked her about that as I got her settled. She said something like, 'Looks like it's just me,' and collapsed onto the bed. I thought she was going to fall asleep any minute, so I told her she'd feel better in the morning, turned off the light, and left."

"I knew Shea for more than twenty years," Kat said, "and I've never seen her unable to walk. She might get silly after a few drinks, but I never saw her so much as stumble."

"So, she didn't seem depressed? Did she seem upset by this friend not coming?" Tori asked.

Mary thought about it. "No," she said. "Not visibly upset. I think she was a little embarrassed, actually. She mumbled something about how she should have eaten dinner. The next morning, she never came down to breakfast. Checkout is at eleven. That's when I finally went upstairs to look in on her."

Tori reached for Kat's hand, both bracing for the tragic finish to Mary's story.

"She wouldn't answer the door. I became concerned, so I let myself in." Mary stopped then, her eyes closed, and she shook her head.

No one spoke. Kat stared vacantly out the picture window behind Mary.

"I'm so sorry for your loss," Mary finally said. "I can tell she meant a lot to both of you."

Kat refocused on her, sensing the end of this interview. "What about the other guest who saw her? I wonder if he might have talked

56

to her a little more. It's so unlike our friend to come here without telling anyone, or to drink alone and get that inebriated. We can't understand it."

"Well, like I said, he was there, but I can't imagine they spoke much. He was just arriving at the same time and opened the door for her, I believe. When they came inside, we both helped her up the stairs, and I took over getting her to her room. He went to bed."

"And there is no way someone could have visited her after you left her?" Kat asked.

"I locked up the house after I left her and turned in. The police did some investigation of the room even though it appeared to be an accident. No evidence of anyone else there, far as I know. There was just no reason to suspect anything other than the obvious."

"Was her bedroom door locked when you left her?"

"I locked the door behind me, of course. I assumed she'd fall asleep any second."

The women thanked Mary. They walked back into the grand entry to leave, but Kat stopped, looking up the stairs. She couldn't leave yet. Maybe Shea didn't want her to. Kat didn't know if she believed in such things, but Shea had been here. Maybe some part of her spirit was still here. "Mary," she said, stepping back into the parlor. "Would you allow us to go up to the room where she stayed?"

"I suppose I can do that," Mary said. She stood and walked to the main desk to grab her keys. "I can't imagine why, but . . ."

"I don't know how to explain it. I feel like maybe it'll help."

They followed Mary up the stairs. "There are only four guest bed-rooms," she said.

"And do you sleep up here as well?" Kat asked.

"Oh no. I have the whole back of the house on the main floor."

She unlocked the door and walked inside. Kat and Tori followed. It was a beautiful, large room, with plush beige carpet and a four-post bed.

Kat walked through the room and into the large bathroom, eyes fixed on the black-and-white mosaic floor tile. She stared at the tub's claw feet, then up along the smooth, white porcelain. In a flash, she saw Shea's face, her body, lying there. She imagined Shea resting her head on a towel. But then, like her mind was a slide show, the picture suddenly changed, and she saw her friend under the water, her hair floating on the surface. Kat gasped, threw her hand to her mouth. It was impossible not to imagine how it must have happened. Tori's arm curled around her. "We should go."

Mary was still standing at the open bedroom door, and Tori and Kat walked back toward her, arm in arm. Kat stopped one more time, as if it would help to envision Shea's last moments.

She looked at the inside of the door. The door lock and a dead bolt.

"Mary, when you came up to check on Shea last Sunday, you said you unlocked the door. Do you remember if the dead bolt was engaged?"

Mary paused for a moment. "No. No, it wasn't. It's a separate key. I remember that I just had a room key in my hand. I wasn't carrying my full set."

"And you said that when you left her the night before, you locked the door behind you. Did you lock the dead bolt?" Kat asked.

Mary didn't answer right away. It felt like an eternity, waiting for her to think back.

"You know," she finally said, "now that you mention it, I think . . . no, I'm sure. I locked them both from the outside when I said good-night. I was carrying my set that night. Huh."

"But you definitely remember that the dead bolt was not engaged in the morning?" Kat said.

"Yes. Right. She must have unlocked it. Do you think that matters?" Mary asked. "She obviously got up to take a bath after I left her. Maybe . . ."

None of the women finished the thought. Finally, Mary said, "I suppose I could tell the police about the locks, if you think it might matter."

"Sure, yes, that seems like a good idea," Kat mumbled. "Thank you so much, Mary," she said. She quickly descended the stairs and left. She suddenly couldn't get out of there fast enough.

Tori followed Kat outside. "You okay?"

"Not really. Shea opened the door, Tori."

"So what? Maybe she heard a noise."

"Maybe she let someone in. And who was the friend she was expecting?" Kat asked. "She did not come here to kill herself."

"I agree."

"You do?"

"I mean we know why she came now. But what's obvious is that she was upset after going to the memorial, she got drunk, she filled a tub, and she took a bunch of pills."

"But she might not have been alone." Before Tori could answer, Kat pulled at her elbow. "Come on."

"What?"

"It's only been one week. She sat at a bar and got hammered, right here, probably not far from where we are standing right now. Someone had to see her. She's not exactly a wallflower. Every time we come to this island, we go to the same three bars. And it's early in the season. It couldn't have been too crowded, right?"

"True," Tori said. "The ferries only resumed service a couple of weeks ago."

"Let's go."

CHAPTER 10

KAT AND TORI WENT INTO THE TAVERN, the bar closest in proximity to the inn. Kat pulled up Shea's Facebook profile picture on her phone and asked every member of the waitstaff if Shea had been there the week before. No one recognized her picture.

"Come on," Kat said, leading Tori outside and heading toward Rudolph's.

"What about the girls?" Tori asked.

"Just send them a text. We'll bring them snacks for waiting."

It was nearly three o'clock; Rudolph's was now packed, and a musician was setting up near the front. Blake's friends were nowhere to be found. Kat and Tori made their way up to the bar, but every stool was taken, every nook filled with people wedging their way forward to place an order with the bartender.

Finally, Kat maneuvered into an opening. It was too tight for Tori to fit beside her. A woman stepped in front of Kat. "What can I getcha?" she said. Before Kat could even respond, she'd lined up three glasses, filled them with ice then vodka, tossed bottle caps into a garbage bin, and reached into a fridge for beers.

"I have a question," Kat said, leaning forward. "Any chance you were working here last Saturday?"

"Yep," she said. "Always working now that the ferries are running." She took off to deliver beers and drinks and collect cash before Kat could get another word out.

Kat sighed, having wasted precious time with pleasantries. When the woman was back within earshot, Kat raised her voice and asked for a Miller Lite. Maybe ordering something would garner a little more time. The woman grabbed one from below the counter within ten seconds. "Four bucks," she bellowed.

Kat reached for her purse and got the money, and the woman stood by, finally frozen until payment was received.

Kat handed her a twenty. "This is kind of a weird question, but our friend died on this island last Saturday. We were wondering if she might have come in here during the day."

"Are you talking about the woman from Humphrey House?"

"Yes," Kat said. "You know about her death?"

"It's pretty big news when something like that happens around here. We heard Mary was pretty broken up about it."

"Yeah," Kat continued. "We know she'd been drinking that day so we just wonder if she came here. This is one of the places that our friends always visit when we come to the island."

"You and millions of others," the woman said. "Anyway, she was here. Hold on." Several other people were vying for the bartender's attention.

Kat took a sip of her beer and looked around the room. Tori was now waiting by the door. Kat caught her eye and offered a thumbs-up. Shea had been here. Right here, maybe standing on this spot. Kat's right hand still gripped her phone, ready to share Shea's picture with whomever she could find. She scrolled through the hundreds of photos on Shea's Facebook page while she waited. Shea was smiling or offering a silly face in every picture. How had this woman been so sad and no one knew? Even if it was an accident, something was pressing her down.

The bartender returned, now getting something for the man beside Kat.

"So, you've seen this woman?" Kat asked, leaning in, pushing her phone toward the woman, so she could see Shea's photo.

"Well, sure."

Finally, some progress.

"But that's because her picture was in the paper. I didn't wait on her. Hold on," she said, departing again to help others.

A few minutes later she was back.

"Do you know who waited on her?" Kat asked.

"Doug thought he recognized her. That's what he told the cops, anyway. But he didn't overserve her, if that's where you're going with this."

"No, not at all. We're not trying to blame anyone. We just wonder if anyone talked to her."

The woman looked around. "Doug's around here somewhere. He's probably getting stock in the back."

"I'd be so grateful if you could get him. I'd just like to ask him a couple of questions."

"Kind of a full house," the woman said. "And as you can see, I've got about a dozen people trying to get my attention."

"I know, I'm sorry. I'll wait. As soon as you have a minute."

The woman moved a few steps away and began getting more drink orders. Kat remained frozen, hoping her presence would be a constant reminder, the silent pester.

A few minutes later, a bearded bald man with enormous biceps came out of the back with two cases of beer in his arms and set them on the counter nearby. The bartender nudged him, and pointed toward Kat.

He smiled and stepped over. "Hey, there," the man said. "I'm Doug. How can I help you?"

After introducing herself and her connection to Shea, she confirmed, "So you waited on her?"

"I did. Cape Cods. Two, maybe three max. Like I told the cops. Didn't seem like too much to serve over a couple of hours."

"Sure, no, she wasn't a lightweight. Did you talk to her at all? We don't understand why she was here alone."

"She wasn't alone. Like I told the cops, she was with this guy."

Kat's breath caught in her throat. "Who?"

"Well, I wouldn't know, would I?"

"I'm sorry. Of course. Could you describe the man?"

"Good-looking, about late forties, or fifty, I'd say. I don't know," he added, like Kat's questions were beginning to bore him.

"Did it seem like they knew each other?"

"She came in alone, I know that. But he joined her, and they walked out together after he paid. I remember, she seemed a bit drunk. She'd stumbled off the stool, and I looked at the guy as he helped her stand. He said not to worry, that they were just heading over to Humphrey House."

~ • ~

Back at Tori's house, the women were preparing dinner. Dee offered to make cocktails for everyone. She was feeling no pain. It was no wonder—she'd barely eaten all day and had been drinking her weight in wine since their return to the house.

The women chatted about their upcoming schedules. Tori was busy with college prep and sporting events for her youngest, and Evelyn was heading out of town for a couple of days, setting up some new computer network for a company in Denver.

Kat had work to do, too, but her priority was to visit Ryan and pay her respects, though what she really wanted to do was ask about Shea. Did Ryan think Shea intended this? Did he know about some alleged affair after Christmas that Dee mentioned? Was she really addicted to Vicodin? Did he know about the man at the bar on Put-in-Bay? But how could she ask? Even for close friends, there were limits to what felt appropriate.

Dee turned the discussion toward when the women would gather next. They threw dates around to one another, no one needing or asking for Kat's availability. She wasn't a part of this group anymore. She found her phone and went into a bedroom to call Mack. It had been too late to call when she'd finally gone to bed on Saturday night, but now, getting no answer, she guessed it was too early. He was probably still on the golf course. It was an hour earlier in Texas. They hadn't had a conversation since late Friday night, which was typical these days. Usually, she could blame international time zones for the disconnect. But, given the tension in their last conversation, the silence between them took on new weight.

When the women sat down for dinner, Tori stood at the head of the table. "To Shea," she said. "I'll never forget you." Everyone raised their glasses in agreement.

"To Shea," Kat said, keeping her glass high in the air. "Moving in next door was one of the luckiest events of my life." She began choking up. "I . . . miss you and . . ."

"Hear, hear," Lina said. They all sipped again before Lina pointed outside and raised her glass again. "To Shea—thanks for getting me to swing from that rope!" They laughed and agreed.

"To Shea," Evelyn said. "You were a really good friend, and . . ." She shook her head, apologized, and ran off to the bathroom.

Dee turned to the others. "Get that girl a diaper!"

"What is wrong with you?" Lina asked.

"What? It's funny! She didn't hear me," Dee said.

Dee then stood and raised her glass to offer her own tribute to Shea. "To Shea," she practically yelled. "Good riddance!"

Everyone gasped, and Dee swatted the air, drunkenly insisting that it was a joke. The dinner conversation turned uncharacteristically quiet.

"Come on, guys, I'm just kidding. We're getting so maudlin here. I thought this was supposed to be a celebration of her life!"

Everyone ate their dinner, and as Evelyn rejoined the table, Dee spoke up again. "I know. Who here has seen someone else's husband naked?"

"Okay, why would you ask such a bizarre question?" Tori asked. Everyone responded with nervous giggles.

"I just think the truth should come out," Dee said, surveying the women like she had a secret.

Kat looked around the table for someone's eyes to meet her own, for someone to share her dismay.

"I think it's safe to say no one has," Lina said.

"Wait, I've seen Ryan naked!" Tori said. She started laughing and turned to Dee. "You have, too!"

Dee turned red. "I have not!"

Now they were all laughing.

"It was here," Tori explained to Kat and Evelyn. "Like six years ago. We had Shea and Ryan, Lina and Bill, and Dee and Charlie up for a weekend. It got a little wild."

"Oh!" Dee said. "That's right!"

"My God, what are you talking about?" Kat asked. With Dee involved, anything was possible.

Dee took over Tori's story through her laughter at the inside joke. "We all drank too much."

"Oh, stop," Lina interrupted. "Now it sounds like we played some stripping game. Ryan and Shea obviously got romantic after everyone went to bed, that's all."

Tori leaned forward, taking over the story. "And I got up in the middle of the night for water and went to the kitchen. Dee was in there, too. Out of the blue, Ryan strolls in without a stitch of clothing on!"

Everyone howled at the image. "What? Why?"

"It was like he was sleepwalking," Tori tried to explain through giggles. "He looked dazed and confused and stumbled into the room. I was like, 'Hello, Ryan, what are you doing?' He turned back and went to bed. The next day he didn't remember it happened!"

"*Anyway*," Lina said, far less comfortable with sharing Ryan's embarrassing secrets, "I guess we can all take some solace in the two decades of memories we'll always have. Shea was one in a million."

~ • ~

After dinner, Kat cleaned up with Tori, Dee, and Evelyn, but Dee's intoxication put her on edge. Dee seemed angry about something. Evelyn had asked if she was okay, and she'd swatted at her and said, "You don't even know me."

Lina was on the back deck sitting under a knit blanket, looking up at the stars. Kat took her glass of wine and joined her. As she relaxed into the seat beside her, Lina offered a drag of her joint, but Kat declined. Her brief college affair with pot led only to some missed assignments, too many Taco Bell visits, and disturbing paranoia.

"You doing okay?" Kat asked.

"Así, así, mi amiga. I'm hangin' in there. And this," she said, lifting her joint and offering a mischievous grin, "es muy bueno."

"If you need anything," Kat began to say, though she stopped herself. What could she do, really?

Lina put her hand on Kat's knee. "Hey, we all die sometime. And I'm luckier than most. Worse case, I get to see Bill sooner than I planned."

Lina's husband, Bill, had suddenly died of heart failure two years earlier. Another life that ended too soon.

"What about you?" Lina asked. "You looked pretty pale back on the island. And that boat ride home was painfully quiet."

"Yeah, I can't stop thinking about Shea."

Evelyn pulled open the sliding glass door, popping her head outside. "May I join you two?"

"Please," Lina said. "Yes, sit."

Evelyn took the open chair. "I figured I should get out of the line of fire."

"Oh, boy. Well, you're safe with us."

Kat's contact with Dee had always been limited to large group gatherings, so they weren't close, but she had seen that Dee's tone could turn as an evening wore on, that her good-natured teasing could become more like true insults depending on the number of drinks she'd consumed.

"Tori was telling us inside that you two spoke with the innkeeper and bartender on the island," Evelyn said.

"That's right." Kat shared what they'd learned, what Shea had told Mary about expecting a friend. "So, she didn't tell those guys at the memorial she was with a friend because she was nervous," Kat said. "Someone was planning to come to the island with her. And she met up with a man at Rudolph's, and they left the bar together."

"So, I guess that man was the friend," Evelyn said.

"That's what I'm wondering. The bartender said the man mentioned that they were heading to the inn."

"But the innkeeper never saw a friend?" Lina asked.

"Nope. The other guest at the inn helped Shea inside and went off to bed. Unless—maybe that man was the other guest at the inn? But that doesn't make sense. When Mary put her to bed, Shea gave Mary the impression her friend wasn't coming. So if the man at the bar was the friend, then maybe they argued or something, she went to the inn alone, and the other guest helped her inside. Mary seemed sure that Shea never left her room again. She figured Shea would be asleep within minutes, that she was very intoxicated."

"But the bartender only gave her a couple of drinks?" Lina pressed.

"But the Vicodin . . . maybe that's why she was such a mess," Evelyn said. "Could the bartender give a name for the guy she was with?"

"No. I asked if he used a card. He paid cash."

Lina took a drag from her joint and held the smoke in her lungs.

Kat let her head fall back against the cushion, gazing at the stars high in the sky. "Doesn't it seem weird that whoever was supposed to join her never came forward to say anything?" she said to herself as much as to them. "And why in the world did she want to return to the island for the memorial of a stranger?" Blake's death had brought her to the island, she'd intended to go with a friend, and, somehow, she'd ended up alone. Kat had to know more.

Lina blew the smoke into the sky, watching it dissipate. "You know," she said, "you should talk to Georgia."

"Why Georgia?"

"After Shea left the bar with Blake, Georgia told me she didn't think it was safe. All his friends were still sitting around with our group, and he seemed nice enough, but Georgia thought she should go out and look for Shea. I didn't really see any danger. Shea's a grown woman, and I figured she could take care of herself. Besides, I thought perhaps Georgia was feeling jealous."

"Why jealous?"

"Oh, she was the one who pointed out the group of men in the first place, commenting on how cute Blake was, but he only had eyes for Shea. I watched Georgia several times trying to get involved in their conversation, but it was like she was invisible. I mean, really, it's Shea versus Georgia. Let's be real."

Georgia was attractive, but in a Betty Crocker kind of way. Shea oozed sexuality even in a pair of sweatpants. All she had to do was smile and expose that dimple, and men were mesmerized. "So, Georgia went after Shea. And you said they came back together, right?"

"Yep. Blake wasn't with them, and they both seemed oddly quiet. I doubt the others even noticed, because everyone was involved in conversations and they'd all had several drinks by then, but of course I was sipping my water. Shea looked like she'd been crying. I leaned over and asked if she was okay, but they both brushed it off and said, 'Of course—just tired.' I figured she might have simply broken down outside with Georgia about her marriage falling apart."

"And no one ever spoke of the guy—of Blake—again?"

"Not to me," Lina said.

"Me, either," Evelyn agreed.

Lina continued. "I didn't give it much thought after we all got back home. It was Thanksgiving. The kids were home. Everyone went back to life as usual, and I think we all hoped that whatever was going on with Shea and Ryan would resolve itself."

"Where is Georgia, anyway?" Kat asked. "Why didn't she come this weekend?"

"She said something about her husband's work schedule and kid issues," Lina answered. "I don't buy it, though—I don't think she wanted to come back here. She's taking Shea's death pretty hard."

CHAPTER 11

December 24

SHEA WAS IN THE KITCHEN making pancakes for the eighth time in two weeks while drafting a grocery list for the next store run, her fourth that week. Leigh and Stephen's return home a couple of weeks earlier had brought the normalcy, smiles, and laughter she'd been desperately craving. The kids' friends were back, too, bursting into her kitchen, raiding her fridge, entertaining her with college escapades, allowing her to ignore the mounting evidence that things were falling apart, despite Ryan's statements to the contrary.

Their brief rekindling had faded fast, and for the last two weeks, his days had been spent in his home office or away visiting his sick father in Detroit. She'd later find the office trash can filled with empty beer bottles, or he'd come home with the glazed eyes of a few martinis. The kids were oblivious, and she wasn't prepared to shatter illusions. It was easier to pretend, and Ryan was onto something: martinis helped. She'd successfully laughed and joked through three Christmas parties without anyone seeing the cracks.

When she popped into Ryan's office before heading out to the store, he jumped, quickly shutting the laptop. She turned and walked out without a word. He didn't try to stop her.

Later, when he left to do some last-minute shopping, she reviewed his search history. And there it was, two screens back from the more recent Netflix and sports news pages: a video of a woman in her bedroom, performing for the camera. Shea watched the woman's moves, her melodramatic portrayal of arousal. It was almost laughable. What was so enticing? Suddenly, a pop-up ad appeared. The raw and sordid message hit her like a punch in the gut: fuck buddy: 3 miles away. call me. Other women were not just out there, somewhere in cyberspace, far from their real life. Their tentacles reached out to entice viewers from their homes. And now where was Ryan? Supposedly shopping for the family? Or with a prostitute just three miles away? It seemed both absurd and possible.

When Ryan came to bed, she pretended to read her book. She couldn't look at him. He turned off his bedside lamp and climbed in, facing away from the dim of her light. "It doesn't mean anything, you know." She could hear his irritation. "It's nothing, really."

Shea shook her head and closed the book. "Where did you go this afternoon?"

He finally rolled over to face her. "I went shopping."

She didn't know what to believe. Was that pop-up some crazy advertisement that appeared during any pornographic content, or did it appear because the user of that particular computer had used that service or searched for that before? There seemed to be no way to know, but she was often struck by how anytime she was online in the days after searching for a product on the computer, pop-up ads would try to entice her back to those items, as if some unseen nefarious power always knew what she wanted and what ads were most effective.

She felt sick at the thought that Ryan could have done far more than watch videos, especially after her Herculean dedication to digging out of their rut, as he'd called it at Thanksgiving—bringing him coffee each morning, reaching for his hand when they watched television, and constantly initiating sex. It wasn't like it used to be, of course, but she'd been trying, and what had *he* been doing? Getting drunk, watching porn, and who knew what else.

"I read that e-mail you wrote last month," she said. "It's not just sex." Ryan had opened up to that woman, like she was someone he knew, someone he cared about it. "I thought you were going to stop."

"I was—I am," he stammered. "I will." He rolled onto his back then, looking up at the ceiling of their room, like he couldn't face her anymore. "You're the only woman I want to be with. I swear."

"You're drinking too much."

"I know."

Neither of them said another word. She put her book on the table, turned out the light, and remained with her back to him. He rolled toward her and put his hand on her thigh.

"I'm tired," she said, her eyes wide open. He removed his hand and rolled away.

Was it all nonsense? Maybe she was making too much of the porn. Maybe lots of men did that. And was that all it had been? Or was she just desperate to believe him?

She stared at the dark wall, unable to calm the storm inside her mind, the fear, the anger, the sadness that they might not fix whatever was happening. And she was not perfect, either. She had her own secrets. She'd made some terrible mistakes. She thought back to that night on Put-in-Bay, the blood on Blake's face, the moment he'd dropped to the ground.

She rolled toward Ryan, facing his back. "I don't want us to fall apart," she whispered.

He turned to her, and they looked at each other, though in the dark he probably couldn't see the tears streaming onto her pillow. He reached for her again, pulling her close, and they kissed, tentatively at first, but then intensely, desperately. She frantically pulled at his clothes and removed her own.

~ • ~

The next morning, Shea set the table and put some cinnamon buns and a casserole in the oven while Ryan and the kids slept in. Ryan later shuffled into the kitchen and, as she stood at the island, folding napkins, with the scent of cinnamon in the air, he stepped behind her and wrapped his arms around her, kissing her neck with a "Good morning" and "Merry Christmas." She lingered in his arms, relishing the illusion that everything was okay.

The snow was falling outside, a perfect backdrop to the perfect Christmas she was trying to create. Ryan built a fire in the living room and when the kids came down, everyone got coffee and sat around the tree to open presents. Shea had asked that they focus on sentiment more than stuff this year, assuring the kids that she and Ryan didn't need anything. She'd challenged Ryan to give her something that money couldn't buy. Leigh and Stephen, in a rare cooperative gesture, had conspired to gather years of bad photos—unintended double chins, red eyes, falls, and fails, rejects that would never be shared with the online world—and presented a picture book to Ryan and Shea, entitled *The Real Walkers*. Every photo brought laughter and vivid retellings of the captured moments.

Ryan gave Shea a new neon-green phone case. He said it glowed in the dark, which they both knew would come in handy because she so often misplaced her phone. It was a perfect gift—thoughtful, practical, and cheap. That would have been enough, but he passed her one more badly wrapped box.

Inside, she found a date book, the kind she hadn't used in a decade, thanks to smartphones. She leafed through the pages and found dozens of notes written throughout the year in Ryan's chicken scratch: *January 4, drink some wine with Ryan by the fire, January 12, watch Ryan do all the laundry, March 7, foot massage, thx to manservant Ryan.* She marveled at the time he'd spent coming up with all the entries, giggling and sharing only those rated PG and G with the kids. She finally stepped over and gave him a long hug, whispering, "Looks like it's going to be a great year."

Shea's gift to Ryan was similarly aimed at romance. Kat had offered her three vouchers for all-expenses-paid hotel stays in Chicago, New Orleans, and Las Vegas. She said Shea could use them for a girls' getaway or run off with Ryan for the weekend. But Kat insisted that if Shea used them, she had to order room service, eat at the hotel restaurants, use the spas, and report her findings on the in-room survey. It was part of Kat's job to analyze and address customer feedback, and Shea was thrilled to oblige. "We're booked downtown in three weeks," she said with a wink after he'd opened the envelope.

She stuck to giving the kids the essentials they'd asked for, clothes and gift cards for some of their go-to spots near campus. Everyone seemed content, laughing about the fact that only at Christmas could someone wrap socks and sweatpants and call them gifts.

Ryan suddenly excused himself and returned with more wrapped boxes. Shea tried to remind herself that this was a good sign—he obviously *had* been shopping yesterday. But the looming financial unknowns pulled at the smile she had painted. Her stomach tied itself in knots again as Stephen opened his gift, a MacBook, and Leigh opened hers, a fancy new camera. Both kids squealed with delight, but Shea's heart began pounding, and heat rose into her cheeks. It was insane, an illusion. He was unemployed! Still keeping secrets and pretending that nothing had changed.

"I'll get a bag for the trash," she said flatly, trying not to spoil the moment for the kids. She stood to leave, but Ryan jumped up, grabbing her hand. "Babe, don't worry. I know what you're thinking, but it's fine. I swear. Here, I have a little something for you, too." Before she could say another word, he presented her with a small box, the trademark Tiffany blue with white ribbon.

Leigh jumped up. "Oh, Dad, what did you do? Mom, open it!"

Shea opened the box to reveal a diamond infinity ring set in platinum. It was identical to the wedding ring she already owned. She'd joked once about the fact that she should have another one, to sandwich the engagement ring on her finger, though she never meant it and never even cared about jewelry. But Leigh swooned at the sight of it and Stephen patted his dad on the back. "Way to go, Pops."

Ryan took the ring from the box, slipping it onto Shea's finger, and said, "This is because I wish I could marry you all over again. Here's to another twenty-five years."

~ • ~

Ryan and Stephen spent the afternoon watching football and drinking beer, and Leigh hung out with her friends most of the day. Shea tried to let her anger wash away, focusing on the good in the house, but she'd finally gone upstairs to bed, exhausted by the effort.

She looked out the window, and she could see Kat and Mack in their living room, cuddled up on the couch. They were probably watching a movie. She was tempted to knock on their door, to break up their relaxing evening and unload on Kat over a bottle of wine, to finally tell her about Ryan's job loss, and her fears, and his drinking, and the porn, but it was Christmas.

Kat would soon be gone, anyway.

Shea stood in the bathroom, brushing her teeth, wondering if she and Ryan were strong enough to weather whatever was happening between them. She smiled and frowned at her reflection, at the wrinkles that appeared with each expression, reminding her that nothing lasted, not her looks, maybe not even their marriage. She searched the medicine cabinet for eye cream, something to help stave off the outward signs of her slow march toward decline. She couldn't find it. Instead, she found her Vicodin prescription from last spring. Those magic pills had taken away the shoulder pain, made her a little loopy, maybe too relaxed. She opened the bottle—still half-full. Perfect.

She lay in bed with a book but was soon rereading the same pages several times. The Vicodin was kicking in. When Ryan came up soon after, she could see the buzz in his eyes. It wasn't the time to talk, but as he climbed into bed, she couldn't stay quiet. "What are you doing?"

"Going to sleep," he said, grinning, refusing to match her tone.

"How can you spend all that money—"

"Stop," he said, his anger sudden and sharp. "Haven't I always taken care of us?"

She didn't respond.

"Do you see the lights? Do you feel the heat? Do you see any reason to panic?"

"Ryan . . ."

"Please, Shea, just trust me. I'm not an idiot."

"But how can I when—"

"Jesus," he yelled. "It's Christmas. Can't you just be happy?"

Before she could answer, he pulled off the covers. "I'm going to watch some TV."

CHAPTER 12

April 10

ON MONDAY MORNING, KAT, EVELYN, and Lina left in the first car to return to the real world. Evelyn was driving, and Kat took the backseat. Tori needed to stay behind to deal with some maintenance guy, and Dee volunteered to stay with her. Dee was undoubtedly hungover and probably still sleeping after last night's record-breaking, college-level intoxication.

Everything about Dee during the weekend felt off. She'd suggested dares and outrageous stunts for laughs last night, but she'd seemed angry. It was hard to know if her behavior was entirely about Shea or not. Dee was another recent empty nester, and Kat wondered if that was its own struggle. For two decades, Dee's world had centered on her kids and volunteering at schools, and suddenly it was over. Kat's job had often made her feel like a bad mother—the missed games, the unmade lunches, those days when Peter was sick and she was out of town. But after Peter headed off to college, she'd become thankful for the escape from their suddenly quiet home.

As Evelyn drove along the highway, Kat imagined Shea's last hours in reverse, her arrival at that memorial, her ride over on the ferry, her long drive to Ohio alone. She hated driving long distances, always saying that two hours was her limit. Beyond that, she'd joked once, it was like she had narcolepsy. Ryan did most of the driving during family road trips, and she'd never volunteered to drive on any of the women's previous getaways to Ohio. Five hours alone in the car was a long time.

Kat let her head fall back and took another deep breath, loudly expelling the air. Maybe she was subconsciously trying to channel that yoga mantra: "Good air in, toxins and stress out."

"Dee was a little loco last night, huh?" Lina said.

An understatement.

"You missed her rapid-fire roasting while we cleaned up the dinner," Evelyn said. "Let's see, she made fun of Tori's clothes . . ."

"Well, that's easy," Kat joked. They all thought Tori was the only woman in the entire Chicago area aware of, and wearing, the latest New York and Paris fashions. The Midwest was at least a year or two behind the trends. She'd shown up in startling combinations for so many years, they were no longer startling.

"I said something about liking Tori's shirt, and Dee looked at me with a deadpan expression and said, 'Why are you here, again?'"

"Ouch," Lina said. "I hope you didn't let that get to you. Some people just get mean when they drink too much. I'm guessing I was spared because of the cancer?"

"Probably," Evelyn smirked. "Tori even said something about how I had obviously dealt with suddenly losing a spouse, asking how I got through it, but Dee cut me off and said, 'Getting dumped is not the same.'"

"Holy crap, what is wrong with that woman?" Lina asked.

Dee wasn't wrong, it wasn't the same, but they all knew that Evelyn's husband had left her, after twenty years, without a word. Weeks later, she heard from a lawyer. No explanations. No warning. In that way, it was easy to see the parallel.

"Dee was hammered last night," Lina said, "and there's just no excuse for that behavior, but let's not give it another thought. Whether

78

a spouse walks out or drops dead on your kitchen floor in the middle of breakfast, it's not easy."

The women fell silent. Evelyn and Lina had pulled those painful, heavy boxes of loss out of storage, and no one knew what to do with them.

Kat suddenly felt lucky, despite the last several months. A husband she loved, who was alive, in good health, and missing her right now. She pulled out her phone. Miss you. Heading back to Chicago now. Talk later? She hoped he'd see it as the olive branch she intended. She was determined to plan something special upon her return, a romantic gesture to show Mack that she wanted to fix things. Maybe they could shake off the residue of arguments and hit reset.

When they finally neared Chicago, Kat asked Evelyn to drop her at her hotel downtown.

"Don't do that," Lina said. "You should stay with me this week, at least until your meetings on Thursday and Friday." Kat considered it. "You still haven't seen Ryan or Georgia. Just stay with me. I'd love the company. That house is too big and empty with the kids off at school."

"Thanks, Lina. That sounds perfect."

"Well, all right, then," Evelyn said. She bypassed the exit ramp for the city and turned west on the Eisenhower Expressway.

~ • ~

For most of the afternoon, Kat sat at Lina's dining room table, laptop open, cell by her side, absorbed in e-mails and conference calls. At six o'clock, she walked up the street to Georgia's house.

The air was crisp under a still-pink sky. She'd been to Georgia's several times over the years—book clubs or cocktail parties or happy hours—but they'd never done a one-on-one, and she suddenly felt nervous. Georgia was unlike Kat in obvious ways—a soft-spoken southern transplant who'd married her high school sweetheart and excelled with grace as a domestic CEO and Martha Stewart–level crafter. There was something about Georgia's accent, her tenor, that always reminded Kat of Shelby in *Steel Magnolias*.

When Georgia opened the door, Kat found a frazzled woman, nearly unrecognizable compared to the never-without-makeup mask she'd come to expect, even at yoga. Georgia looked like she hadn't slept in days, her eyes puffy and circled in darkness.

"Am I too early?"

"No, no. Come in!" Georgia said in that soft southern lilt, pulling her in for a hug while the chaos of shrieking children poured from the home. She smiled, patting her haphazardly tied-up hair. "Just don't look at me. I'm a wreck." She was barefoot, wearing yoga pants and a T-shirt partially covered by a dirty apron—a far cry from the woman who, even at the grocery, looked perfectly groomed. Georgia had one in college and two in high school but had startled the neighborhood with a surprise pregnancy at forty-two.

Her eight-year-old, Tess, ran past them with two friends into the front yard, like caged animals that had spotted an open gate. Despite the season, each child was dressed in a Halloween costume. It made Kat momentarily nostalgic for those moments—the silliness, the laughter of children that disappeared far too quickly—but Georgia's exhaustion was clear when she embraced Kat a little too long, as if holding on helped hold her up. Kat finally broke free, and Georgia yelled for the kids to get back inside.

The kitchen table, mostly covered with crafts, offered two wine-glasses and a plate of cheese and crackers at one end. Even in chaos, Georgia was the eternal southern hostess.

"Please, sit. I'm dying to sit," Georgia said.

Kat shared a few stories of the weekend at the lake, and Georgia embarked on what seemed a well-rehearsed excuse for missing it. She wasn't a great liar. She looked at her glass while explaining how her husband's work crisis had prevented her from joining them. When

Kat shared what she'd learned about Shea being on the island for Blake's memorial service, Georgia turned pale and took a deep breath, moving her focus to the windows. She then drank most of the wine in her glass.

"What is it?" Kat asked.

Georgia turned to Kat and smiled. "Huh? Oh, nothin', hon," she said before turning her attention to an imaginary hangnail that she began to gnaw on.

"Listen," Kat continued, "Lina told me that you went out to look for Shea back in November after she left the bar with Blake."

"True. Why?" Georgia poured more wine for them both, took another sip, and peered past the kitchen into the family room, where the girls were now playing.

"She said that you two returned together and both seemed upset. She thought Shea looked like she'd been crying."

"No, that's not true," Georgia said. Her voice actually cracked, as if she were truly the worst liar on the planet.

"It's not like it matters now," Kat said. "She's gone, and Blake is gone. I just want to know what was going on with her. Please, just tell me what happened in November. It doesn't make much sense that she'd go to his memorial unless there was more to it."

Georgia took another sip, put down the glass, and took a deep breath before rising from the table and walking to the doorway. "Tess," she said to her daughter, "could you and your friends head down to the basement, please? It's just a little loud up here." Georgia returned to her seat, and the women silently looked at each other while the sounds of laughter and footfalls faded slowly down the stairs.

"I did go out looking for her," Georgia began. "She'd been incredibly flirtatious, to put it mildly, and they were both drunk. It seemed like a bad choice."

"And did you find them outside?"

Georgia took a cracker, breaking it into pieces. "I looked around out front and didn't see her. I started walking through the park. I didn't see her . . . but then," she said, her focus firmly on the broken crackers, "she was running toward me. I was sitting on a bench." She finally looked up, took a deep breath, and ate a cracker.

"What happened?"

"Shea collapsed, crying. She said that he took her down to the docks to his boat. It was pitch-dark, she was alone, and she suddenly realized she was in over her head. She said she'd kissed him but had literally lost her balance when she closed her eyes. She'd wanted the harmless flirtation but never intended to sleep with him. I guess he didn't like being turned down."

Having just walked through that park, with the mass of small boats parked along piers that would have been entirely cloaked in darkness after sunset, Kat could almost see the fear on Shea's face as she listened to Georgia's story.

Georgia offered a cracker and cheese. Kat took it, and Georgia took another for herself before continuing. "Shea said he'd become aggressive and angry when she tried to pull back. It had become a fight, and she hit him over the head and ran. She left him at the boat. She was horrified that she'd gotten herself into such a situation."

"She hit him over the head? With what?"

Georgia thought for second, chewing her food. She took another sip. "She didn't say. I said we should go to the police and report the attack, but Shea wouldn't have it. It was her word against his. She said she'd brought it on herself, and she begged me not to tell anyone. Not even Tori or the others. She wanted to go home."

"And so you went back to the bar and everyone left?"

"Yes." She began wiping at the table, scooping up the crumbs from their crackers, carefully dropping them back onto the tray.

"And did you ever ask her if she thought he was okay?"

Georgia looked out the window.

"Please, Georgia, just level with me. They're both dead. It doesn't matter. I just need to know."

Georgia finished the remaining wine in her glass. "Shea brought me the article Tori showed her a couple of weeks ago. She was terrified that . . . that she'd been responsible."

"By hitting him on the head? Did she tell you any more about it specifically?"

Georgia shook her head. "She'd searched online for any details of how he died or when he'd last been seen, but she couldn't find anything. And when she found out about the memorial, she wanted to go. She said his friends would know if he ever returned to the bar that night. And if he had, she'd know it wasn't her fault. She said she couldn't live with the idea that he might have fallen into the water, or passed out on the boat and somehow it became unmoored. She said she hadn't slept in days."

"Why wouldn't you tell Ryan all this? Don't you think it would help him to know why she went there?"

Georgia picked up the tray of cheese and crackers and walked to the sink, ready to be rid of the mess. "It's not like the truth would help the situation," she said before dropping the tray on the counter and turning back to Kat. "How would it help to know that Shea went to the island because some strange man she'd hooked up with was dead and she felt responsible? And what if that man's family found out? What if they decided Shea *was* responsible? If they decided to go after Shea's estate for wrongful death or something? How could any of this get any better by telling Ryan?"

Kat didn't respond. It was difficult to imagine how the dominoes could fall with so many unknowns.

Georgia came over and poured more wine into her own glass. "I mean, if that happened," Georgia continued, "I could be forced to testify about what she told me. How could I live with that?" Georgia lifted her glass with a trembling hand as she took a sip.

Kat stood and took Georgia's wineglass, set it on the table, and took Georgia's hands in hers, wordlessly guiding them both back to sitting. "Stop. It's okay. It was an accident. No one knows what happened to him, and no one ever will. Shea hit him in self-defense, and frankly, we'll never know if she even hit him very hard. We saw Blake's friends on the island. There's no investigation. It's over. All of it."

Georgia's eyes welled with tears as if there had been some relief in sharing the secret.

"Come on," Kat said, pulling her in for a hug. They both took cleansing breaths during the embrace. Kat was not the only one gasping for air these days.

Kat poured herself a bit more wine, and they both sipped in silence.

"Were you planning to go with her?" Kat asked.

"No!" Georgia stood from the table, like it was the most outrageous question, went to the sink, turned on the water, and began rinsing dishes. "I didn't go. I was here. Ask anyone."

"Okay. I only ask because she told Blake's friends at the memorial that she was with someone, and she told the innkeeper she was expecting a friend. I was just curious."

Georgia finished rinsing the plate, turned the water off, and dried her hands before returning to the table. Something was weighing on her, and it was obvious she had no idea how to respond to Kat's questions.

Kat put her hand on Georgia's. "No one blames you for anything. No one is even inquiring about any of this. I'm just trying to get my head around it all. I want to understand what Shea was going through, what she might have been thinking about."

Georgia dabbed her eyes as they filled with tears. She shook her head and focused on the table, unable to look at Kat. "She wanted me to go with her. We talked about it. But I thought it was a mistake, I thought she was looking for trouble, and I begged her not to go. I said that I wouldn't go, hoping that would convince her to drop it. I . . ." She couldn't speak or catch all the tears before they trickled down her now flushed cheeks.

"Hey, this isn't your fault."

"But if I had gone with her . . ."

"Stop." Kat pulled her into another embrace. Georgia had obviously been holding it all in for more than a week now. "It's not your fault."

After a long hug at the door, Kat left and walked back to Lina's, grateful to have gotten some answers. She had known Shea's friends would be heartbroken over Shea's death, but it had never occurred to her that any of the others would feel the same guilt that she did. Kat's torment over Shea's call was just like Georgia's. They were both feeling the weight of knowing things might have gone differently, if only . . .

Hearing what really happened in November, what pulled Shea back to the island, explained a lot—certainly Georgia's hesitation in returning to the island, and her reticence in sharing the truth. But Kat was left with new nagging questions: Could Shea have accidentally killed that man—or at least contributed to his death? And what if someone knew what happened between them? Maybe someone at the memorial saw Shea and sought revenge. The fog was lifting around why Shea had returned, but now there was something even more troubling, a possible motive to harm her. What if that man at the bar was connected to Blake?

Like a child telling herself ghost stories, Kat's adult, rational brain continued to insist that Shea had been alone in her room, with no sign of foul play. She could have simply been upset by the memorial. Perhaps she blamed herself, and the alcohol and pills were evidence of a woman desperately trying to wash away the stranglehold of guilt.

CHAPTER 13

April 10

BACK AT LINA'S, KAT PHONED Mack. It had been almost three days since they'd had a conversation, but she was determined to have a good talk and put the argument of Friday night behind them.

"Hi," she said when he picked up the call.

"Hey, babe," he said. And that was all it took. She heard his tone and knew that things were okay.

"Sorry I haven't been able to reach you until now," she said.

"It's okay. I know you're having fun."

It was a tiny dig, like a needle prick. "I wouldn't say it's fun. I *am* here because Shea's dead."

He didn't respond, and she immediately regretted her words. She'd sounded defensive. The residue of Friday's argument was still there.

"I wish you were here," she said.

"Me, too. How was Catawba?"

Kat shared what she'd learned about Shea's death, why Shea had gone to the island, as well as her nagging need to learn more.

"It sounds like you're looking for an explanation, but . . . it sounds obvious."

Now it was her turn to stay quiet. It wasn't obvious.

"You know why she went. You know why she might have been upset. You just don't like the idea that someone you idolized for almost twenty years could be a drunk or a drug addict."

He'd found a way to put them both down in one fell swoop. "One, I didn't idolize her; two, she was not a drunk or an addict; and three, we have no idea what she was thinking that night."

There was a long pause. "Listen, I'm sorry. I don't mean to be insensitive. Can we just talk about something else for a moment? How's your room?"

Sometimes her hotel put her up in the swankiest suites; other times, just the basics. She was supposed to have a sense of all options. "Actually, I'm at Lina's. She offered, and I thought that would be nicer, at least until my meeting on Thursday."

There was a beat of silence before Mack said he had to go and quickly disconnected.

Kat stared at her cell. What was that? What did she do now? Here she was trying to understand Shea, and she couldn't even understand Mack. She knew he'd been annoyed that she would be in Chicago all week, but what did it matter whether she was downtown or at Lina's?

Kat had made a career of managing people without being terribly good at confrontation. But she tossed all night, arguing with Mack in her mind, going through all the things she'd wanted to say but hadn't. What came out morphed into the real problem. Mack should have come with her. Both Shea and Ryan had been his friends, too. Kat was heartbroken, and Mack had returned to Chicago three times for work since they'd left in January. Why wouldn't he come with her on this trip? *He should be with me*, she thought. They should be mourning Shea together, offering support to Ryan together, talking through all of this together. They used to do that.

~ • ~

On Tuesday morning, having slept only a few hours, Kat was still irritated by her conversation with Mack. She took care of the daily onslaught of e-mails and returned several work-related calls before Lina offered a welcome distraction—cranking up her music and schooling Kat on how to make a proper empanada. They figured Ryan had received enough lasagna at this point. Lina said he'd be ready for some Cuban love.

At two, Kat brought the food to Ryan. Lina wasn't up to making the delivery, but Kat had to see him and was glad to not arrive empty-handed. After all, Shea had rallied the entire neighborhood to bring meals to Kat's house four years earlier when she'd had knee surgery and been unable to walk for three weeks. In fact, it was Shea's thing. Every time a friend faced a medical crisis, from broken bones to cancer, Shea started the e-mail chains and got the troops organized to help the affected family. And now Ryan was alone. Kat assumed the kids had returned to school, and she hoped someone else had taken on Shea's role of looking out for the wounded.

Everything about passing the walkway between her old house and Ryan and Shea's house stung. She looked at Shea's north-facing window that faced Kat's south-facing window. Thousands of conversations had bounced through those openings. "Get over here," Shea once said from that window as Kat walked toward her front door one evening. "You've got to see this." When Kat entered Shea's, the living room had been transformed. She could only see blankets, at least six of them, propped and perched on top of a new furniture arrangement like a roof. "They spent all day on that," Shea said with pride.

The boys had created a fort across the entire living room. Little Peter heard Kat's voice. "Mom, Mom, come in!"

"Well," Shea said, getting down to her knees, "come on. It's awesome." Of course, Kat had followed.

Now, as Kat rang the bell, she feared finding Ryan in a dark corner, shades drawn, Chinese takeout strewn all over the coffee table.

Instead, Ryan answered the door in workout clothes, his face flushed, his hair wet with sweat, a water bottle in hand.

"Kit Kat!" he said with a big smile. He looked surprisingly well. He'd always had a little extra weight in his face and belly, nothing too serious, just the markings of a man who said yes to beer and burgers with regularity, but he looked about twenty pounds lighter than when they'd said good-bye in January.

"I'm sorry to pop in on you like this," Kat said. "I just needed to hug you and bring you food." She raised the tray. "Lina's homemade empanadas."

"Come in, Kat, please. I'm so glad to see you. I'm sorry I'm such a mess. I think we should skip that hug for now. I stink." She laughed and agreed, and he led her into the kitchen. Kat explained that she was in town for work all week and staying with Lina for a few days.

When Ryan opened the fridge, Kat realized the troops had obviously rallied. Every shelf was filled with Tupperware, Pyrex, and tin pans. "I guess you didn't need that, did you?" she said, nodding toward the dish he was now shoving into the tiny bit of unused shelf space.

"Why do you think I just went for a run?" he joked. "I've never been presented with so much food in my life. And, as luck would have it, I'm a stress eater."

"I don't know about that, Ryan. You look great. I hope that's not awful to say."

"Thanks," he said, shutting the fridge and pounding his belly. "Pretty good, right? I lost a little weight before all this happened. Part of a New Year's resolution. But I'd really like to avoid putting it all back on. Look," he said, opening the freezer drawer to share the additional ten containers covered in frost. "I'm set for, like, three months."

"Are you busy right now? Because I could make us some coffee while you go shower. I'd love to catch up. Or I can come back if you'd—"

"No, that's a great idea. Thanks, Kat. I'll be quick. You know where everything is. Make yourself at home."

Kat got the coffeemaker started and browsed through the tinfoil-covered containers while she waited, amused by the labeling so many friends had provided. Each explained how long and at what temperature to heat the dish; some even included tips on what to have with it: *Pairs well with a Caesar salad.* It seemed absurd. He was not a child, and it was not a contest for who could present the best meal. But everyone's heart was in the right place, she knew. And if it was a contest, it was clear that Evelyn would win. It had barely been a week, and there were three dishes from Evelyn in separate containers. Maybe she knew that daily casseroles were the best tonic.

A small mountain of condolence cards sat on the kitchen counter. Kat sat at the table and waited.

When Ryan returned to the kitchen, she stood, waving toward the cards. "These must make you feel good."

"Yeah. That woman was loved by a lot of people. I don't even know half those names!"

"Sorry I didn't send a card, but I'm just . . . heartbroken," Kat said. Her voice cracked, and she swallowed hard, determined not to cry.

"Me, too."

They hugged and both took deep breaths before Ryan finally pulled back. "Come on."

They went to the patio with their mugs. The flowerpots had not yet been filled for the summer season, and there was a good chance they never would be, but Shea had already put out all the summer furniture, done the spring cleanup, and readied the yard for entertaining. The air was humidity-free and crisp, and the budding greenery was hard to resist.

Ryan sipped his coffee, staring into the yard. "Had you spoken with her recently?" he asked.

"No." She couldn't say any more than that. She had nothing to offer, only questions. And she wasn't even sure she had a right to ask them.

"So, you're in town all week?" he asked, as if they could keep the conversation light.

"Yep. I've got some meetings at the hotel at the end of the week, but I'm staying with Lina for a few days."

"Oh, speaking of, thank you for the hotel vouchers. Shea surprised me with those at Christmas. That was really generous."

"My pleasure. Did you get to use any of them?"

He nodded, like he needed a moment to recall. "We did."

Men. No details, just the facts. "Where did you go?"

Ryan looked toward the yard. "The one downtown," he finally said. Staying at Kat's hotel with Shea was probably the last thing he wanted to think about.

She didn't want to make things worse or upset him, but since she had relevant information . . . She took the plunge.

"Ryan, do you know why Shea went to the island?"

"I know what you're thinking, Kat. What everyone's thinking."

"What do you mean?"

"She lied about where she was going, she went somewhere by herself, far from home, and the pill bottle was empty. But it was an accident."

"I agree. I can't believe . . ."

His brows furrowed as if he didn't even want Kat to use the word. "It's what everyone's thinking. Even the kids. They're all looking at me, wondering if there were signs. It's not what happened."

Finally, someone who wasn't dismissing this as suicide.

"As soon as we get the tox screen back, it'll show that I'm right. It had to be an accident. We were fine. We were good, Kat. None of it makes sense . . . I can't even believe she did that drive alone."

"I know. She joked to me about highway narcolepsy."

"Well, there was actually more to it. She never told you about her mom?"

"Yeah, she died when Shea was a teenager, right?"

"She fell asleep, driving alone on the highway. Shea had an irrational fear of doing that to her family. She never went more than a few hours. In twenty years, never . . ."

It was the right opening. She needed to tell him what Georgia had shared. Blake's death had obviously been weighing heavily enough . . .

"But," Ryan continued, "I'm never going to understand it. The innkeeper said she'd mentioned real estate."

"And you didn't know about that?"

"No. But that doesn't mean anything. It was her business. She loved to look. And I've learned that someone drowns in a tub every day in America, and out west, where people are drinking alcohol in hot tubs, it happens like three times as often. People fall asleep or pass out and just slip under the water."

He made it sound plausible.

"Did you know about the pills? Evelyn said something that suggested Shea was addicted."

Ryan shook his head. He frowned as he sipped his coffee.

"I hope you know none of us are spreading rumors. We just miss her and spent the weekend together. It was hard not to share a little information, trying to make sense of everything."

"Well, I'm surprised Evelyn said that." His irritation at the rumor was obvious.

Kat suddenly felt guilty for even sharing it.

"I didn't realize she'd shared the pill issue with anyone."

"So it's true?"

"Yes and no. Yes, there was an empty pill bottle, but no, she was not an addict. She got a prescription last spring, but she stopped because they made her feel a little too good. As far as I knew, she hadn't had any pills in more than eight months. She wasn't a drug addict, Kat."

Kat nodded. "I'm sure it was an accident." She didn't know what else to say. She wondered if she should mention the man at the bar and whether he might have been a friend, but despite their twenty years of history, she felt like she was crossing a line. And how would it help? It might only make Ryan feel worse. Besides, the police had probably already told him.

The silence between them hung in the air, and Ryan's gaze was frozen, focused on the fire pit deep in the yard. She couldn't imagine being in his shoes, the utter devastation he must be feeling.

"Did you learn anything from her cell phone?"

"I couldn't."

"What do you mean?"

"It's gone. It wasn't in her room."

"The police can get those records, though, right? They go to the cell company or something?"

"Yeah, they mentioned that. We'll have to see. I think that takes a while, maybe months. And frankly, none of it really matters, at least to the police. Suicide or accident, I'm guessing it's not a high-priority situation."

Kat would be following up daily, trying to nudge the police to dig. He had to wonder if Shea had made calls or texted with anyone that day, if there'd been anything on her calendar, any notes or pictures. But nothing was going to bring her back. Maybe it was unfair to pull him into these spiraling inquiries.

She thought of Georgia, the panic in her eyes. It was possible that Shea had told Ryan about what happened with Blake back in November. Wouldn't he feel better knowing why she'd returned to the island?

But maybe not. Maybe none of it mattered. Maybe telling him would just cause more pain.

"Well, it was nice to be back at Tori's with everyone. Everyone shared stories—memories of meeting Shea, some of our silly antics. She was so important to so many of us, Ryan."

Ryan nodded but remained quiet, drinking his coffee.

"Did Shea tell you much about that last girls' trip in November?" she asked, attempting nonchalance.

"You weren't on that trip, were you?"

"No, but the girls told me about it." She couldn't tiptoe anymore. "Okay, Ryan, I'm so sorry that I'm probably totally crossing the line, but it doesn't feel right to act like I don't know things that I know. Shea told everyone that weekend in November that you two were in trouble. She was pretty upset. I guess it got a little wild."

Ryan took another sip of his coffee. Kat suddenly felt like a meddling busybody and quickly backpedaled. "I'm sorry, none of this is my business. I heard that things were better with you two, though, that's my point. I don't know why I keep talking."

Ryan patted her knee and smiled. "It's okay. Here's the deal. You probably heard a different version from the women because, well, when Shea went to Ohio in November, she thought I was having an affair."

"You weren't?"

"No." He avoided her eyes. It was starting to feel like no one could look her in the face. "This is a little embarrassing."

"Ryan, I don't want to pry."

"It's okay. I'd rather have friends know the truth than think I was cheating on her. Shea found some e-mails on my computer. She thought it was a relationship. But, actually, I'd fallen into a bit of a dark hole. I guess I figured that I wasn't doing anything wrong, because I never physically touched anyone."

"So, like an emotional affair?"

"Not exactly. Let's just say some late-night online stuff became some live-streaming and conversation."

Kat winced. "We're talking *porn*?" she said carefully, embarrassed to suggest it if she'd misunderstood.

Ryan laughed. "Your reaction lets me know you're not exactly up on the adult Internet world."

Kat let out a giggle as well. "Not exactly. I think Facebook is as much online interaction as I can handle. Sometimes that's too much for me."

"Well, it's out there. It's easy to find, and it really screwed with my marriage."

"But you guys worked through it?"

He nodded. "We did," he said before looking away again.

"Well, that's good." She'd pried enough and felt like she was on the wrong side of the fence that had separated them for years. "None of this is my business, Ryan, and I'm glad that you two were doing better. Maybe that's a comfort. I'm just not handling it all that well. I'm sorry for all the questions."

"It's okay." He offered a weak smile. "So, did Dee go to Tori's?"

"Yeah. She's not handling this too well, either."

Ryan nodded. "Did she tell you all about what's going on?"

"What do you mean?"

"Charlie left her."

"Oh no."

"Yeah. I'm betting she blames Shea, too, so I'm guessing her emotions are pretty complicated right now."

"Why?"

"Oh, Kat. If I were to tell you, you'd never look at me the same."

"What do you mean?"

"Let's just say that you always had a way of staying above the fray. This town can get pretty wild."

Kat didn't know what to say, and before she could decide, Ryan stood. "More coffee?" he said, arm outstretched.

She handed over her cup, and as he went to the kitchen for more, she walked into the yard for a better view of her old house, just beyond the cedar fence and blooming lilacs. The old pass-through they'd cut into the fence between them, back when the kids were little, was barely visible behind a new shrub. It was like a dog door for kids. At a happy hour a few years back, Dee had proved that she could fit through the door, too.

Kat noticed that the new owners had painted the siding on her house's back addition. She and Mack had agonized about picking just the right shade of red to blend with the brick when they had that addition constructed. She was not a fan of the new owner's choice. She wondered what else they might have done to her house.

When Ryan returned, he enlightened Kat on the wildness he had referenced before going for their refills. She listened, mouth agape, like a child being told there was no Santa, her illusions shattered. She'd lived twenty years in this town, feeling like she'd made such close friends, especially with Shea and Ryan, and yet in just the last few days, she'd realized there was so much she didn't know. His stories reminded her of the car trip to Catawba, of Tori's stories of her daughter's escapades that made Kat appreciate her own ignorance. Houses had curtains and blinds for a reason, after all. She supposed he was only sharing now because there was safety in gossiping with an outsider—and that's what she'd become.

But did Dee really blame Shea for losing Charlie? Could any of that have had something to do with Shea's trip to the island? Someone knew something about that day, and it seemed like that person was a friend.

CHAPTER 14

January 7

AFTER THE KIDS WENT BACK to school, it was Shea's turn to host the quarterly dinner party. She and Ryan were at their best among friends, laughing and relishing the escape from their quiet home, putting on their best faces. It was easy to throw all that baggage in the closet when friends came over. Even the thought of the party made Shea brush issues aside.

She'd tried to convince Kat and Mack to stay an extra week for the dinner, but Kat said it wasn't possible. Shea had watched with sadness and envy as they drove away in their overstuffed van, away from icy sidewalks and assaulting cold air.

She'd planned the menu and set the table for eight two days ago. She loved nothing more than escaping into the world of hosting the perfect gathering, of attending to every detail. How bizarre that the girl who'd spent her teens lying on the grass, staring at the sky, pondering the meaning of life, and creating bucket lists of countries to explore would someday relish creating the perfect centerpiece.

But yesterday, cancellations started coming in. Tori said she had the flu, and Georgia had mistakenly double-booked. Shea didn't buy that one, as it seemed Georgia was intentionally avoiding her. Left with just Dee and Charlie as guests, Shea wanted to reach out to both Evelyn and Lina.

Ryan was sitting in the living room, feet up, beer in hand, watching a game on TV. He scoffed at the suggestion to include the women, saying it would be like he was at a girls' night. He muted the television. "Besides, it's Saturday night. Don't you think the singles have dates?"

"I doubt that," Shea said. There was no way romance was among Lina's priorities right now, and Evelyn had recently declared being sick of all men. "Evelyn told me she'd fallen for a married man. So she's given up on the dating scene for now."

Ryan took a sip, as if he was considering the suggestion. "Well, let's not tempt either of them with this," he said, slapping his chest like Tarzan.

Shea laughed. "No woman can resist that, I suppose?"

"Whatever," he chided. "Just because I'm not Tom Selleck anymore."

"What, are you sixty now? You need some new references, buddy."

"Ha-ha. Let's just have a quiet dinner with Dee and Charlie. It'll be fun." He took the TV off mute, ending the conversation.

Another night with just the two of them. And the thought of Charlie—of whatever he might have been implying at the club a few weeks ago—had sat at the pit of her stomach for weeks. Shea had finally been able to push that night with Blake away from the front of her mind. She could finally close her eyes without thinking about his hands digging into her arms.

Though perhaps this would be the chance to find out what Charlie knew. She could ask Dee. What could he know, anyway? Georgia would never have said anything. Maybe that was just Charlie being Charlie, making some general comment about "women gone wild."

When Dee and Charlie arrived, they all worked together in the kitchen. Dee offered to chop the salad while Shea worked the side dishes. Charlie made the drinks while Ryan focused on the tenderloin. When Shea looked over at Charlie and Ryan in the corner about thirty minutes later, laughing and whispering like two adolescent boys, tension began rising into her neck, as if she was getting in over her head again. But looking at Dee, oblivious to any whispers and happy to talk about the kids, the holidays, and everything else that had them stressed out, she told herself to calm down, that she was panicking for nothing. Ryan was obviously feeling no pain; his close talking and those telltale flushed cheeks told her the drinks had kicked in. With a fresh martini in hand and three blue-cheese olives, her anxiety began melting away.

The dinner was a success. Everything was hot at the same time, and the foursome lingered at the table over the wine. Ryan pulled out the cognac afterward while Shea got some sweets to pass.

When Charlie began to reminisce about the antics of their last foursome dinner, Shea laughed along with the others. Perhaps it was the alcohol making her relax, but these were friends of nearly twenty years. A few weird kisses were not going to ruin that.

Charlie held up his glass for a toast, looked at Dee, and winked at Ryan before speaking. "So, my dear friends, I have a little proposition."

Shea looked at Dee, wondering if she knew where this was going, but Dee was now focused on downing her drink.

"Dee and I discussed this, and I hope you both know that we would never suggest this to anyone else, and if you're against it, we don't ever have to speak of it again."

Shea's stomach dropped. She looked at Ryan, who was smiling broadly, like he knew exactly where this was going, eagerly awaiting the finish.

"I don't know about the two of you, but Dee and I are always looking for ways to keep some excitement in our life, right?" He looked at Dee for affirmation. She was midgulp and pulled her glass from her mouth, nearly choking down the liquid as she concurred.

"And here I sit with the two most beautiful women in this town, and the best friend a guy could have. Ryan and I have shared stories and laughs, so why not share a little more . . ."

Shea looked to Ryan for help, but before she could say a word, Ryan held up his glass, as if to toast, and smiled at Shea. "I'm up for it if you are, babe. Time to get a little wild, right?"

"Exactly," Charlie said. Dee laughed, looking over at Shea. It seemed like everyone at the table knew this was coming, and they were all okay with it.

"I need a drink," Shea said.

"Oh yes, let's all do a shot," Charlie suggested.

Shea stood to clear the dishes, and Ryan followed her to the kitchen. "What are you thinking?" he asked.

"Are you telling me you want to have sex with Dee?" she whispered. Before he could respond, she added, "And you're okay with me sleeping with Charlie?"

Ryan took her hand and squeezed. "Maybe just this once."

Shea didn't know what to say. Her head was spinning in a mix of rage, shock, confusion, disbelief. It took her breath away.

"Hey, babe," Ryan said. "I don't love anyone else. This is just fun and games with our closest friends."

Dee walked up to them with two shots as an offering. "Charlie and I have already had ours," she chided. She was obviously drunk. Shea's buzz was gone.

Ryan grabbed his shot and swigged before taking Dee's hand. "Okay, everyone, we'll be back!" He pulled Dee out of the kitchen and headed downstairs, to the guest room, she assumed, before Shea could say anything else. Her head felt ready to explode. She looked over at Charlie, who stood smiling at her like some schoolboy hoping for a kiss, and she swigged the shot.

"Wanna go upstairs?" he asked. She didn't know what to say. Everything felt off-kilter, and this voice in her brain, the twenty-year-old, who was still trying to be cool and fun and wild and exciting, said, *Go for it. You can have sex with someone new! What woman, married to the same man for more than two decades, wouldn't want that? Charlie's gorgeous!*

But the other voice in her head, the one that wasn't completely drowning in alcohol, knew it was reckless and dangerous and not the way to bring spice into their love life. She simply did not want to do it. She'd never looked at Charlie that way. She'd fantasized about Ryan Gosling, maybe, but not the neighbors. She turned from Charlie as he came toward her. He must have taken her hesitation as shyness, and he leaned over and kissed the side of her neck. She felt anchored to the floor, her shoes suddenly filled with cement, unable to move or react.

"Ryan and Dee are having fun right now. Don't you think it will be harder if we don't do something? Otherwise, you'll feel like he cheated on you. Come on, just sit with me."

Shea suddenly felt sick, almost like a little girl being pulled somewhere she didn't want to go. She stumbled forward, resisting, silently shaking her head. He pulled her into the living room as her mind swirled, focusing on Charlie's hand holding hers. Her husband was downstairs taking off her friend's clothes. Kissing her, looking at her. Nothing would ever be the same.

"I've fantasized about you for almost twenty years," Charlie said. "And ever since that night when you gave me just a taste of what it could be like—"

That was it. She stood, trying to pull her hand from his grip. "I'm sorry, Charlie. This can't happen. Please don't be offended, but we're just friends. I love my husband."

He wouldn't let go of her hand. "And I love my wife."

"This can't happen." She broke free and ran toward the basement stairs. She called out as she descended. "Ryan?"

When she got to the bottom of the stairs, Ryan and Dee were standing in the middle of the family room, not the guest room, still fully clothed, laughing nervously. "We couldn't do it, either," Dee said.

"We were just about to come back upstairs," Ryan added.

"Oh, thank God," she said. Charlie had followed behind Shea and after some nervous laughter and bad jokes, everyone agreed that it was a silly idea and promised not to speak of it again. Of course, it wouldn't be that easy.

CHAPTER 15

April 12

ON WEDNESDAY MORNING, KAT AND Tori accompanied Lina to the hospital for her ninety-minute chemotherapy appointment. The nurse readied Lina for treatment, and Kat and Tori sat in nearby chairs, sharing magazine articles and focusing on lighter topics— good books and new shows to binge on Netflix. Within the hour, Lina fell asleep.

Kat leaned toward Tori and, in a low voice, she asked, "Can you keep a secret?"

Tori smiled. "Hell, yeah."

"For real."

"Okay, now you're insulting me. I know I enjoy a little celebrity gossip, but I'm a great secret keeper. You wouldn't believe all the dirt I have locked up here," she said, pointing to her head.

"I saw Georgia on Monday night. She knew all about Shea's plan to return to the island for Blake's memorial. She'd asked Georgia to go with her."

"What? Why hasn't Georgia told Ryan?"

Kat explained in more detail what had apparently happened between Shea and Blake and Georgia's fears about saying anything.

"What I don't understand," Kat said, "is why Shea told the inn-keeper that she was expecting a friend if Georgia told Shea she wouldn't go."

Tori tossed the magazine from her lap and gripped both armrests of her chair. Her eyes darted around the room like she was looking for something.

"What is it?"

Tori went to the window and turned back to Kat, leaning onto the sill behind her. "I think Georgia's lying," she said, her voice booming through the peaceful room.

Kat briefly glanced at Lina, who was still asleep under a heavy blanket. Kat joined Tori at the window. "What do you mean?" she said softly, leading Tori back to a library voice.

"That night in November," Tori said in a near whisper, "after our excursion to the island, I woke in the middle of the night for some water. I found Shea in the living room, sitting in the dark, crying. She told me about the attack."

"But—"

"Shea didn't say anything about hitting the guy and running off. What she said was that she'd gone with him to his boat, she'd had second thoughts when she realized what was really happening, and that things got scary when he got angry."

"So—"

Tori turned more directly to Kat, crossing her arms. "And then she said"—volume rising—"'Georgia saved my life.'"

"Maybe she meant, by being there . . ."

Tori shook her head. "I pressed, but she refused to elaborate. The implication was clear that Georgia helped her get away from the guy."

They stood in silence for several minutes. Kat turned her focus out the window. Finally, Kat said what Tori had to be thinking, too. "If Georgia saw the struggle between Shea and Blake and she ran up to help . . ."

"Georgia may have hit Blake over the head," Tori said. "Oh my God," she said back at full volume before catching herself and resuming her whisper. "What if *Georgia* killed Blake?"

Kat shook her head. "First of all, this is Georgia we're talking about. That woman probably doesn't even kill spiders in the house. Second, there's no way that Shea and Georgia could have acted normal and returned to the bar pretending like nothing happened if they'd knowingly killed a man. That's insane."

"You're right," Tori said, nodding. There was a beat of emptiness between them before Tori turned to Kat. "But I shared that news story with Shea just days before she left town. They could have suddenly realized what they'd done."

Kat left Tori at the window, returned to her chair, and sat, looking at Lina, so peaceful. Of course Georgia wouldn't have wanted to go with Shea if she'd been the one responsible for Blake's death.

Tori began pacing. "If Georgia hit Blake, and then she found out that he died that night, she would have been terrified of being implicated."

Kat froze, stunned by the thoughts that were forcing their way inside. Georgia had seemed nervous when they spoke on Monday and relieved when Kat said no one was investigating. "What if Shea had convinced Georgia not to involve police at the time, just like Georgia said?" She finally got up and moved toward Tori, now back at the window. "If all that were true, I can't imagine how Georgia would have felt when she heard that he was dead. Accident or not, her whole life would be in jeopardy if anyone found out, right?"

Tori looked at Kat, eyes wild. "She might blame Shea for all of it. But now . . . Georgia is saying Shea hit him, and there's no one to say otherwise."

Kat winced. It was an outrageous leap. Georgia couldn't hurt Shea. She was about as violent as a monk. It just wasn't possible.

Kat offered to get them both some coffee. She needed a moment alone. It was a disturbing theory, and she wanted out of that room.

When she returned, Tori was sitting by Lina. Kat took the open chair beside her. They sipped in silence. Finally, Tori said, "What are you thinking?"

"I have no idea," Kat said. It was true. A topic change was in order. "Do you know what's going on with Dee?"

Tori nodded and blew on her coffee.

Kat waited.

"She's going through a rough time," Tori said. "Charlie left her."

"Yeah, Ryan told me."

"After you all left the lake house, she told me it was Shea's fault, though she didn't say why."

Kat took another sip, wondering if it she should say anything to Tori, her friend who enjoyed gossip more than anyone. Shea was dead, and it seemed wrong to share what she'd learned from Ryan. But, then again, maybe it was relevant. If Dee blamed Shea . . . could any of that craziness Ryan had told her about be a factor in Shea's death? "I think I know why," Kat finally said. "But, seriously, this has to remain between us."

Tori promised, and Kat shared what she'd learned from Ryan about their escapades with Charlie and Dee. Tori's jaw dropped, just as Kat's had when Ryan told her. The whole idea of Shea and Ryan swinging, or even attempting to—with Dee and Charlie, no less—was stunning. Kat's idealized image of Shea had been shattered. She'd been struggling in her marriage and taking pills. Suddenly, the possibility of Shea having an affair sounded plausible. There were so many secrets.

"I don't know what I thought I'd learn when I came back. I wanted to make sense of Shea's death, to understand what was going on. She was my closest friend. How did I know so little of what was happening in her life?"

"How well do any of us really know each other?"

"Until this week, I would have said I knew Shea better than anyone. I've assumed we all know each other very well. We've got twenty years of history."

"People know what we want them to know. Look at me. You probably wouldn't guess that I'm seeing a therapist."

"Really?"

Tori just chuckled and nodded. Tori's life appeared to be filled with fabulous trips, excess money, and lots of free time.

"Why?"

"Nothing is what it seems, Kat. I know what you see, this fabulous woman." She gave a dramatic head toss.

"I do, you're right."

"But I'm alone a lot, my husband and I are very different . . . there's just stuff. There's always stuff."

"I guess I do that, too," Kat admitted.

"What do you mean?"

"Well, I haven't told anyone that Texas sucks so far, that Mack resents me for the move and I resent him for not trying harder to make it work. That I'm jet-lagged a lot, hoping to come home and find boxes unpacked, and he's irritated that I come home and sleep. That I've worked for this kind of opportunity for years and much of it is great, but I can't share any of it because he's miserable. And we fight. A lot."

Tori reached for her hand.

"Does that mean we're not good friends, after all?"

"Of course we are. We're there for each other. If any of you want me, I'll be there. But we can't read each other's minds."

"Have you been in therapy long?"

"Only ten years."

"Seriously?" Kat chuckled.

"No one's life is sunshine and roses, Kat."

"I spent the last twenty years thinking Shea's life was. I unloaded my stress on her because it always seemed like nothing got her down, like she was my laid-back, wine-sipping surfer girl who just coasted on top of every wave."

"Everyone has crap. It's universal. But no one wants to complain or be a downer."

"So now Shea's gone, and we realize she was taking pills. And she said nothing to me about trouble with Ryan last fall. Though she was pulling away by then." Kat had felt it, the distance that came once they were both sure Kat was moving.

"She obviously didn't want us to know," Tori said.

Kat watched Lina sleeping peacefully. "You know, I couldn't stand the idea that Shea might have intended this. It was just too painful to bear. But now . . ."

"What?"

"You're going to think I'm crazy."

"Hey, which one of us is in therapy?"

Kat smiled. "Well, after I spoke with Ryan yesterday, I did a little research. He told me about how common it was to fall asleep and drown in a bathtub. I'd never heard that. So I looked it up. I found some articles that said much the same, but I also read a quote from a prosecutor that I haven't been able to get out of my mind. He believed many tub drownings could be unsolved homicides—it's a difficult crime to prove, and a relatively easy crime to commit."

Tori seemed to be taking it in, considering it.

"What if someone was in that room and caused her death and walked out, knowing exactly what it would look like?"

"Come on," Tori said. "That's nuts."

"She was expecting a friend. She had drinks with a man we don't know, who told the bartender they were staying at the inn. It seems like she opened her door after Mary put her to bed."

Tori didn't respond.

"I left Georgia's with this sinking realization that someone might have known what happened between Shea and Blake. Someone who would blame Shea. At the time, I thought of Blake's friends. I mean that big guy at the bar, Dave, he seemed a little scary to me. And he was on the island that day. He saw her."

"Yeah, but they say they left the memorial and got on the ferry. They never went to Rudolph's that day."

"I guess." She couldn't look at Tori. "You just implied that Georgia could have benefited from Shea's death. And Dee apparently blamed Shea for the end of her marriage. No one has come forward to say they were the friend who was supposed to go with her. That makes me think a friend is keeping a secret. Why?"

"No way," Tori said, shaking her head. "I mean, if you're going to start throwing out these theories, what about Ryan? He's jobless. I mean, money alone can make people kill. Spouses kill for life insurance all the time. And if Shea did break up Dee's marriage, maybe that wife swap became something more that he's not talking about."

Kat shook her head, not even considering it.

"Well, what about Evelyn? What about me? What about Lina over there?"

"Now you're being crazy."

"That's how you sound. These are our friends, Kat. You think one of them killed Shea, and in some perfect way so that it looked accidental?"

"I know. It doesn't make sense. And I would never say that to anyone else. But someone knows something. She had drinks with someone at Rudolph's and walked out with him. He paid cash, so we can't know who that was. It's possible Shea had something to do with Blake's death. What if someone drugged her?"

"And said, what, 'Now, go home and take a bath'? Not much of a theory." Tori chuckled.

It was absurd. But she wasn't crazy.

CHAPTER 16

February 17

SHEA ROSE FROM A HEAVY sleep facing Ryan's side of the bed, but fortunately, he was already up. She dragged herself into the bathroom and shut the door before brushing her teeth and getting a pill from the medicine cabinet. Thank God for those pills, the only reason she was finally sleeping at night. It had been four weeks of constant insomnia, spending at least three hours a night on the couch, binge-watching Netflix, before she'd finally sleep. And then her back began to hurt.

It wasn't about addiction. But she knew enough not to tell Ryan about the pain or the pills, sure that he'd use it against her, somehow comparing his porn habit with the drugs, like she was some addict. She wasn't an addict. She just needed some sleep. And she needed to get through her days without the pain.

Shea sat on the toilet, looking out her bathroom window at the snow covering Kat's green-tiled roof. Everything had fallen apart since Kat left. Maybe it just felt that way because she'd hosted the dinner party from hell just days after saying their final good-byes. Since then, the hand-holding, the coffee offerings, certainly the sex had all stopped. And to make it worse, Ryan acted as if everything was normal, or at least the new normal. He didn't even question Shea when she told him she'd canceled their hotel reservation in the city, that romantic gift she'd presented at Christmas. He didn't care.

Every time she looked at him, she'd recall his shit-eating grin with Dee and Charlie that night, his willingness to run downstairs with her friend, and his complete indifference to her potential tryst with *his* friend! And he was losing weight, probably getting himself date ready. He didn't love her. It was the only explanation that made sense. He said he did, but how could she trust anything he said anymore? He'd also said he was heading to work, for weeks, when he wasn't.

She was so tired of his superiority and his secrets about money. It used to seem chivalrous. He felt duty bound to take care of his bride, and she'd loved it. But now, she realized he'd been treating her like a child.

The house had become so quiet. It was like a death, the life drained from the air. How bizarre that in just six months, everything had changed so radically. The energy was gone, her life of focusing on caring for her kids—clothing, feeding, driving, supporting, loving— was gone. The whole neighborhood felt quiet. Too quiet. It seemed like it was more than just cold weather that had caused a collective hibernation.

Georgia and Dee were both avoiding her, and Tori was busy with her youngest child, her charities, her vacations, her ridiculously easy life. Lina had real problems, fighting to stay alive. And Evelyn was nice, but they didn't know each other that well. She had a big job and was trying to enjoy a fresh start. She didn't need to hear about Shea's marriage falling apart.

Every time Shea spotted the new owners coming and going from Kat's house, it hurt a little. Not only that Kat and Mack were gone, but that life went on as usual. She wanted so much to invite Kat over, or go for a walk together, or sit in the yard like they used to, back when the kids were little. But Kat was traveling the world, going to all these places Shea had only read about. She'd moved on.

Shea would scan her Facebook feed, peering into her friends' lives, seeing their happy faces, their busy schedules, their trips, their date nights. Everyone else was fine, and she was a walking cliché, an empty nester struggling with the start of whatever was to come, a mother who felt lost when her kids grew up, a wife whose husband had lost interest, content to live a lie. It was all such nonsense. There were people starving in the world, for Christ's sake. And here she sat, in her big, beautiful home, wanting to run away, without any idea where to go.

When she finally went downstairs and poured some coffee, Ryan was at the table, engrossed in the sports page, chomping on an apple as if he had no worries.

"What are you up to today?" she asked. She dropped her phone on the table and took the seat beside him, focusing her attention on wrapping both hands around the hot mug.

"I've got a few meetings," he said without looking up.

She had no response. Lies and evasive answers were Ryan's MO. That was a nice side effect of her magic pills: it was just a little easier to let the tension in her neck roll right off. Like yoga without the yoga. *Actually, I should probably do some yoga*, she thought, trying to remember how long it had been since she'd shown up for a class.

Her phone pinged. The screen lit to display another text from Charlie. She ignored it and glanced at Ryan. He briefly looked at her phone before returning focus to the newspaper. Didn't he see that the text was from Charlie? Didn't he care?

Charlie's texts had been coming in a slow and constant trickle since that dreaded night. Initially, they were odd, but harmless: What are you up to?, How's it going?, Just checking in. Hope you're having a good day. Her responses were curt but polite: nothing, fine, Thanks, you too. No chance of being misinterpreted, no interest in engaging in any real conversation. But then she got a private message through Facebook. Charlie said they should try again, that he'd talked to Dee and she was okay with it. He had a plan. Shea couldn't believe what she was reading. It was as if she was the only one who didn't understand the punch line of some elaborate joke. Why was Dee fine with this idea? Didn't she care? Did she have a thing for Ryan?

Shea tried to remember Dee and Ryan's body language when she'd descended the stairs that night. They were both standing—moving, actually, probably five feet apart. Had they simply pulled back when they heard her coming downstairs? Had those nervous laughs been faked? Maybe they didn't want to upset her by admitting they were into it. Maybe Ryan and Dee had started something. Was that why Dee was avoiding her? She and Dee used to walk together at least once a week when the weather allowed, but ever since that night, Dee always had some nonsense excuse. And Charlie's most recent message had suggested a rendezvous in Michigan, with Dee's blessing. Shea hadn't even responded.

That afternoon, Shea came home from the grocery as another snowfall began. Ryan was asleep on the couch in the living room with an old horror movie on television in the background. So, these were the meetings he had lined up. Ryan's cell pinged, and the screen glowed. A text from Dee: We need to talk. Why did Dee want to talk to Ryan when she wouldn't talk to Shea? What the hell was going on? What if they were sleeping together? Was this why he was losing weight? Was Dee the reason he seemed indifferent at the change between them? He'd said he was visiting his father in Detroit at least three times since that night in January. A father from whom Ryan had been estranged for years. He'd always said his dad was a small and insignificant presence in his childhood, that he'd drunk too much, that he'd never been around for Ryan as a boy. He hadn't even been at their wedding. But ever since last September, Ryan had made regular visits to Detroit.

Jesus, she thought, *what if none of that was true?* She'd assumed Ryan was finally making peace with his dad, now that the man was dying. But when she'd volunteered to go with him a few times, he said he preferred the time alone. Was it all a lie? What if all those overnight trips were trysts? She wanted to throw that phone in his formerly fat face.

Maybe no matter what they'd once had, it had gotten stale. Maybe it was inevitable. Maybe it was just human nature, after all these years with the same person, to want something different. And her friend had offered. She couldn't believe Dee would betray her like that. It didn't matter that Charlie had pulled the strings, that Dee seemed incapable of saying no to his ideas, ever.

But it suddenly all made sense.

She stomped up the stairs and grabbed a suitcase.

Maybe everything was a lie. Maybe she forgave Ryan's affair the first time, not because of love. Maybe she just held on all these years because it was easier than starting over, easier than being alone or breaking up a family.

She left a note on the kitchen counter, explaining that she'd gone to her sister's place in Grand Rapids for the weekend. She asked him not to call or text, said she needed some time to herself. She wrote, "I know you'll understand." He'd better understand. He had caused all of this.

It was more than two hours later when Shea reached the exit for Saint Joseph and released her death grip on the wheel. The snow had continued during the entire drive, and her heart had raced with every passing car. Once on the east side of the lake, the snow had exploded into giant lake-effect flakes.

Shea pulled up to the cottage on Lake Michigan and saw the SUV, blanketed in four inches of fresh powder, parked in the gravel driveway. She cut the engine and shook out her hands. Charlie was there, waiting for her. She pulled a pill from her bag, swallowing it down with the remains of her Diet Coke, and got out of the car.

CHAPTER 17

April 12

THAT EVENING, KAT WORKED AT her laptop at Lina's dining room table, prepping for tomorrow's meeting downtown. It had been a long day with Lina and Tori, but she'd been so glad to be there for her friend, so glad to have her friends. Her phone rang. A snapshot of Mack's sleeping face filled the screen. Kat had snapped the photo years ago, in the early morning, to capture Mack's huge smile, like he was enjoying the best day of his life. When he woke and she shared it, they both laughed because he'd had no recollection of what he'd been dreaming. Every time he called and she saw that sleeping grin, it made her smile.

"Hey," she said as she picked up, holding her breath to see what kind of call it would be.

"I'm sorry," he said.

Kat exhaled. "Thanks. I am sorry, too." She knew he was struggling. It was her job that had dragged him to a new town and then left him there alone most of the time. The move hadn't been easy on anyone.

"I'm sorry I hung up on you the other day," he said. "It's just that I had decided to surprise you by jumping on a plane and spending the week in that hotel with you downtown and then, when you said you were at Lina's, I got pissed."

"I would have loved that, babe. I'd still love that."

"No. You'll be home in a couple of days. Let's just plan to do something together."

"You read my mind. I'm sorry that we're apart so much. I know that no one plans for tragedies, but the timing of all this was pretty bad."

"It's okay. It's good that you went. I probably should have gone, too." He was saying all the right things. "How has it been, seeing everyone?"

She wanted to tell Mack more about what she'd learned from Ryan and Tori and these disturbing revelations about her friends. But she didn't want to hear his likely response that she was creating problems. He might say that her concerns could ruin their friends' lives, and certainly ruin their friendships if she shared some of the more outrageous theories with police, putting their relationships under some sort of spotlight. She knew all that. Besides, she and Mack were having a good talk. She didn't want to spoil it. "They're all okay."

The doorbell rang. "Oh, hold on a second. Someone's at the door." Kat didn't want the bell to wake up Lina, who'd gone to bed at seven.

She opened the door to find Dee smiling, holding a giant tin tray of food. "Hi," Kat said, suddenly feeling awkward and guilty about all the gossip she'd just learned, and shared, regarding Dee in the last twenty-four hours.

"Here," Dee said, offering the dish to Kat. "It's a chicken and rice dish. One of the few things I make without burning. It's, like, enough food for eight. Let's hope Lina likes it."

"One sec," she said, and put the phone back to her ear. "Mack, I'm gonna call you back, okay? Dee just walked in."

He agreed, and she disconnected the call while opening the door wider and waving Dee inside. "Come in, come in. Lina's sleeping. I was just finishing up work." The food delivery reminded Kat that she'd never eaten dinner. It was after nine. "I'm starving, have you eaten? You want a drink?"

"No and yes," Dee said. "Let's eat this. It's too much for Lina. You can tell her if it's any good."

Kat chuckled, put Dee's dish in the oven to warm, and poured them both a glass of pinot.

"I saw Ryan yesterday," Kat said, having quickly decided that it would be disingenuous to act oblivious. After all, Ryan had felt comfortable opening up; maybe Dee would find it easier to talk to her as well, now that she was an outsider. "He told me about you and Charlie splitting up. I'm so sorry, Dee."

Dee sat at the kitchen peninsula. "Yeah, well, it's been a roller coaster, but I may actually be turning the corner. I think I'm finally seeing the good in all of it."

Kat reached across the counter, putting a hand on Dee's. "If you need someone to talk to, I'm here."

Dee blushed. Her eyes began to water. "So, I guess you know about our idiotic escapades?"

Kat gave a half smile, trying to indicate knowing without any pleasure in being privy to the information. "Sorry."

"It was all so dumb. Just some drunken kisses. But Charlie wanted more. He always wanted more." She sipped her wine, and Kat remained silent. "I don't think I could have ever told anyone this stuff before, but I'm finally feeling like perhaps I'm the lucky one. It's funny—just a few days ago, I was still so mad at Shea, at the world, feeling like everyone came in and ruined my marriage. But I'm starting to see that Charlie was just a bad husband." Dee chuckled, as if she finally got the joke.

Kat drank her wine, not wanting to agree or disagree. Dee's new attitude could just be another stage in the grieving process.

"I shouldn't have been surprised. Charlie always let his gaze linger on Shea. She was a beautiful woman. And when we got back from Catawba in November and I shared with him our antics on Put-in-Bay, he was so entertained by the idea that Shea was wilder than he'd realized. I didn't give it much thought. He loves *wild* women. That's what Charlie always said he loved about me most, my wild and adventurous side."

"We all love that about you," Kat said.

"But that's the joke. It's not me. At least that's not who I always was. Charlie brought it out in me. When we met, he said he bored easily."

"What does that mean?"

"That was just his veiled way of warning me that he would cheat and eventually break my heart. And he did."

"He's cheated on you?"

"Oh yeah. At least twice that I know of, but they were always strangers, at least to me. Women he met while traveling for work. But we've been married for twenty-three years. We have a family. It's hard to just toss it all aside because of a few . . ." It was like she wasn't sure what to call it. "But, you know, when he said that about getting bored easily back when we were dating, I thought of it as a challenge. It never occurred to me at the time that it was Charlie's problem—*his* attention span that needed work. I was twenty-four, and I simply decided that I was never going to be accused of being boring. He was the most exciting—certainly the best-looking—man I'd ever dated."

Dee began recounting her wild adventures in the name of keeping Charlie happy: taking mushrooms with him on that camping trip, jumping off that cliff on their honeymoon, pretending to be someone else at a restaurant to snag reservations. Everything outlandish had been Charlie's idea, but most of the time, she enjoyed it. And after a while, she thought she *was* wild and adventurous, even though, prior to Charlie, she'd never broken a rule or taken a real risk.

When they finished their wine, Kat excused herself to check on Lina and found her sleeping soundly in the bedroom. She'd probably sleep through the night. Kat plated up a couple of servings of the casserole Dee had brought.

Kat ate, and Dee talked. She seemed glad to be sharing.

"When the actual swap happened," Dee said, "Ryan and I panicked, giggling at the absurdity of it, and backed out. I was so relieved."

"Yeah, that's what Ryan said, too."

"But after that night, Charlie started acting weird. I'd walk into a room, and he'd be looking at Shea's Facebook page. I'd find calls to Shea's number on his phone. I'd see texts he sent to her. And he didn't come anywhere near me after that for more than a month, not normal for the guy who treated sex like a workout—in the mood or not, it had to be done at least twice a week." Dee stared at her plate, moving the food around with her fork.

"But Ryan said that Shea was the one who ran downstairs that night to stop it. She obviously didn't want to do it, either."

"I know. But then in February, Charlie said he wanted some time alone to think and said he'd work out of our place in Michigan for a while. I just knew that something was happening between them."

"Did you talk to Shea?"

"I couldn't."

"Why? She was your friend."

"I don't know why. Now that she's gone, it seems even crazier, but my husband had fallen for her. I knew it. I could see it. How could I talk to her about it? I'd even said I was okay with the stupid swinging idea!"

"But do you have any reason to think she returned those feelings? Did you ever see any texts from Shea on his phone? Anything?"

"No. But if she never did anything to encourage him, I don't know why he'd continue to text her. I even reached out to Ryan. I mean, I didn't know what to do or what I could say. They were supposed to be good friends. Ryan seemed fine with the idea that night, so for all I knew . . . It was all so weird. I wasn't sure what to say."

"But you talked to Ryan?"

"I sent him a text on a Friday, back in February, the day Charlie told me he was going to Michigan. Ryan didn't respond, so I called him that night. My first question was if Shea was around, and he said she'd left a couple of hours earlier for Michigan, to see her sister. As soon as he said it, I just knew Shea and Charlie were together. Did you see the way Charlie fell apart at the funeral?"

"No."

"He was a mess. It was ridiculous. Like, inappropriately ridiculous. Like it was his wife who'd died. Something was going on between them. He was obsessed with her."

"Do you think Ryan knew about it?"

"I don't know. I practically hung up on Ryan when he said Shea was in Michigan. I didn't know what to say. She stopped trying to reach me, and I certainly wasn't going to call her. I knew they were together. We didn't speak for, like, six weeks. Then she killed herself. I saw her death as proof. Like at least she felt guilty for what she'd done."

"I still don't believe that she intended to die," Kat said.

"Well, maybe we all see what we need to see. I need to believe she was sorry."

~ • ~

After Dee left and Kat cleaned up the kitchen, she went off to bed and called Mack. It rang three times before he finally picked up.

"So, how is Dee?" Mack asked.

"That's a loaded question. Hey, please promise me you'll never cheat on me. No matter what, okay?"

"Wow, where is that coming from?"

"I'm just overwhelmed by how naive I've been. I'd never think that could happen to us, but I travel a lot, and you're alone a lot. I didn't think it could happen to my friends, either, but I was wrong."

"We both know it's a miracle you ever fell for a tech nerd. I'm not about to screw with that. I take it you're referring to Dee and Charlie?"

"Yeah."

"That's not surprising, though, right? I mean, it's Charlie. It's not as surprising as some of the others."

"Like who?"

Mack didn't answer.

"Mack. You have to tell me! You're my husband! We share secrets, remember. That's the rule!"

He chuckled. "Okay, okay. I guess it doesn't matter now. Ryan and Shea. I know he stepped out, you might say."

"When? Why have I never heard this? Was it Dee?"

"Dee?" He chuckled. "That seems like a crazy leap."

"You'd be surprised. Dee believes Shea and Charlie were having a thing, too. That's a whole other story. Why didn't you ever tell me about this?"

"Because Shea was your closest friend. That would have put you in a terrible position. Ryan told me at the luau party, last summer. We were smoking cigars in the backyard around midnight, and he asked me if I ever cheated. I said no, of course."

"Good answer."

"Right. And he said, 'Well, don't do it. Disaster. That's all I'm saying.' I didn't press. I didn't really want to know the details. I think I said, 'Okay, I'll remember that.' We laughed, and he chugged his drink and walked off."

The luau party had been such a happy occasion. Everyone was in a great mood, a celebration of Leigh and all her friends heading off to school. And Shea and Ryan were smiling, laughing, arm in arm as

Ryan toasted his daughter. Why would he even think about such a thing that night?

Unless something—or someone—reminded him.

Lina said Shea had found an *undergarment* in his drawer after that party. Kat had sat in Ryan's backyard just yesterday, and he'd been so sincere, assuring her that there had never been an affair, that Shea had been mistaken when she suspected something last fall. That it had been about porn. Was it all a lie?

Kat wished she could go back in time, to walk through that evening again, to notice what she might have missed.

CHAPTER 18

February 17

WHEN CHARLIE OPENED THE DOOR, his smile was wide, like a kid on Christmas morning. Shea's mouth began to dry. Her heart was racing. She tried to remain stone-faced, even though her tendency in moments of nervousness had always been to smile or even giggle.

"Come in, come in," he said, waving her toward the living area. Shea dropped her purse by the door and walked toward the roaring fire in the center of the cabin. "I'm so glad you're here," Charlie said, like this was some agreed-upon rendezvous. "I was starting to think you weren't coming." She heard a hint of a slur. There was an empty glass in his hand. An open bottle of scotch sat atop the console table against the wall.

Shea stepped to the coffee table, to the open bottle of cabernet, the two glasses already filled. She picked up the glasses, and, without saying a word, walked to the kitchen. Charlie put his empty glass on the console table and followed her like a curious dog.

She went to the sink, paused, looking at the wine, and took a big swig from one.

"What's going on?" he asked.

She ignored the question and poured the wine from both glasses down the drain before turning around to face him.

"You prefer scotch?" he asked with a grin. "I've got some good stuff."

She took a deep breath. She'd been preparing for this moment during the entire car ride. "You have to stop this. I don't know what else to say to you. The texts, the calls. This nonsense has already messed with my marriage and my friendship with Dee. I've tried to be nice, but this is never going to happen."

"But it can happen," Charlie said, walking toward her with that confident grin. "And I think you just don't want to admit that you want it to happen because you feel guilty."

"That's not it."

"But you came, just like I asked."

"Because you won't leave me alone, Charlie."

"I know you're attracted to me," he said, walking closer, invading the few feet of space between them. "You just don't want to admit it. But we don't even have to tell them."

Shea put up her hand to stop him from getting any closer. "Listen to me. You've built up some fantasy about this, but I love my husband." It was true, she'd realized during that long, tear-filled car ride. She wasn't ready to give up yet. Things were terrible between them right now, but for most of their twenty-seven-year history, he'd been her best friend. She couldn't just toss it away. Not yet. "And I love Dee. I don't understand why the three of you have lost your minds, and I don't know what's going on with any of you, but I'm not going to be the one to wreck everyone's lives."

Charlie stopped, cocked his head, almost like a dog trying to understand a human. "I love them, too, Shea. No one needs to get hurt. I told you, Dee is cool with everything."

Shea began shaking her head. "I don't believe that."

"I'm telling you," he said, leaning closer. "She doesn't care."

"Are they together?" It was barely a whisper. She was as afraid of asking the question as of hearing the answer.

Charlie's confident laugh emerged. "I don't think so. He's not her type. No offense."

For a moment, this thought gave her some comfort, until Charlie stepped forward. "I don't think you should worry about Ryan. He's no saint, you know."

Shea turned her head, unable to look at him, terrified of what his expression was suggesting, and whatever else he was about to say. She didn't need to hear that Charlie knew all about Ryan's infidelity a few years ago. It was horrifying enough to think about, much less hear that others knew about it. And he'd sworn that it was the one and only time, and that her assumptions last fall were mistaken, that what she'd found was just online nonsense. She'd already walked this road, making huge mistakes of her own based on a fictitious affair. And she didn't trust Charlie, anyway. "Don't," she pleaded, putting her hands up, suddenly exhausted by the anxiety, the stress that had consumed her for months. "Please don't do this, Charlie. My marriage is not your business."

Charlie bridged the remaining space between them. "Come on, you're acting like you don't enjoy a little harmless flirtation, but we both know that's not the case. And Dee told me all about you on Put-in-Bay."

Shea was horrified. She'd finally pushed that memory deep enough that it no longer plagued her nights, but just like that, Charlie brought it back. She invited these disasters.

"Just give in, Shea. You're here. There's snow falling, a roaring fire in the living room, wine. Besides, don't you think it's only fair that you *both* get to have a little fun on the side?" He quickly gripped her hips, as if she wanted to be convinced or overcome.

Shea pushed against his chest, breaking free, and crossed to the other side of the room. "Don't Charlie. I'm serious. That's not why I'm here."

"Yeah, right," he said, coming at her before she could say anything else, pressing his face against hers, pinning her against the wall, forcing a kiss.

She pushed him away. "Stop!" she cried. "I came here to beg you to stop!" She walked out of the kitchen and went to the front door. "This was a mistake."

Charlie followed her. "Shea. Stop. Please," he begged, his tone softening. "I'm sorry. Please."

Shea grabbed her purse, then the doorknob.

"What about me? You're okay with wrecking my life?"

She whipped around. "What are you talking about? I don't want to hurt your feelings, but you are out of line, Charlie. This is nuts, and I am not interested."

Charlie took the scotch bottle on the console and quickly poured more into the empty glass beside it before stepping toward her. "You don't understand. I can't get you out of my mind. Seriously, this has never happened to me before. I think I'm in love with you."

"Bullshit," Shea said, raising her hand again to stop him from getting any closer. "I can't even dignify that with a response, Charlie." She pulled the purse strap to her shoulder. "I came here so we could finally talk face-to-face without Dee being aware of any of this. You need to hear me. If you text me again, I'm going to tell Ryan and Dee everything."

"I wouldn't do that if I were you," he said, suddenly angry. He stepped back, looked away, and swigged the scotch. "Not unless you want them both to know when this all really started." He walked back to the console and refilled his glass again.

Shea's shoulders collapsed; the purse strap slipped off. She let it fall to the ground and braced against the wall. The night she'd buried long ago. A Christmas party at least twelve years earlier.

She looked back at him. He smirked, raised his brow. "I had a taste of you then, and I've always known how good it could be between us." And then he added, with some feigned sincerity, "And the kids are grown now."

"You're insane. How can you even bring up that night? You don't want to go there, not unless you want me to tell everyone my version."

"What?"

"Are you kidding me? I was asleep! I went upstairs to the bedroom for my coat at midnight and fell asleep. None of that was consensual."

"But you woke up."

Bile rose into her throat and tears came, recalling the moment. Her insides soaked with champagne and vodka, she'd been curled up on the bed, lying on her side among the coats. She'd felt the weight of another body suddenly behind her on the bed. Arms wrapping around her waist while the stubble of a beard brushed against her cheek. Ryan had been growing out his beard for a few days, and Shea had told him it was sexy. Her stomach fluttered as she felt kisses on her neck; her toes curled when she felt his breath in her ear. She giggled, eyes still closed, when his hand moved along her waist, cupping her breast through her dress.

"I was hoping you'd find me," she had said softly. It had felt wild and spontaneous and a welcome end to an evening when they'd barely been in the same room. But then he whispered in her ear, "You're so beautiful," and she'd stopped breathing.

It was Charlie. Charlie's lips on her bare shoulder, his hands all over her . . . Her whole body froze.

He had turned her face to his and kissed her. She didn't stop him. But she wriggled away, laughing it off, unwilling to make a scene, terrified of saying something that could cause so much damage between him and Dee, or between him and Ryan, or her and Dee, or her and Ryan, or her and everyone she knew.

She'd quickly escaped to the bathroom, collapsing onto the closed toilet seat in the dark, the feeling of his hands all over her, the kisses on her neck. Had she invited this? Dancing around him, basking in the attention, the whispered compliments on her dress, the innu-endos. He'd come up behind her by the bar and slipped his arm around her waist, reeling her in. "You're driving me crazy," he'd said. She thought they were just playing. Ryan always said she was a flirt, though he never seemed to mind—he was, too. Her friends teased her about it, about how whenever they were out together, Shea was always the target of strange men's affections. She'd deny it through laughter, but Georgia had once said Shea liked to toy with them, always making them think they stood a chance.

Shea was crying now that she was finally speaking about it after all these years. "I thought you were Ryan," she whispered, still choked from the memory.

"Please," Charlie said. "I kissed you. Your eyes were wide open. You just can't admit that you enjoyed it."

She shook her head, sniffling. "I didn't want that. I never wanted that."

"You're lying. You were just afraid we'd get caught."

Shea shook her head. "No, Charlie. I didn't know what to do. What to say." It had reminded her of the times in her college years when she'd simply gone along, finding herself in uncomfortable places, never wanting to spoil the fun or dampen the mood, never wanting to be called a tease or a bitch, allowing herself instead to be used, convincing herself that she enjoyed her effect on men, that she had some sort of power. But of course, that wasn't it. It was fear. Paralyzing fear, hidden under the blanket of confidence. Fear of rejec-tion, of judgment, of everything.

She'd considered telling Ryan what had happened that night, but she couldn't speak of it. She hadn't reacted quickly, or raised her voice, or acted offended. And everyone had seen her behavior that night. *It happened, it was nothing,* she later told herself. It was over, and she'd decided alcohol was to blame. She had kept her distance for a couple of years and, over time, let it go.

Shea bent down for her purse, wiping at her face before grabbing the doorknob. "Leave me alone, Charlie. Please."

She walked to the car, nauseated by the confrontation, and tried to control her shaking hands as she put the key in the ignition.

The windshield was covered in fresh powder. She turned on the wipers, putting the gear into reverse.

"You're a fucking tease," Charlie yelled from the door.

She ignored him and looked over her shoulder before pressing the gas. Something shattered on the front hood, and she jumped, whipping her head around. Charlie was closer now, standing there with a smirk on his face. His hands were empty. The snow on the hood had cratered from the impact of his glass, the amber liquid now splattered across her car.

She said nothing but turned and began backing out of the driveway.

"Bitch!" he shouted. A final farewell.

CHAPTER 19

April 13

On Thursday morning, Kat went downtown to the Chicago office for her morning meeting. As various hotel managers shared details and problems at their properties, hotel business—her business—began to creep back into the forefront of her mind, a welcome distraction after spending the last several days consumed with theories about who might have wanted to hurt Shea.

Kat remained in the conference room after the meeting. As she created to-do lists and jotted down notes on how to address the staffing issues and reservation system hiccups, her usual work stress was missing. She didn't second-guess the ideas as they came to her, and she wasn't tormenting herself with worry that she might fail to fix what needed fixing. She knew how to do this job, and she could do it well. It was entirely different from dealing with Shea's death. She wasn't an investigator, she obviously didn't know all the facts, and learning all that she had over the last week had only made her feel worse. Perhaps the best move would be to wrap up these meetings and get on the first possible plane home. She had a life that needed attending to and a husband she was beginning to miss more than ever. Nothing she learned would bring back her friend, anyway.

A knock on the conference-room door finally pulled her attention from a slew of e-mails. "You asked for these?" It was one of the administrative assistants, Martin, with the documents Kat had requested.

"Oh, great, thanks." Martin left, and Kat went through the spreadsheets detailing the first-quarter customer reviews for amenities at five of their hotel properties. Looking through the graphs, the Chicago spa seemed to have some hiccups. The last page included the reservation number associated with each guest's review. She wondered which of these comments had been Shea's. Shea had promised to use and review the spa when she used those vouchers, and Kat would be embarrassed if her gift had been a bust. Maybe Ryan was just being nice about their hotel stay. He had shared very little when she'd asked about their experience, she remembered. Kat pulled up the Chicago hotel's reservation database and searched for a Shea Walker.

She didn't see her name. Kat's phone pinged with a text from Tori. She was in the city for some morning appointments and suggested they meet for lunch. Kat was starving. Yes! Where/When? she wrote.

> Panera. Next to your hotel. I'm heading there now. See u in 10

Kat stacked her materials and sent a quick e-mail to Martin.

> Re: reviews of Chicago property in first quarter . . .
> Pls find reservation for voucher assigned to Shea Walker. Asap. Thx.

Tori was easy to spot—ever the model of high fashion and high heels—removing her giant sunglasses as she stepped inside the restaurant.

"So, what brought you downtown today?" Kat asked once they'd sat down with their orders.

"Just a meeting with my banker," Tori replied. Her banker. Kat couldn't imagine having a relationship with a banker. "Oh, and a little consult with my doctor regarding what to do about this," Tori joked, lifting the skin along her temples.

"You're kidding," Kat said. "Come on, Tori. Do you see you? You don't need that."

"Oh, my naive friend, you say that like this is natural," she said, swirling her hand in front of her face. "I've had this guy on speed dial for years."

Kat laughed. "Really?"

"Every woman has her secrets," she said, playfully raising one brow.

"Well, then, I guess you know what you're doing. You look great all the time."

"Thank you, da'ling," Tori replied in a Zsa Zsa Gabor–style accent. "Anyway, how is work?"

"Fine. It was kind of nice to be consumed by work again—a welcome change after this last week. And you're right, by the way—"

"About what?"

"Dee. I was crazy to suggest that she could have had something to do with Shea's death. She came over to Lina's last night with dinner, and we talked. She couldn't possibly have done anything."

"Well, I'm glad to hear you say that. As much as I called you out for sounding crazy, I could barely sleep last night, thinking about our conversation. Did she tell you anything about Charlie and the whole marriage collapse?"

"'Fraid so. And I gotta say, I've never had a strong opinion about Charlie. But, boy, I am *not* a fan." Kat shared more about Dee's belief that Charlie had become obsessed with Shea in the months before her death.

Tori took another bite of salad and sipped her tea before chiming in. "I'd believe it. He is such a flirt. We just can't trust beautiful men, can we?" she joked. "Why do you think I married my man?"

"Stop. Herman's cute!"

"Of course he is. But he doesn't stop traffic. I'd prefer that the head turns be directed my way, thank you very much. And Charlie seems entirely too aware of his looks. He's definitely a guy that would make you feel insecure."

Kat thought about this, about how Mack had often joked that Kat was far out of his league, and that, luckily, she lacked the self-confidence to realize she could have done better. It wasn't true, but she loved that he thought so, and it always made her laugh.

"Jesus," Tori continued. "What if Charlie had something to do with Shea's death?"

Kat shook her head. "No way. To hear Dee tell it, he cried like a baby at the funeral."

"Yeah, I saw that," Tori said. "It was weird."

Both women took a break from the conspiracy theory to finish their salads, but as soon as Tori took her last bite, she continued. "What if Charlie was the friend Shea referred to on Put-in-Bay?"

"But that would mean Shea was having an affair with him. I know that's what Dee thinks, but Ryan said he and Shea were doing fine near the end."

"But let's just assume Dee is right. You just said Dee thinks Shea and Charlie may have been in Michigan together. Perhaps Charlie and his charm eventually got to her. Maybe she felt betrayed that Ryan wanted to do the swap in the first place. Maybe it justified the outcome."

Kat shook her head. "No way." She could not believe Shea would betray Dee like that.

"Let's just play this out. If she had an affair with Charlie, he could have been the friend. He'd obviously be the last person to judge her for misbehaving with some guy while on the girls' trip. Maybe she confided in him. Maybe she was with Charlie in the bar, they had a fight, and that's why she told the innkeeper her friend wasn't coming."

"It sounds crazy. Besides, there's no way to know. Shea's gone. And even if you are right, it doesn't mean anything. It certainly doesn't mean Charlie's a murderer, and the innkeeper told us that Shea's friend didn't come."

"Unless you're right and she let him in later."

As she pictured Charlie walking Shea home from the bar, she thought again about Mary's comment that the other guest had brought her inside. What if the man from the bar was the guest?

Kat suddenly felt sick to her stomach as she thought about this. Dee had said Charlie was obsessed. Kat didn't believe Shea would have planned to go away with Charlie, but . . . "What if Charlie found out Shea was going to Put-in-Bay? If he was obsessed, he could have followed her, wanting to surprise her, maybe getting a room in the inn." It actually sounded possible. It explained why she might have gone into the bar alone but left with the man. And it would explain why she might have opened her door after she went to bed.

Tori pulled out her phone and searched the number for the inn. The lunch rush had passed, the restaurant now quiet. "Let's find out," she said as she called the inn and put the phone on speaker in the middle of the table.

Both women leaned forward. Mary answered the call on the third ring. Tori started the conversation, reminding Mary of their meeting a few days earlier, asking if Mary wouldn't mind sharing the name of the other guest who was registered when Shea was there.

"Well, I guess it's not a secret. The police asked as well. His name was Ted. Hold on," she said, returning to the line a few seconds later. "Here, I just wanted to pull out my book so I didn't misspeak. That's right, Ted Baker."

Kat sighed, relieved. She wanted answers but certainly didn't hope to find a murderer among her old friends.

"Can you describe what he looked like?" Tori asked. *Fake name?* she mouthed to Kat.

"Well, he was very good-looking, I can tell you that," Mary offered. "And a bit of a flirt, too," she added with a chuckle. "He made me blush; that's for sure."

Kat and Tori stared at each other while Mary spoke.

"I'd say he was about six foot two, dark hair, a bit of some gray in there. He looked, I don't know, midforties or maybe fifty."

Mary's description easily fit Charlie. "I don't suppose he told you where he was from?" Kat asked.

"Indianapolis, I think. Actually, I couldn't tell you much more than that, because, like I told the police, he paid cash. Usually I copy IDs and get a credit card imprint, but he'd lost his wallet on the way to Ohio, so I really don't know any more."

"And you said he was the one who came in with Shea when she was a little tipsy?" Tori continued.

"That's right."

"And it was after he had come down for breakfast and checked out that you went to check on Shea?"

"Oh no. He didn't come to breakfast. But I didn't expect him. I knew he had plans to fish in the early morning, so he was up and gone before I ever woke up."

"One more thing, Mary," Kat said. "You said you locked up after Shea and the other guest came in, right?"

"That's right. I like to go to bed by around nine o'clock when the place is empty. Since they were both in, I probably locked up about twenty minutes after they arrived."

"And if Shea had let anyone else in . . . ?"

"Oh no, I think I would have heard that."

"Okay, then, thanks for your help, Mary."

Tori disconnected the call. "Oh my God," she said. "Could that guest have been Charlie? Could he have appeared at Shea's door after Mary left?"

"Just hold on," Kat said. "That was a general description, and the man was from Indianapolis. Maybe it really was some guy named Ted Baker." She took Tori's phone and did a search for the name *Ted Baker* in Indianapolis. Within seconds, there were several search results. She clicked on the White Pages. "Look at this, fifteen men by that name in that city."

Tori grabbed the phone and scrolled through the results. "Yeah, but the man paid in cash and had a story about losing his wallet. Maybe that was so he could use a fake name."

Kat felt overwhelmed. There was no way she could let this go and get back to work. "I should talk to Ryan again. But how can I do that?"

"Just tell him what Dee told you, that she thought Shea and Charlie were together and that Charlie was obsessed. He has a right to know."

"His wife is dead, and Charlie is one of his best friends. And Dee could be wrong."

"Or Charlie might have killed his wife."

CHAPTER 20

February 19

SHEA ROLLED UP THE SNOW-COVERED drive and pulled into their detached garage on Sunday. She cut the engine and sat in the darkened space. Looking at the wire shelves in front of her, the tears came quickly. The shelves were stacked with boxes of Christmas lights and holiday decorations, ski equipment, skateboards that hadn't been touched in a decade, sand buckets filled with sidewalk chalk, a catcher's mask, and those two folding chairs she and Ryan had used for years on the sidelines of the kids' games. This was their life together. A family, two decades of adventure and memories, of laughs and triumphs, and they'd done it together. The shelves were a mess, just like their marriage, but the weekend had helped. After sharing everything with her sister—the swinging nonsense, the Charlie stuff, the text from Dee that caused her to run out on Friday night, Shea had realized there was no proof. She might have been jumping to conclusions when she stormed out. That was what secrets did. She took a deep breath and grabbed the door handle.

She trudged through the snow and stomped her feet as she entered the quiet house through the kitchen door. "Ryan?"

No one responded.

It looked like there had been a party. Empty beer bottles and open food containers sat on the island. She walked into the hall slowly, fearing what she'd find next. The television was on in the living room, couch pillows on the floor, along with popcorn kernels. More beer bottles and an empty bowl on the table.

She walked into the front hall and put her hand on the banister to head upstairs but stopped when she glanced toward the mess in the dining room, the mail strewn across the table, a package opened, its contents—a bunch of Victoria's Secret lingerie—thrown around the room.

She moved closer. The mail had been opened. It was bills. Lots of them. Slowly lowering herself into a chair, she examined each statement. The kids' colleges, the cable company, the credit cards, insurance companies, bank notices, their mortgage statement, even a maxed-out home-equity line Ryan had opened three months earlier that she knew nothing about.

She turned to stand, her worst fears confirmed, and was assaulted by one more disturbing discovery. A hole—like someone's fist had punched a crater into the drywall. She felt like that wall.

She found Ryan asleep on their bed, facedown and naked, without even a sheet covering his body. The bedroom was a mess.

"Hey!" she yelled. He didn't respond.

She kicked at the mattress and shoved him in the back. "Ryan! Wake up."

He groaned and rolled over.

"What the hell is going on here?"

He opened his eyes. "Shea?"

She turned away, crossed the room, and sat in the chair in the corner while he slowly sat up.

"I thought you left," he said. He looked around, confused, like even his nudity was unexpected.

"So, what, you have a party or something? What the hell is going on here?"

He grabbed his boxers and went to the bathroom. She could hear him turn on the sink faucet.

She followed and stood in the doorway. He was throwing water on his face.

"Don't you have anything to say to me?"

"What are you doing here?" Ryan asked without even looking at her. He opened the medicine cabinet and tossed back some pain relievers.

"What the hell is wrong with you? Why does it look like you had a party down there? Why are you naked?"

He ignored the question and brushed his teeth. And then it hit her like a punch in the gut. A woman. She turned back and surveyed the bed more closely. Had someone been here, in her bedroom? The sheets were twisted up, the duvet was on the floor, a towel by the bed. She looked in the closet, walked the space, checked the floor for more proof. She felt sick. Maybe Charlie was right. Maybe Ryan was doing something. Maybe it was Dee . . . maybe . . . She couldn't stop tears from falling. She went to the side tables, looking for evidence, anything to prove the last thing she wanted to believe. All she saw was that envelope of hotel vouchers from Kat, the Christmas gift of romance they'd never even used. It sat on her bedside table, like some cosmic reminder of what was missing. She dropped onto the bed, taking the envelope in her hand. It was empty.

"Where are my vouchers?" she yelled.

Ryan said nothing. She took the empty envelope and walked back to the bathroom door, waving it in the air, aware that she sounded hysterical. "What did you do with my vouchers?"

He looked at the envelope, looked back at Shea, and said, "I didn't do anything." He turned back to the sink.

She walked out, refusing to let him see her cry.

She was in the hall, at the top of the steps, when he appeared, standing in the doorway.

"I know where you were, Shea," he said. "So excuse me if I went a little nuts. I don't think you're in the position to act so righteous."

"What are you talking about?"

"How was your sister's?" His tone was laced with sarcasm.

"Fine." He was acting like this was her fault somehow. She turned to face him. "What's wrong with you? Who was here?"

He stopped and looked back, scanning the room, like he didn't even know.

"Don't you even care that Charlie has been actively pursuing me right under your nose? You don't talk to me, you don't tell me what the hell is happening. Ryan, I just went through all those bills in the dining room. What is going on?"

Ryan didn't answer. He walked back into the bedroom, and she followed, ready to battle. He ignored her and started stripping the sheets off the bed.

"You were the guy who scoffed at my credit card balances when we were young, scolding me on the evils of debt. We've got nearly maxed-out credit cards and some maxed-out home-equity loan I knew nothing about; you lost your job months ago; you don't tell me anything; you're buying things we obviously can't afford. It's like you're trying to ruin our life here. What the hell is going on with you?"

"Maybe too much has happened."

"Just talk to me. I'm supposed to be your wife."

He turned to look her in the face, finally, his eyes weary. "But you're sleeping with my best friend."

"I am not."

"Don't lie, Shea. Don't make this worse. I know where you were this weekend."

"I know you do, because I left you a note."

"Bullshit!"

Now Shea was yelling, too. "I went to my sister's. I told you that."

He grabbed the jeans and T-shirt from the floor and got dressed. "What is wrong with you?" she pleaded.

"I was so stupid. You left me some message about *needing time* and *you'll understand*," he said, tossing the balled-up sheets in the corner. "Here I was thinking I had screwed things up between us. I'm thinking, oh shit, maybe I should jump in the car and follow her and tell her I love her!"

Shea quietly walked back to the chair in the corner.

"And then I think of that FindMyPhone app you put on my phone so I could help you find your phone when you lost it. I stood there, watching that little dot moving around a circle over and over while the GPS located your phone, and then—boom. It finds you. Not at your sister's in Grand Rapids, but in Saint Joe. So I'm thinking, she must be on the way. And I zoom in, and then I see that blue dot—smack-dab on Charlie's lake house."

Shea took a deep breath. She'd have to tell him everything. She'd wanted to spare him. She didn't want to ruin friendships, but it was too late for that. "Charlie has been trying to have an affair with me, Ryan. Ever since that dinner party. That stupid night. He's texted me constantly. He even said he'd gotten Dee to agree to the idea."

"And so you finally gave in." He sat on the bed, looking at her now, like she was the liar.

"No." She leaned forward, her elbows on her knees. "Listen to me. I went there to beg him to leave me alone, and then I went to my sister's to think about us."

She told Ryan what happened when she got to Charlie's, how she'd pleaded with him and told him that she loved Ryan and didn't want to lose Dee's friendship. She told him how Charlie became angry. "Ryan, there's something else. I'd never wanted to tell you. I didn't want to hurt you." She finally shared what happened at the Christmas party all those years ago. Another secret between them. She'd been so good at burying the truth.

He didn't say a word for more than a minute.

His face turned angry. "Jesus Christ, Shea. All these years you let me be friends with a guy that groped my wife? How could you do that?"

Shea couldn't hold back the tears. "I just thought he was being a creep. And it was a party. Everyone drank too much. I'd been a flirt. You know he's a letch. We all think that. But you liked him so much, and I really loved Dee. I didn't want to upset anyone. It was just the one time, more than a decade ago. It was in the past. At least until all that stupid kissing and swinging madness."

Ryan fell back onto the bare mattress, his head in his hands.

Neither spoke for a minute, letting the truth soak in.

And then, as much to himself as to Shea, he said, "I thought it was over between us. I thought I'd played a dangerous game and had been punished for it."

"What happened here?" she finally said, sniffling, tears streaming down her cheeks. She looked around the room, at the sheets now balled up in the corner. "Are you sleeping with Dee? Was she here?"

Ryan looked up. She glanced away. She wasn't sure she could watch him admit it. "No. Of course not," he said.

"She texted you on Friday. And she's been ignoring me, and you've been losing weight and ignoring me. Charlie said she was fine with whatever he wanted with me . . . Something was going on. I walk in here and you're naked. Was someone here? In our bed?" She could hardly say the words.

Ryan stood, walked to the window and surveyed the room. His eyes were fixed on the mattress, like he was trying to process everything. "So, you're not having an affair?" he asked again, the expression on his face lifting, like a glimmer of hope was emerging. He looked at her. "What about all that lingerie that came yesterday? I opened that box and it felt like you were throwing it in my face."

Shea wiped the tears that kept coming. "That was for you, you shithead," she said, chuckling at the absurdity. "Your birthday is next week. Remember? I was trying to add a little spice without bringing in other people, for Christ's sake!"

"Jesus," Ryan said. "I am an idiot." He looked back out the window. "I can see Charlie's house from here." He turned to Shea. "Well, that friendship is over." His tone had lightened like they'd worked it all out, like their fictional infidelity was the only issue one the table.

"What's with the sudden weight loss?" Shea asked. "Is this a midlife crisis? Are you freaking out about getting old or something?"

"No." Ryan chuckled, shaking his head. "I was trying to be better. For you. God, I feel stupid. I knew that I screwed up at that dinner. I should have been the one to stop it. And I thought the best thing to do after a night like that was to never mention it again. My dad always said, 'Act as if. Fake it till you make it.' I figured I'd act as if everything was fine, and, eventually, like every other wrinkle, it would smooth out. I'm pretty good at avoiding, as you know. And I thought maybe if I dropped a few, you'd see me for the hot man I am."

"You're ridiculous."

"No argument," he said.

"So, no one in this house is sleeping around?" Shea begged for confirmation.

Ryan shook his head and then put his hands to his face, squeezing his eyes shut. "I got so drunk yesterday."

It wasn't an answer. Shea looked at the bare mattress. "What are you saying? Ryan? What happened?"

He didn't stop shaking his head, but he removed his hands and looked at her. "Nothing," he said. "I got overwhelmed. I got drunk. I punched a wall, and you found me in all my glory."

Shea exhaled. Ryan did, too.

"We can't keep living like this," Shea said. "I'm not your child. You're supposed to talk to me. You're living in denial, racking up debt. What is wrong with you?"

"I know," he said, sitting on the bed. "Here's the thing."

She couldn't move, terrified of whatever he was holding back.

"I hate being an accountant."

She grinned and took a breath. "Okay, but that doesn't really explain any of this."

"I kind of panicked when I lost my job last summer. Leigh was about to go off to college. You were planning this big party and feeling so emotional about our baby leaving. It wasn't the time to talk about it. I didn't want to worry you."

"So, you just pretended it didn't happen."

"Sounds stupid when you say it," he joked. "I always kept six months of cash available for emergencies—at least until the crash a few years ago, and then it got tighter. But I was ready for a least a few months of crisis. But then, with the kids' tuition due, we had to replace those pipes in the basement, the car broke down . . . Anyway, it got tight. I figured I'd find something else quickly and then share the news. I didn't realize how difficult it would be to find something. I didn't realize that after turning fifty, I'd be competing against kids."

"But it seems like you stopped looking. And you kept spending money, insisting that everything was fine."

"There is something I haven't told you."

Shea held her breath again.

"You know I've been visiting my dad a lot."

"Yes, or so I hoped, anyway. For a while there, I began to worry that you were with someone else, just pretending to see him. I mean, in all these years, you've never been close. And suddenly he's sick and you're at his side constantly."

"Yeah, I know. It's never been an easy relationship. But I guess impending death softens a guy."

"Well, I'm glad, but how does any of this relate to our life?"

"My dad and I talked. Really talked. I told him about losing my job, and I admitted how much I disliked it, and how hard it was to find something new. How I felt like I was failing. Funny how much easier it is to talk to him when he can't move. You know what he said?"

"What?"

"He said, 'So don't do it.'"

"What do you mean?"

"He said he'd done the same thing. Worked a job for thirty years, surviving two heart attacks, popping antacids for decades from stress and years of traveling to meet impossible quotas, feeling like Willy Loman. He said, 'Life is too short.'"

"Okay, well, I guess to a certain extent your dad is right, but what you've been doing isn't about finding a new direction."

"I'm afraid of what you'll think of me. That's why I didn't say anything."

"What aren't you telling me?"

"When I was with him just before Thanksgiving, the doctors told me that I should probably say good-bye, just in case. He'd become very weak. I said I'd be back again after Christmas and asked that they call if something looked imminent, and I'd jump in the car to be there at the end. I think he sensed that the end was near, too. That's when he told me that I wouldn't have to worry, that when my mom died, he'd been her sole benefactor, but now that he was dying, everything would go to me. Her parents left her a lot of money."

"So . . . ?"

"Jesus, please don't think I'm the worst person on the planet."

"What, Ryan? What did you do?"

"My dad said I'd soon have enough to take care of our family and try something new. I knew it would take months to land a new job, and I assumed the inheritance would come in by then. So, I got the equity loan to help cover us until . . ."

Shea sat back and looked away.

"I know it sounds awful. That's why I didn't tell you. I wanted to take care of you like I always have. It's my job."

"You made it your job, not me. Do you know how insulting it is that you hide stuff from me, that you handle everything and keep me in the dark? How is that supposed to make me feel like a partner?"

Ryan didn't say anything.

"Why didn't you tell me any of this? All these conversations with your father. Why haven't I heard about any of this? That's not a marriage."

He didn't answer.

"So, you've just been waiting for your father to die?"

Ryan wiped his eyes. "I thought it was the end," his voice pleading. "I thought we'd made peace, and he'd given me words of advice, and suddenly the gift of starting something new. But he's still hanging on, and I find myself waiting for him to die. And when I called at Christmas, the nurse told me that he'd taken a turn for the worse. Part of me was sad, but part was just relieved to think that we'd be okay."

"Jesus, so you went off and bought those outrageous Christmas gifts."

"I know, it seems disgusting. I'm not a monster. I don't want him to die. I just wanted . . ."

"What?"

Ryan broke down. He covered his face, trying to hide. She didn't move.

"I couldn't tell you. I'd made such a mess of things. How could I tell you that?"

"I don't understand. Is everything gone? What about our retirement savings, the kids' college funds?"

"The college funds were short, so I dipped into retirement to pay for tuition back when I assumed I'd be working my old job for another ten years. I've just been living in denial."

"You should have told me."

"I know."

"I feel like I don't even know who you are right now."

He came over to the chair and knelt on the floor in front of her.

"I'm a terrible communicator."

Somehow, that made her laugh. "That's an understatement."

"But, Shea, I swear to God. I love you. I've made a lot of mistakes, but I did what I did because I was afraid of letting you down or losing you."

They were more alike than she admitted. "I could have helped. And we're not going to go on pretending life is fine, waiting for your dad to die."

Ryan stood up and extended his hand. She took it, and he quickly pulled her to standing, dropped into the seat, and pulled her down on his lap. "Please, don't leave me. I don't want to lose you." His eyes welled with tears.

"You are such an idiot," she said.

He pulled her tight. They both held on. It felt good, despite everything. It felt like home. Wasn't that all it was supposed to be? Having someone to hold, someone who held on tight, someone to ride through the peaks and valleys together?

"I'm sorry," Ryan whispered.

Shea pulled back from the embrace. "I'm not ready to give up on our life together. No more secrets and lies, okay?"

He looked away from her eyes. There was more.

"What?"

"I found your new Vicodin prescription this weekend, too."

Shea dropped her head onto his shoulder, melting into him. Now she was the one who couldn't face his eyes. "We are a mess, aren't we?"

"It appears that way."

"I haven't been sleeping. My back was hurting." That wasn't it. "I was escaping."

"Can you stop?"

"That depends. Are we going to be okay?"

"Yes."

"Then, yes, I can."

They sat in that chair, in silence, surrounded by the mess. Shea finally sat up and looked around the room. "We're going to sell this house."

Ryan shook his head. "You love this house. I always thought our kids would come back here with their kids and we'd always be here."

"It's just a house, Ryan. It's a beautiful house that has served us well. But the kids are grown. We don't need all this space. We're lucky we've been here twenty years and we can make this move. I'm not some frail little woman. I can handle things. I can handle change and stress and difficult situations if you'd just quit trying to protect me like your child."

Ryan looked around.

Shea followed his gaze. "There are some things we need to do to get it ready first, like maybe you should patch that wall in the dining room."

He smiled, and she did, too.

"But we're going to sell the house, pay off these credit cards and this equity loan, and get the hell out of here. The best time to sell a house is spring. Fresh start, smaller house. Things aren't good, Ryan, but it's not the end of the world. We have our health, we have this big, beautiful, valuable home. And your dad is right. You don't need to continue doing something you hate. But you must do something. We can't sit around waiting for some magic bag of money to appear."

Suddenly, it seemed like a great idea to Shea, too. A fresh start. They'd start a whole new chapter.

"Maybe we could even start a little business. Think about it—we're only fifty-two. Well, I am. You're an old man now at fifty-five." She smiled. "We may have another fifty years to go, if we're lucky. Let's do something new. Let's be like Kat and Mack and get the hell out of here. It's time for reinvention. You and me."

Ryan took Shea's hand in his as the tears streamed down his face. "I always knew you were too good for me."

"Me, too," she said, leaning in to put her head on his shoulder.

CHAPTER 21

April 13

KAT AND TORI RETURNED TO Maple Park after lunch in the city. Kat could handle the remaining work crises from Lina's dining table. Fortunately, Lina said she was enjoying Kat's company, and Kat was happy to be there. The time for getting answers was slipping away quickly. She was supposed to leave tomorrow afternoon after her last meeting.

As Tori turned off the expressway, Kat stared at the familiar Maple Park landmarks, the same ones she'd noticed just five days earlier. The historic homes she'd always admired, the ice cream shop she'd biked to with her son, the pool where he'd learned to swim, the parks, trees, shops. Everything had been softened by distance, perfected in memory. But, today, she noticed peeling paint on some of those beloved homes, lease signs in the windows of stores she'd loved, and patches of park grass that had been muddied to destruction from spring showers.

You can never go home again, she thought, remembering the first time her mother had said that to her. Kat had finished college and was back in her childhood home, feeling rootless, depressed that everything had changed since she'd moved away.

A part of her had wondered if she had made a mistake leaving Maple Park, if perhaps they should return. If she had to travel so much, perhaps it had been unfair to uproot Mack.

But coming back no longer felt viable. Every town had its charms and its issues, just as everyone in them did. She was beginning to look forward to getting on that plane. She and Mack just needed more time to adjust. He was one of the good ones. He was home. All the problems they faced now seemed trivial.

~ • ~

Later that afternoon, she walked the six blocks back to Ryan's house, quietly talking to herself along the way, practicing what could be said, what would be least damaging. Everything she wanted to ask was out of line. Ryan's marriage was none of her business. But Charlie, and Dee's stories, hovered in her mind. Shea had opened her bedroom door at the inn. She'd had drinks at the bar with a man, and a man had walked her inside Humphrey House. Someone else had been with her when she died. Kat knew it.

When she got to the front walk, Ryan was at the door in his sweat-pants and a T-shirt, picking up delivery boxes off the front porch. "Hey, Kit Kat!" He stopped as she came up the walkway. "I was hoping I'd get to see you before you left town. Come in."

"Thanks. Here, let me help," she said, grabbing the remaining box from the stoop. "What's all this?"

"Not sure," Ryan said. "I'm not sleeping all that well, and I find myself scrolling the Internet in the middle of the night. I guess I'm trying to avoid the fridge."

It was impossible not to wonder, seeing all the boxes, if there were still financial issues going on here as well. Kat looked around the room and for the first time realized that there were a couple of new pieces of furniture and a new, larger television in the living room.

Had Ryan gotten a new job? And if so, why was he home at four o'clock in the afternoon? She knew it was wrong to ask, wrong to even wonder, and she stood in the front hall feeling more and more like an intruder.

"Come on, come sit in the living room. Want a drink?" he asked, walking toward the dry bar in the corner of the room.

Kat sat in a chair and looked at the table, covered in dirty dishes. The afternoon light streamed through the window, highlighting a thin layer of dust on the glass surface. "Oh, thanks, but I've still got some work to do when I get back to Lina's."

Ryan stepped over the throw pillows strewn across the floor and collapsed onto the sofa, lifting his glass to avoid spilling what appeared to be a scotch on the rocks. "I get it." He chuckled. "Well, that's not true, is it?" he muttered to himself.

He seemed a little buzzed. Was that a reference to being unemployed?

Kat didn't know what to say. Should she offer condolences for his job loss—that she only knew about because of gossip? Should she ask if he was all right, when he obviously wasn't? No one would be okay two weeks after a spouse died.

Ryan's head was now resting against the top of the sofa, his eyes closed, a full glass in his hand. He took a deep breath.

Kat took one, too. "Ryan, it seems stupid to ask if you're okay. Can I do anything? I'm sure this is so difficult. I wish I could make it better."

"I'm gonna move," he said suddenly, lifting his head and opening his eyes.

"Really?"

He took a big sip from his glass. "Yeah, there's nothing left for me here."

It was the perfect opening. "What about work? What about your friends?"

"My job is over. You know I always hated being an accountant?"

"Really? Okay, well, then I guess it's a good idea not to do it, right?" She trod carefully, wondering if she could handle what he might say next.

"That's right," he said, smacking his hand against the coffee table. He took another swig and finished the drink. "And good riddance."

Good riddance. What an odd phrase. Dee had used it, too, in her dark and drunken attempt at humor, joking that Shea's death had been a good thing.

At least Dee had moved on to some healthier perspective about her own collapsing marriage. After all, marriages were destroyed from within.

"We had a plan," Ryan continued. "We were going to get out of here. A fresh start."

"You and Shea? You were going to leave Maple Park?"

"That's right. And now she's gone. I shouldn't stay here," he slurred.

Kat sat forward. "This must be so difficult, Ryan. I totally understand wanting to run, but you are surrounded by friends who love you."

"Well, that's bullshit, isn't it? I have no friends. Zero. I'm telling you, Kit Kat, you were a smart cookie, getting out of here." He put his glass down and resumed resting his head against the top of the sofa.

Kat didn't know what to say. She looked around at the space that had appeared kept and tidy just days ago but was now beginning to fall apart. Suddenly, she heard Ryan breathing deeply. "Ryan?"

He was asleep. She stood and quietly walked out of the room and into the kitchen. Dishes were piled high in the sink. Food meant for the refrigerator sat out on the counter. She returned the cereal boxes and chips to the pantry, put the juice back in the fridge, and moved a half-eaten casserole to the trash. It was impossible to know how long it had been sitting out.

Kat pushed her shirtsleeves up to her elbows and washed the dishes, then moved on to the kitchen table, the only remaining sign of chaos in the room. Even the mail was scattered around, the condolence cards no longer in a neat pile. She stacked the junk mail and gathered the cards. It was amazing how many people had reached out. Kat wondered what would happen if she died suddenly. She had a few good friends in the world, and certainly counted some of these neighbors among them, but she could probably count on two hands those who might mourn her. She shook off the thought, feeling silly. How could she continue to look at Shea as if her life were better? She was dead. And, obviously, Shea's life had been far from ideal. All these years, Kat's lens had been distorted. Shea's endless positivity, her smile, her breezy, flowing dresses and bare feet projecting this laid-back, "life's a beach" persona. But everyone wore a mask of some kind. No one escaped life's rough waters.

She noticed a card from Dee and Charlie. Their return address label was on the back of the envelope: Charlie and Dee Goldman, but Charlie's name had been scratched out. The front of the envelope, addressed to Ryan, was obviously Dee's handwriting. Kat opened the card and skimmed past the prepackaged well wishes from Hallmark, to Dee's personal message: *Regardless of everything, I'm here if you need me. Dee.*

Suddenly, Ryan was standing in the doorway to the kitchen, rubbing his eyes. "Hey again. Boy, you're seeing me at my best."

Kat tossed the card onto the pile, embarrassed to be snooping, and walked over, hugging him before he could resist, holding on tight. "You're gonna be okay. I know it's not the same, but when my father died, I fell apart for a while. We never get over it, but we do get on with it."

"I wish this was about my dad dying," he said, pulling out of the embrace. "He's the one that's supposed to die, for Christ's sake. The fucker's still holding on, though."

Kat smirked, assuming this was an attempt at humor. "Well, that's good, right?"

"Not really. But that's another story," he said, walking toward the fridge. He pulled out a tinfoil-covered Pyrex dish and put it on the island. "At least I'm not starving to death," he added. "Anyway, I know you're right. I'll be fine." He looked around the clean kitchen. "Thanks for doing this."

"No problem. Ryan, I know that nothing is going to make any of this better, but if there's even a small chance that someone out there did something to Shea, I don't want them to get away with it, you know?"

"Kat, no one did anything to Shea. You've got to let this go."

"I'm sure you're right, but before you fell asleep you said you had no friends. I'm guessing that means you and Charlie are on the outs." He didn't disagree, so Kat pressed on. "Dee thinks Charlie may have been obsessed with Shea." She stopped to gauge his reaction, and he looked away, staring vacantly out the window.

"I'm not sure you should trust what Dee has to say," he said.

"Shea had been drinking with a man at the bar on the island, you probably heard that. But they left together, and the man told the bartender they were going to the inn. The innkeeper saw her walking in with a man, who was her other registered guest."

Ryan didn't speak, so Kat pressed on.

"She didn't assume they knew each other, but the man used cash and said he'd lost his wallet. The innkeeper's description of that guest sounds like—"

"Kat, what are you doing?"

She said nothing.

"Charlie's a piece of shit. Yes, that friendship is done. But to suggest that she was there with Charlie? That she'd ever let him into her room? You're dead wrong. She wanted nothing to do with Charlie."

"I'm sorry. I just keep hearing these things. Evelyn said you didn't know Shea had been looking at real estate on the island. It seems like there was a lot more going on with her than any of us knew about. And if there's any chance some man out there killed her, we can't let him get away with it."

"Evelyn doesn't know what she's talking about. Shea and I were both looking at real estate listings. I didn't know she'd looked at Put-in-Bay, but we were looking. They were for us, for our plan to start over."

"So, you didn't think . . . ?"

"Shea was not having an affair with Charlie. Don't go starting some crazy rumors, Kat."

"No, of course," Kat said, her eyes welling. She didn't want to make it worse.

"I told you before," he said, his voice louder. "I never cheated on Shea. She never cheated on me. We were *fine*. It was an accident. I'm sure of it. Now, stop, please."

But Ryan had cheated on Shea. He'd told Mack. She stepped back. "I'm sorry, Ryan. I didn't mean to offend you."

"It's okay," he said, his tone softening. "I'm sorry to snap. I'm just tired."

It was none of her business, and even if he had once cheated, how could that matter now?

He began walking to the door, and Kat took the cue to follow.

CHAPTER 22

March 29

SHEA WAS SITTING ON THE window seat in the living room, cradling her warm coffee. Ryan had just replaced the storm windows with screens, and the house could now breathe. She could finally enjoy the cool breeze and the sounds of birds gathering in the trees outside, their conversations filling the house with life. Living in Maple Park during winter felt like walking through an old movie—nothing but black and white and gray. In spring, it was as if someone hit the switch, as if she'd landed in Oz: green lawns, blue skies, tree buds, perennials breaking through the hard sod, magnolia blooms. It all seemed to happen overnight. It was enough to confirm the beginning of their fresh start. Things were finally turning around.

When the doorbell rang an hour later, and Shea found Tori standing outside her door, she suddenly realized how long it had been since she'd seen her friend. Other than sitting with Lina at a chemo treatment a couple of weeks ago, she and Ryan had spent the last month in their own cocoon. She'd stopped making plans with friends, not wanting to make small talk, not wanting to share anything about what was really going on in their lives.

"Hi," Tori said. "I haven't seen you in ages, Shea. I miss you."

"Me, too. I've just been busy. Come in."

Shea led Tori to the living room. She'd dumped everything from cabinets and shelves onto the floor. After nearly two decades in the house, there was a huge amount of purging they needed to do.

Tori looked around. "Wow, what's going on here?"

"Spring cleaning. It seems things get worse before they get better, right? I decided to dump everything on the floor to figure out what I really needed. Maybe not the best method, but it's mine." She wasn't about to tell Tori what was going on. No one needed to know the dire straits she and Ryan were in, or why. It never helped if word got out that a couple *really needed* to sell their house. When it was time, they'd tell everyone about their plans. But not now.

"I should do that, too," Tori said. "We have so much stuff we don't need."

"Don't we all. Anyway, what's up?" Usually, when a friend popped in without warning, she was out for a walk, but Tori was in jeans and heels.

"Actually, I just got back from Catawba yesterday, and I was thinking of you," Tori said.

"Oh?"

"Can we sit?"

"Okay," Shea said, gesturing toward the sofa. "What's going on?"

Tori climbed over the piles on the floor and sat on the sofa. Shea sat beside her. "Remember that guy you met when we all went to Put-in-Bay before Thanksgiving?"

Shea instinctively looked toward the hall, looking out for Ryan, who was in the basement storage area working on his own sorting and purging. "Yeah." There was no chance Shea would ever forget that night, as much as she wanted to, but reminding Ryan of the pain they'd caused each other in the last several months was the last thing she wanted.

"Well, I saw this in the paper when I was out there. Isn't that him?" Tori asked, handing the paper to Shea, folded to show the man's picture and the story she'd read.

Shea looked at the picture of Blake. His smile, those unmistakable dimples. "Why?" she asked before answering.

"He disappeared the night we were there. That's him, isn't it?"

The last moments with Blake were right there in her head. His face, the blood, the screaming. She'd just wanted to get away. Something inside Shea told her to wait, not to share with Tori. "I don't know," she said, staring at Blake's picture. "I'm not sure I remember exactly what he looked like."

"Really? Because as soon as I saw it, I thought of him. I didn't remember what his name was, but I could have sworn that was the guy you hooked up with."

Shea looked toward the hall again before chiding her friend. "Tori," she said, lowering her voice. "I didn't hook up with him. I just flirted."

"Okay, flirted."

"I don't really remember him all that well, honestly. This guy is good-looking, and so was he, but that's about it."

"Oh, okay. I just thought—"

"What's the article about anyway?"

"Dangers of Lake Erie. Several deaths that occurred last year. This guy disappeared, and his boat washed up on one of the islands. He was last seen the night we were there. I thought it looked like your guy."

"He wasn't *my* guy," Shea said, glancing away. "I don't know if it's him." She tossed the paper onto the coffee table. Heat rose in her face as she thought back to those last minutes with Blake. He'd been knocked down, but she thought he'd get up. Did he get up? "Hey, I'm sorry to push you out, but I've got a doctor's appointment in like thirty minutes. I've got to get dressed."

"Oh, no problem," Tori said, rising from the couch. "Anyway, let's get together soon. Coffee? Happy hour? Whatever works."

"Absolutely. I'll call you."

After Tori left, Shea went to the couch and read the story about Blake. No amount of alcohol could protect Shea from remembering every detail of what had happened on that boat.

Ryan appeared then, looking filthy. And cute. "Was that Tori?" he said, looking toward the front door. "I thought I heard her voice."

"Yeah, she was just stopping in to say hi."

"How'd you explain all this?" Ryan waved at the disaster they called a living room.

"Spring cleaning."

"Good one."

"How's it going in the basement?" she asked, folding the paper as if it were just another item in the mess needing organization.

"I think it gets worse before it gets better. I've really made a mess of things, though."

"So have I," she said.

"Wanna take a break? I never ate lunch."

As he stood there, covered in dirt, looking thinner than he had in years, wearing that work belt Shea had bought him back when they first married, back when he'd pledged to be a Mr. Fix-It around the house—which he never became—she smiled, feeling more connected than they'd been in a long while.

They'd been waking each day with purpose, planning the end-game to get top dollar for the house, and despite the uncertainty of the future, she'd felt . . . hopeful. It reminded Shea of when they were young and she was pregnant with Stephen and they were trying madly to get the old house fixed up before the baby arrived. They were finally getting back to who they used to be. And Tori had just casually dropped a grenade in the living room. She'd pulled the pin and walked out, leaving Shea to wonder if it would destroy everything.

"I can't eat right now," Shea said. "I've got to run some errands. I'll see you later."

She brushed past him, but Ryan grabbed her and pulled her close. "Wait a second," he said. "How you like my work belt?" He raised his eyebrows like he stood before her in a tux.

"Love it." Shea kissed his cheek. "Total turn-on, but I gotta run."

She went upstairs, got dressed, and grabbed the newspaper article before she went over to Georgia's.

CHAPTER 23

April 13

Back at Lina's, Kat was making some dinner when the doorbell rang. Before Lina had the chance to get up, Kat answered the door.

Tori came barreling into the house. She saw Lina on the couch and leaned in for a quick air kiss before collapsing onto the seat cushion beside her. Kat followed her into the living room. "What's going on?"

"I spoke to Dee," Tori said. "Charlie was not in Maple Park when Shea went to Ohio. He'd been staying at their Michigan cottage a lot of the time, ever since asking for space. And guess what?"

"What?" Kat and Lina asked in unison.

"Charlie asked Dee for a divorce the day before Shea was found on Put-in-Bay."

"That doesn't mean anything," Lina said.

"But Dee drove to their Michigan house to speak with him about it," Tori continued. "That was April first. She was devastated and not ready to give up on them."

"And?" Lina asked.

"He wasn't there. She called his cell, and he didn't answer. She sent texts, he didn't answer. She sat around waiting, and he never came back."

"But it doesn't mean that he was on Put-in-Bay with Shea," Kat said. "If he wanted a divorce and wanted space, he may simply have been avoiding Dee."

"True, but she stayed the night. He never came home. Dee said she felt like a fool, certain he was with another woman. She assumed it was Shea."

"I still don't see how Dee was so certain Shea had been with Charlie."

"Actually, she said she found a wineglass in the dishwasher at the cabin. It still had remnants of lipstick on the rim. One of those bright shades Shea always wore. Dee took it as proof."

Kat sat on the arm of the sofa. "What are you saying?"

"Two thoughts. One, Charlie and Shea went to Put-in-Bay together, or two, Charlie somehow found out Shea was going to Put-in-Bay and followed her. If he was obsessed like Dee said, and Shea had been rebuking his advances, then I'm thinking he'd want to tell her that he was leaving his wife."

Kat and Lina looked at each other. Neither commented.

"Think about it," Tori said. "He secretly checks in to the inn under a false name, shows up at the bar, they drink, he brings her back, lets Mary assume they're strangers and that he found her outside, and then later knocks on her door. Who knows? Maybe she finally succumbs to his advances, being slightly drunk. We know she may have been upset by Blake's memorial. Maybe Charlie was sleeping in the room with her when she accidentally drowned in the tub and he panicked and left. It would certainly explain his over-the-top blubbering at her memorial. Or maybe she refused his advances and he snapped and held her under the water . . ."

"Take a breath," Kat finally interjected. "Your imagination is in overdrive. I spoke with Ryan earlier today. He said there was no way Shea was having an affair with Charlie. I got the sense that he might have even known more about Charlie than he wanted to tell me. They are obviously on the outs, but he bit my head off at the suggestion that Charlie could have been there. Ryan certainly knows him better than we do. If anyone would have a reason to suspect Charlie, it's Ryan, and he doesn't."

"You should talk to that innkeeper again," Lina said. "She's the only one who saw the man who stayed at the inn."

"Yes, and the bartender," Kat agreed. "We'll get a picture of Charlie and settle this." She got up, grabbed her laptop, logged on to Facebook, searched for Charlie's profile page, captured a picture, cropped, and saved. "Here," she said. "We'll send this." She found the website for Humphrey House and drafted a message to Mary, attaching the photo. She found the website for the bar and sent an e-mail to the attention of Doug Avery, along with the photo, and asked him to call her.

"And now," Kat said, hitting "Send," "we wait!"

Lina put the dinner Kat had prepared in the oven and went to the sofa and collapsed. "Well, chicas, that's about all the excitement I can handle today. You two are making my head hurt."

"Sorry," Tori offered with a smile. "I blame Kat. She got me started with all this craziness. How about some tea?"

"Perfect."

Tori put a kettle on the stove, and Kat brought a blanket to Lina and sat in the chair beside her, browsing Facebook. She hadn't looked at her feed in nearly a week, and she had several notifications of posts from friends. The first one was the picture that Tori had taken after the memorial, while the women sat on her back deck in Catawba, toasting Shea.

"Oh, look, that's a great picture," Kat said. Kat had been tagged, as had Dee, who had posted a comment. "To Shea, a true friend. We'll miss you."

Tori piped in from the kitchen, "I hear sarcasm."

"I think you're reading into it," Kat said over her shoulder.

Tori set a tray on the coffee table. She gave one mug to Lina, one to Kat, and picked up the last before sitting. "Am I?" she asked. "According to Dee, Shea was a true friend who might have destroyed her marriage, so—"

"Stop," Kat said. "I think we should cut Dee some slack. How would you feel if you were in her shoes?"

"I would never be in her shoes," Tori said. "If my man ever came to me and wanted to spice it up with other women, I'd tell him to hit the bricks. He wants more than one, he can jump on a plane to Utah and become a polygamist. I'm no sister wife."

"That's for sure," Kat said with a grin.

The women returned focus to the picture of their group on Facebook. "Why didn't you tag the others?" Kat asked Tori.

"Evelyn's not on Facebook. Or if she is, I've never found her."

"Can't tag me anymore," Lina said. "I quit the 'Book."

"Really?" Kat asked. "How are we supposed to keep in touch?"

Lina laughed. "You're going to text and call me like a real person."

"You getting tired of my nonsense posts?" Tori asked.

Lina smiled. "I just don't want my kids and friends to be faced with those reminders of my birthday when I'm gone. It seems cruel."

Kat struggled with how to respond and, instead, squeezed Lina's hand. "You said you're feeling better."

"I am," Lina said.

Suddenly, Kat wasn't so sure. She looked at Tori.

"I am, I swear, ladies," Lina added. "I'm a planner, that's all."

"You're not gonna die," Tori said, tapping her shoulder.

"We're all gonna die, Tori," Lina said.

CHAPTER 24

March 29

SHEA PARKED THE CAR IN front of Georgia's and found her and Tess outside, sitting on the sidewalk, drawing chalk animals on the concrete.

"Hey, neighbor," Georgia said. "What are you up to?"

"Hey." Shea looked at little Tess, oblivious and engrossed in her own drawing. "I'm sorry to interrupt. Tess, this is beautiful. Did you do this all by yourself?"

"Mommy helped me," she said.

"Well, you're both really talented. Georgia, can I talk to you for a minute?"

"Sure," Georgia said. "Wanna sit with us?" She patted the sidewalk beside her.

"Actually, could we talk in private a minute?"

Georgia looked at Tess before looking back at Shea. "Is this about Dee's daughter? I already heard, and I just told Tess."

"What are you talking about?" Shea asked.

"Gina's peanut allergy. But she's going to be okay," Georgia said, patting Tess while she said it. "She used to babysit Tess, so Tess was a little worried. But they got there in time, and everything is going to be fine. Dee is leaving today to be with her."

"I should call Dee," Shea said, looking off in the distance.

"You okay?" Georgia asked.

Shea silently shook her head.

Georgia put her arms out. "Help me up."

Shea took Georgia's arms and pulled her to standing. "I just need to talk."

"Tess," Georgia said, "how about we take a five-minute break?"

"Mom, *no*. You promised."

"I know. I just need to speak with Shea for five minutes. Come on, you can go get a snack. Something to hold you over until dinner."

"Okay." Tess jumped up and ran for the house.

"Food," Georgia said. "Does the trick every time. What's goin' on?"

Shea handed the newspaper to Georgia. "He's dead."

"Who?"

Shea didn't answer but gave Georgia a chance to read and look for herself.

"Oh my God," Georgia finally said before putting her hand to her mouth. "Oh my God, Shea. What does this mean?"

Shea shook her head. "He was okay when we left him, right?"

"We don't know that. Oh my God, we don't know that, Shea. He was bleeding badly, and we did nothing!" Georgia looked back at the house. "I'm going to lose my family!"

"No, you're not. Of course not. It was an accident. It's not your fault."

"It's *your* fault!" Georgia suddenly shouted. "Why didn't you let us go to the police?"

"I know we didn't do this. We couldn't have."

"I'm going to be sick," Georgia said, collapsing back onto the sidewalk.

Shea fell to her knees beside her. "Georgia, don't worry. I won't let anything happen to you. You were protecting me."

Tess suddenly reappeared on the sidewalk with two cookies in hand. "One for you and one for you," she said, handing them to Georgia and Shea. "I had one, too. Ready, Mommy? We need to finish."

"Thanks, Tess," Shea said, getting up. "Georgia, I'm gonna handle this. I promise. I'll call you later, okay?"

Georgia didn't reply. She kept her eyes on the sidewalk and wiped her eyes.

~ • ~

Shea returned home to find Ryan in the kitchen making pasta.

"Surprise," Ryan said, waving his arm toward the dining room, to two place mats, utensils, plates, and a couple of candles.

"What's this?" she asked.

"I know, it's not even five o'clock. I thought a surprise early dinner might be fun since we never ate."

"Wow."

"I've got some french bread in the oven, too. You must be starving."

"I . . . I just got some bad news," she said, standing frozen in the doorway.

Ryan stopped stirring and turned off the burner before walking over to Shea. Tears welled as she considered what might have happened to Blake, what it could mean. Ryan reached out and pulled her in for a hug. "Tell me. What's going on? Whatever it is, it can't be that bad."

Shea wrapped her arms around him, holding tight. She didn't know what to do—tell the police, tell Ryan? What if the police were still investigating Blake's death?

No, she thought. She hadn't done anything. It was dark. Her mind was swirling.

"Talk to me," Ryan said.

She pulled back and looked at his face. "It's Dee. Her daughter, Gina. The one at Indiana University. She's in the hospital."

"What happened?"

"Her peanut allergy. Some contamination. It was a close call, but she's going to be okay. I should go." She started back toward the door. "I want to see Dee before she leaves town. I'm sorry."

"It'll keep. Don't worry about it. Go. Keep me posted."

"Thanks for this," she said, waving toward the kitchen.

~ • ~

Shea sat in the car in the grocery parking lot. She should call Dee. She stared at her phone and began writing a text instead.

D—So sorry about Gina. Please call if I can do anything.

There was so much more to say. So much that had never been said. They had not spoken in almost two months.

IMMF, she wrote. All her friends knew it meant *I miss my friends*. The acronym was usually used in conjunction with an impromptu happy hour suggestion, but hopefully Dee would understand. They needed to talk.

After hitting "Send," Shea began searching the Internet for more news about Blake's death. The article Tori had showed her said nothing about there being an investigation, she realized, reading the story again. Maybe it was a totally unrelated accident. She continued to type search terms, looking for clues, pulling up stories of other lake accidents. She searched for stories printed in the days after their visit and found a video clip of a local news story that ran two days before Thanksgiving. The anchor said only that Blake was missing, as was his boat, after an outing on the island with friends over the weekend. A search was underway.

She found a story from a local paper printed several days later about the search being halted because of dangerous lake conditions but saying that, officially, it remained a missing-person case. There were no other news stories about him.

She searched his name on Facebook and found his page. His profile picture was now simply a shadow of a man's image, perhaps a symbolic indication of his death, but hundreds of family pictures remained, confirming that she'd found the right man. Shea scrolled through them—vacation shots and T-ball games, two beautiful young children and a wife. She couldn't reconcile the husband, father, fisherman, and friend to so many with the man she met, the good-looking flirt who had snapped when she pulled away, whose grip bruised her arms, whose tequila breath, hot on her face, spewed insults and threats when she'd fought back.

Closing out of the pictures, she scrolled farther down the profile. He had more than four hundred friends. Shea wasn't connected to any of them, so she couldn't access their names or profiles. There was nothing else on Blake's page. She moved the cursor back to the search bar and searched his name again, both with a hashtag and then an "at" sign to find any recent mentions of him within the Facebook universe. She found several in the last four months: people offering prayers for the family, people asking for help in the search after he first disappeared, a few poems posted as offers of hope.

The most recent mention had been posted just yesterday. Someone had shared a picture of a beautiful old lighthouse, along with a notice of a memorial service to be held in Blake's honor. The notice said that it was finally time to say good-bye. The service would take place at the South Bass Island Lighthouse on April 1, at three o'clock in the afternoon. Dozens of people had posted their intention to be there.

The lighthouse. Blake had told her about it while they sat together at Rudolph's. He had said the views of Lake Erie from the tower were spectacular. It was one of his favorite spots on the island. He'd wanted her to see it. That was what he'd said when they kissed by the bathroom. It was clearly a ploy to go somewhere remote. "It's dark," Shea had said. "What would we possibly be able to see?"

"The stars," he'd answered.

Stupidly, she'd let him pull her out of the bar. When they got outside and Blake began looking around for a taxi or available golf carts to rent, she knew it was a bad idea. Too remote, too difficult to return to her friends. She'd convinced him to show her his boat instead. The dock was nearby, on the other side of the park. "Come on," she'd said. "I can't leave my friends for that long." He'd pouted a little but relented, and they had walked hand in hand toward the water like a couple. God. It was so stupid.

But maybe that was what happened to Blake. Maybe after she and Georgia ran off, he'd decided to take the boat over to the other side of the island to see the lighthouse from the water.

CHAPTER 25

April 13

KAT WAS ON THE COUCH, finishing a glass of wine, when her phone lit up with a text from Tori. So, Tori wrote.

So, what? Kat replied.

Have you heard from Mary or the bartender? Are you crazy?
I can't stop thinking about it!

Actually, Kat had stopped thinking about it. She and Lina had finished dinner, and after Lina went to bed, she'd allowed herself to get absorbed in a TV show for the last thirty minutes.

Kat didn't want Mary or the bartender to recognize Charlie's picture. The idea of someone taking Shea's life suddenly felt far more horrific now that they were looking sideways at their own friends. The fleeting concern that Shea could have intended an overdose was too painful to believe, both because of the despair that would mean she'd felt and because it would mean Kat had been so oblivious to her friend's pain. The tragedy of an accidental death was not much easier. But now, the reality that someone could have killed her—robbing her family of a mother and wife, robbing her closest friends of her company—brought with it such pain and anger, Kat wasn't sure how to handle it.

She checked the mail app on her phone. Mary had responded.

Kat read her reply, closed the mail, and returned to Tori's text, sharing the news with Tori.

Tori replied immediately. Betsy's game just ended. I'm coming over right now.

Twenty minutes later, Tori rang the bell, and Kat jumped up to get it. Lina was already asleep. It was clear the constant war inside her body was draining whatever energy she could muster.

Tori dropped into a seat at the kitchen table. "So, what do you think?"

"I think we're never going to know what happened, and my head hurts. Charlie was not the guest."

"Though it's still possible he was the man from the bar. This feels like one of those abduction mysteries. If you don't figure it out within days, it's not likely to get solved. It's now been almost two weeks since Shea died. Wow."

Time had both sped up and slowed down. It was as if Kat's life had stopped since she'd returned to Maple Park. She'd been here almost a week, and her new life in Texas felt frozen. But nearly two weeks had passed since Shea left this world, and it still felt as fresh a wound as it did the day she got the news.

"This is what I can't get past," Kat said. "Someone, who she referred to as a friend, knows something. She left the bar with a man, and she unlocked her door that night. We're not talking about a Best Western. It's not like she was walking out to fill an ice bucket. She let someone in, right? And if Mary locked up within twenty minutes, then that someone was probably the other guest."

"Who we now know was *not* Charlie."

"Maybe it was a friend of Blake's," Kat said. "Anyone who went to the memorial could have been staying at the inn, too. Maybe we should notify the police of this. Maybe they'll try harder to find out who that guest was."

"Or, maybe, the guest had nothing to do with any of this," Tori said. "If it was Charlie with her at the bar and they fought and she went inside with the other guest, he could have just followed a few minutes later and knocked on her door. It was twenty minutes after Shea went to bed that Mary said she locked up. And if it was Charlie, and he was in her room, he could have left at any point in the night. He could have simply unlocked the front door and left."

She had a point, Kat realized. "No one would know anyone else had been there, because Mary expected the front door to be unlocked when she got up the next morning. The other guest left early to fish."

"Oh, God," Tori said, slapping Kat's knee.

"What?"

"What if it was Ryan?"

"What? Why?"

"If he thought Shea was having an affair, he certainly wouldn't be honest about it now. It would make him look suspicious. He needs everyone to assume that he and Shea were doing great, that he's the mourning husband."

"But he is mourning," Kat said. "Even Shea said they were doing great. That's what she said to Lina at her chemo, remember? And she didn't tell any of us that there was anything going on."

"I think we've already established that we didn't know much about what was going on with Shea the last six months."

"You should have seen Ryan today. He's a wreck. He's not sleeping, the house is a mess. I think he's falling apart. He . . ." She stopped herself.

"What?"

"Nothing. He was kind of drunk. He's been buying crap online in the middle of the night. I feel bad for him."

"So much for his financial problems," Tori said. "Personally, if I killed someone, I don't think I'd sleep too well, either."

"Ryan said he and Shea were planning to move, that he knew all about Shea looking at real estate. I think we're going a little nuts. He also said he is certain there was no affair."

"You asked him?"

"I didn't have to. He was emphatic that neither of them had ever cheated." Kat didn't tell Tori what she'd learned from Mack. It wouldn't be right.

There was a good chance that nothing they had learned mattered and that wondering if Ryan or Blake's friends or anyone else had been there was nothing more than wild speculation. Shea might have chatted with a stranger at Rudolph's. She might have unlocked that door because she heard a noise that turned out to be nothing—or Mary's memory of locking the dead bolt that night could be mistaken. Shea might have simply fallen asleep. Nothing could be worse than becoming a murder suspect, or even a person of interest, when you've done nothing wrong. Kat could ruin lives if she spoke to police. She had to be certain.

"Let's talk to Evelyn," Tori suggested.

"Why?" Kat asked.

"Shea obviously confided in her, certainly more than she did with us. She made that comment about Shea's pills not being about shoulder pain. I got the sense she knew something, like Shea said something. And you saw her at the island after we met Blake's friends. She seemed like she didn't want to share Shea's secrets with us. Maybe Shea would have told Evelyn if she was having an affair."

It was true and it stung a little, but it was a good idea.

"But I gotta get home. And you've got to go back downtown in the morning?"

"Yep. And I'm supposed to go home tomorrow afternoon. Tori, if Evelyn doesn't have any answers and I have to return with all this looming, I'm going to go crazy."

"I know. Me, too. We'll talk to her tomorrow." They hugged at the door.

CHAPTER 26

March 30

SHEA WOKE TO A TEXT from Georgia suggesting they go for a walk. She quickly agreed and got dressed.

"Listen," Shea said as the women began to walk away from Georgia's house, "I've been thinking about this nonstop. Blake was drunk. He was on his boat, and if he decided to go out into those rough waters after we left, it is not our fault."

"But I told you we needed to report what happened," Georgia said. "Don't you see, if we reported it, he'd be alive. Whatever happened to him after we left would not have happened if we had just called the police." Georgia could barely get out those last words through the tears. "How am I supposed to live with this? What if he stumbled and fell into the water? What if he was so disoriented he untied the boat? Hitting him could have caused his death."

"It's not your fault," Shea said.

"I can't sleep. Do you know what I found out?" Georgia asked.

"What?"

"*I* could get in huge trouble because of this, not you. Me. Even if I didn't mean to kill him. If he died because I hit him, I could go to jail. I looked it up. You can get up to five years for killing someone, even if it's accidental." Georgia stopped walking. "I can't believe this is happening."

Shea hugged her. "Nothing is going to happen. This is my fault, Georgia. There's a memorial for Blake on Saturday. I don't know why it's happening now, after all this time, but we're going to go pay our respects along with probably hundreds of others. We can find out what everyone believes happened. Blake may have even been with his friends after we left. We have no idea. Georgia, you might be worrying over nothing. I'm sure this was simply a tragic boating accident and we're freaking out over nothing."

Georgia didn't respond.

"Let's keep walking," Shea said. The women moved forward without words.

After a block of silence, Shea continued. "What are you thinking?"

"I don't like it," Georgia said.

"Come on. We'll go for the weekend. We don't even have to tell anyone where we're going."

Georgia stopped walking and looked at Shea. "Hey, I don't know about you, but I'm not used to lying to my husband."

Shea didn't know what to say.

"I'm so mad at you right now, I can hardly see straight."

"I know. I'm sorry. You have no idea how sorry I am. I'm sorry for my behavior that night, for leaving the bar with him, for putting you in this position." She paused to wipe her eyes. "I wish I could go back. I would do anything—"

"I gotta go," Georgia said, cutting her off and turning back toward her house.

Shea began to follow her. "Will you think about it? Going to the memorial?"

Georgia stopped and turned back. "Don't follow me," she yelled.

Shea stood on the sidewalk watching her friend walk away.

~ • ~

Shea gave Georgia another day to think about it. She was sure that going to Put-in-Bay was the best way to find the answers and put this all behind them. She finally called her on Friday night. "What do you think?" Shea asked.

"I think it's a terrible idea and there's no way I'm going to show my face at a service for that man. What if people are looking for us? They don't know our names or where we live, and you just want to show up. What if the police have been looking for the women who were drinking with Blake and his friends in the bar that night?"

"That's crazy," Shea said. "We were just a group of women who shared some drinks with them. They probably didn't even notice that I left with Blake for a while. Everyone was in their own world. I really don't think we have anything to worry about."

"Well, that's easy for you to say, since you didn't actually do anything. Please," Georgia begged, "just drop it. It's bad enough I have to live with this. Don't make it worse." She hung up.

Georgia was wrong. There was no way she was responsible. Shea would prove it. She couldn't let Georgia spend the rest of her life feeling like she'd essentially killed a man.

Shea walked around the house, turning off the lights and locking the doors, bracing for the conversation she needed to have with Ryan. She had to go. It was the only way to resolve this and put Georgia's mind at ease. She didn't want to lose her friendship over this.

When she got to the bedroom, Ryan was already asleep. He was probably exhausted from hauling all the junk out of the storage room all day. She sat in the chair in the corner, watching his chest rise and fall, listening to the whistle that escaped with each exhale. She began to play out the conversation in her mind. She'd tell him about that night with Blake, about what happened, and Georgia, and Blake's death.

But if Ryan thought it was a bad idea, too, it would drive a new wedge between them if she insisted on going. And it would probably ruin her plans. And it was a good plan.

She was going to surprise Ryan with a visit to Put-in-Bay in two weeks for an entirely different reason. They were heading to Detroit to visit his father in a couple of weeks, and they were going to visit each of the kids while on the road. They were considering a move that would bring them closer to them. Both kids were investigating job opportunities in their adoptive home states. Shea had stared at a map one day, thinking of them, and she'd homed in on Lake Erie, sprawled almost between Leigh at Michigan State in Lansing and Stephen at Ohio State in Columbus.

Ryan had said he wanted adventure. What would be more adventurous than living on an island? The kids would want to visit, and yet in winter, it would become sleepy and quiet.

Her mind had begun sorting through the possibilities—their new home would be a place the grandkids would want to visit; they could become boaters; maybe they could run a sandwich shop. Tori and Herman would visit. She could sell real estate on the side. It was impossible not to get excited by such a change. She began looking at real estate online. Several little houses on the market were less than a quarter of the price of their current home.

But now she needed to go to Put-in-Bay to be sure she hadn't been involved in a stranger's death, to be sure she hadn't put Georgia's future at risk. This whole mess would taint the hope and excitement of a fresh start just as, finally, things were getting better. Ryan rolled over, and the faint whistling stopped.

She looked at him. He was peacefully oblivious to the mess she'd made.

She couldn't give him a new reason to pull away from her. She'd be back in forty-eight hours, and hopefully she'd have learned that there was nothing to worry about and they could move forward. She grabbed a bag from the closet and began quietly packing.

Sorting through toiletries in the bathroom, she thought about the drive. It would be tough. Five hours alone. Maybe one of the girls would come with her. If only Kat were here. She pulled her phone from her back pocket, shut the door, and called Kat. When it went to voice mail, she hung up and sent a text. Hey neighbor. Whatcha up to? Have time for a catch-up? She waited, staring at the phone.

She wanted to tell Kat everything—the good and the bad. She couldn't tell anyone else. Kat had joked for years that Shea belonged on an island. She meant a Caribbean island, but still, maybe Kat would think Shea's fantasy was a good one. Maybe she'd assure her that everything would be okay.

She sat on the bed, looking at the phone, scrolling through all the photos of her friends, wondering what it was like to start somewhere new at this age. She'd wondered many times how it had it been for Kat so far, but she'd been afraid of the answer. She hit the message app again. No response. Kat was probably in another time zone, traveling for work. Shea sent her one more text: IMMF. She finished packing.

CHAPTER 27

April 13

IT WAS ONLY ABOUT THIRTY minutes after Tori left when the door-
bell rang. Kat jumped up to get it. She checked the peephole and saw
Georgia, staring at the front door with a wide smile, like some Mary
Kay solicitor, ready to pounce on whoever opened the door.

"Hi, Georgia, what's up?" Kat said.

Georgia's face seemed to drop when she saw Kat, but she
regrouped quickly, widening her smile. "Hi, Kat! I thought you'd left
town by now."

"Still here," Kat said. "Come on in. I see you've come bearing gifts."

Kat stepped aside to let Georgia in. Georgia had a foil-covered
bread pan in one hand and a brown bag tied shut with a pink ribbon in the other. She barely resembled the woman Kat had visited
Monday. Instead, Georgia's hair was perfectly in place, her makeup
flawless, her lipstick freshly applied.

"I've got one more meeting in the morning and then I'll be heading home," Kat said. "Did you bake?"

"Oh no," Georgia said, looking down at the pan. "Meat loaf. It was
my night to bring a dinner, but the time got away from me. I know
it's late, but I've got another crazy day tomorrow, and I wanted to be
sure I got this to Lina."

"Oh, don't worry about it. I'm sure she'll love having this tomorrow."

"My family loves it. You wouldn't believe it, but there's cereal in the recipe. Gives it just a li'l somethin' extra."

"Ah," Kat said with a fake smile.

"Anyway, I just wanted to check on Lina and see how she's doing. And I brought her some bulbs, too," she said, raising her paper bag.

"Bulbs?"

"For the garden."

"Oh, bulbs. Here I was thinking about lightbulbs," Kat said with a grin.

"I guess you're not much of a gardener." Georgia chuckled.

"You're right about that. Anyway, come, sit," Kat said, guiding Georgia into the kitchen. "Lina is asleep. But she seems pretty good, actually. We're planning to have lunch tomorrow with Tori after my final meeting, if you'd like to join us?"

"Oh, thanks, but I'm helping at Tessa's school tomorrow."

"You want a glass of wine? Or some tea?" Kat asked.

Georgia hesitated, looking toward the door.

"If you need to go . . ."

Georgia dropped the bag and sat in the kitchen chair. "No, let's sit for a minute. Tea would be nice."

Kat put the kettle on and joined her at the table.

"So, how has it been being back for a whole week?" Georgia asked. "Do you miss it here, or are you dying to get home?"

"Both, I guess. I do need to get back at this point, but I just wanted to catch up with Evelyn tomorrow before I go."

"Evelyn, huh? Are you two good friends?" Georgia asked.

"Not really. We drove back from Catawba together on Monday morning, so I probably know her a little better now, but I think with our jobs being as they are, we've never gotten to know each other well. Are you two good friends?"

"Kind of. I mean, I'm like her personal gardener. Does that count?"

"Really?"

"Well, she lives in that spectacular building in the center of town."

"The one with the window boxes?"

"Exactly. The tenants are expected to maintain the boxes, and Evelyn's always traveling."

Kat had often wondered whether the tenants were contractually obligated to tend to the boxes or whether building assessments paid for the flowers. But she knew the building well. It was only about ten stories high, one of the oldest buildings in downtown Maple Park. It had a green tile roof, copper gutters and flashing, and soft, weathered red brick. Most extraordinary, every window of the building featured limestone sills, and beneath every window on the east and south sides of the building were ornate limestone corbels supporting permanently affixed copper flower boxes. Every summer cascading vines and bright-colored flowers filled the boxes; every fall the mums came out; and in winter each box was filled with evergreen accents, often weighed down with snow. One winter, soon after a blizzard, Kat and her son had been passing the building when he looked up at what appeared to be boxes full of snow beneath every window and said how cool it would be to live there, forty feet off the ground, with a snowball supply out your window. Ever since then, Kat had never passed the building without noticing the changing greenery in those boxes. The symmetry, repetition, and sheer volume of green and bright colors exploding beneath each window was magnificent.

Actually, Kat used to assume that when the kids were grown and she and Mack grew tired of maintaining their yard and house, they'd move into a building like it, staying in the town they loved, living within another form of century-old architecture, growing old with friends. She'd even once entertained the fantasy that Peter would return to Maple Park with his own young family someday, perhaps moving into their house—his childhood home—everyone staying close by, generations of family forever connected. She'd babysit the grandkids, maybe walk them to elementary school, along the same route she'd walked her own son decades before. Kat knew of other local families with such histories. Maple Park inspired multigenerational devotion.

"So you take care of the window boxes, then?"

"Yep. Last summer, she asked me who my gardener was, can you imagine? Like I'd have a gardener. But she said she needed to hire one to deal with those boxes, and I said I could do it. I pass that building every morning when I walk. Besides," she added, "I kind of loved the excuse to get inside."

"It is beautiful."

"Turns out," Georgia said, leaning forward and lowering her voice, "Evelyn is loaded. I'm guessing it's family money. The first time I let myself in to water the plants, I was a little taken aback. I mean, when you walk into that apartment, you'd think she was a Vanderbilt or something. We're talking *Downton Abbey*–style antiques. So yeah, I've got keys to the palace," she joked with a bad English accent. "That's about as close as I'll ever come to being a millionaire. I think I'm the gardener of one!"

"Well, it's nice of you to take care of the plants."

"Why do you want to see Evelyn, anyway?"

"Oh, just something she said about Shea that I've been thinking about." The kettle began a slight whistle, and Kat went back to the kitchen. "I still find it so difficult to let this go. I know I need to. Nothing anyone tells me will bring Shea back, but there's this voice in my head that continues to want more information. Anything to help make sense of why it happened."

"You need to let it go, Kat."

"I know. I just miss her." She wasn't about to share all her theories and gossip with Georgia. It wouldn't be right.

Georgia looked relieved. "It was just a tragic accident."

"Yeah, you're probably right," Kat said. She brought two mugs of tea to the table. "At least I understand why Shea might have been panicked and felt like she had to go back. I can't imagine wondering if I'd caused someone's death." The words had already escaped her mouth when she realized what she'd said.

Georgia winced. "Are you trying to cause trouble, Kat?"

"No."

"Let it go. Our friend is gone. Don't sully her name."

"I didn't intend to."

Georgia stood from the table. "You know, I'm a little tired. I'll skip that tea."

"I'm sorry, Georgia. Did I say something to offend you?"

"No," she said before painting a fake smile on her face. "I'm glad we got to catch up. I doubt I'll see you again before you leave, so have a safe flight."

Kat offered a hug good-bye, but Georgia pulled back from the embrace quickly, restless to leave. The truth was, they were never really close friends.

~ • ~

Kat lay on her bed, staring at the ceiling. Her cell rang, and she looked at Mack's sleeping face on the screen. "Hi," she said. "I miss you."

"I miss you," he said. "When is your flight tomorrow?"

"Actually, I'm not sure. I haven't booked it yet. I've got to see how busy tomorrow is."

"I thought the meeting was in the morning?"

"It is. I just need to do a few things after and I'm not sure how long it will take. I need to say good-bye to Ryan, and Tori and I were going to see Evelyn really quick. I don't know when I'll see any of these people again, so there are just some final good-byes to be had."

She didn't even tell him about all the theories and fears and gossip and clues. "And then I promise, I'll be on the first plane."

"So, you're done with work tomorrow morning, you've been gone all week, you were out of town the week before you suddenly dropped everything and went to Shea's funeral, and now you want to stay longer?"

"It's not like I *want* to," Kat said. "I *need* to do this."

"All I asked is that you go to the funeral and come home. You could have returned to Chicago on Thursday for your meetings and spent the days in between at home . . ."

"I spend far too much time on airplanes, Mack. If I was coming to town and I had to be here a few days later, I was not going to go back and forth."

"Even though I'm here. And we never see each other."

"I asked you to come!"

The line was quiet for a few beats. She heard a deep inhale before Mack spoke. "Why do you have to speak to Evelyn, anyway?"

"She might be able to help us figure out if . . ." Her voice trailed off. Mack wasn't going to understand. She wasn't even sure she understood.

"Please don't tell me you're still trying to figure out if someone hurt Shea."

"I know we haven't talked about this much. Things have been tense, and I thought you'd be annoyed. But I feel like there's a good chance someone could have done something to Shea. I know it sounds crazy, but, apparently, Charlie was obsessed with her. And there was a guy who Shea might have accidentally killed last November. Georgia may have been involved and—"

"What are you talking about?"

There was so much she hadn't told him. And now, as she sorted through where to begin, it all seemed kind of . . .

"Kat, you're not an investigator. No one thinks this was more than an accident, right?"

"Right, but—"

"Ryan thinks it was an accident?"

"Yes. But I'm not sure he is—" *Telling the truth.* She couldn't say it. It was crazy. Twenty years of friendship. Even if he'd been unfaithful, it didn't make him a murderer. And . . .

"Kat, it's none of your business. Your friend died. I loved her, too. It's a tragedy. But you've got to let this go."

"But it's my fault!" she yelled into the phone.

"What?" Mack yelled back. "What are you talking about?"

She shook her head, tears now streaming down her cheeks, at the idea of letting it go, of moving on with all these still-looming questions. "I wasn't there for her."

Mack's voice softened. "Don't you see—" he began.

"Stop! You don't understand. There is some weird stuff that was going on here. There are people who may have wanted to hurt her. And yes, I know these were our friends, and yes, I'm not going to share this with police and try to ruin anyone's life, but I need to know, okay? Someone needs to be asking these questions. Because Shea is dead, and if someone did something, I'm not going to let them get away with it!" Her voice rose to a near scream, and as soon as she stopped speaking, she knew it sounded like she was losing perspective.

"Maybe you're just trying to delay returning. Maybe you're determined to hold on to your life there—"

"Me? What about you? Have you unpacked anything?"

He didn't answer.

"You're the one who's not giving our new life a chance."

Mack took a breath. He was always the one to take a breath— never raising his voice at her, always the rational, calm one. "I think we should hang up before we say anything else."

"Fine," Kat said.

"Fine."

The line went dead. Kat stared at the phone.

CHAPTER 28

April 14

KAT TOOK THE TRAIN INTO the city on Friday morning for her final meeting. She lingered in the conference room, gathering notes and files. Mack was right. Her own life was a mess. It was time to focus on that for a change. She waved at Martin on her way out. "We can do whatever remains via e-mail, okay?"

"No problem," he said. "Have a safe flight."

On the train heading west to Maple Park, her head against the window, she breathed deeply. It was that anxiety again. But it wasn't about Shea's death this time. It was about her own life. She was feeling rootless once more. Just like after college. Everything was different, and it was hard to know where she fit. Was that house she and Mack bought a mistake? Was the neighborhood? Was the job? All she knew was that despite everything else, she missed her husband. He was her best friend. The fighting was about loneliness. He was alone—so was she.

She reviewed her e-mail and found the latest from Martin, with a subject line: Voucher Information Request.

Oh, right, she thought, clicking open the message.

The Shea Walker voucher for Chicago hotel was used on March 25. Room 44a, King Deluxe, Riverview. Reservation No. 46586, in the name of Ryan Walker.

Oh, good, Kat thought. At least Shea and Ryan had enjoyed a romantic night together in the city, and in a top-floor suite, no less. Ryan could cherish that memory. And, she realized, if they'd used the voucher, things had been good between them. Despite whatever had happened in the past. Tori was crazy to point the spotlight at Ryan. He loved Shea, Kat was sure of it. Twenty years of living next door to their marriage had to mean something.

Kat got off the train in Maple Park and walked the three blocks to a pub in the center of town for a late lunch with Tori and Lina. She and Tori would drop by Evelyn's later, but no matter what they learned, it was nearing the time to say good-bye again. Tori kept the conversation light, entertaining them with more of her daughters' escapades. Tori's youngest, Betsy, seemed to be the wildest of the bunch. Her license had recently been suspended, and now Tori was back to chauffeuring the seventeen-year-old, who hated every minute of it. And tomorrow she was sitting for the SATs for the second and final time. Tori said with Herman still gone, she was warden for the weekend.

"My only goal," she said, "is to keep that girl home tonight, be sure she gets some sleep, and get her to the test center on time in the morning."

It was these kinds of conversations Kat had missed. Nothing of consequence, just sharing the mundane, the highs and lows, with friends. "I'm really going to miss you two," she said after the meal. "I still can't believe Shea's death was the reason I came back, but I guess . . ." She stopped herself, tears welling, feeling silly.

"What?"

"I don't think I realized how much I missed you all until I got here. It's nice to have some girlfriends again. I don't think I've shared a meal or a cup of coffee or a glass of wine with another woman in like three months."

"You and Mack must be getting a little sick of each other, then, huh?" Lina asked.

Kat took a sip of tea before responding. "Mack and I . . . it's been a tough move. We both miss our friends. I mean, before this week . . ." She wasn't sure how to explain. "We're just struggling. Instead of turning to each other . . ."

Tori and Lina both reached out to Kat's hands, laying their own hands on top, like a sports team. "Hey, you don't have to live here to feel connected to your friends," Tori said. "We might not be able to get coffee or share some wine, but just reach out. Don't go radio silent again, okay?"

"Okay," Kat said, wiping her eyes. "I have a hard time letting people know when things aren't good."

"Why?" Lina asked.

"I hate for people to worry about me, or feel sorry for me. Or talk about me."

"I know something about that," Lina said.

"So," Tori answered, "in the name of privacy or pride, you like the world to think your life is perfect?"

"In a nutshell," Kat agreed, smiling.

"But if any of us were to talk about you or worry about you, or feel sorry for you, it would only be because we love you."

"Thanks."

"Good," Tori said, with a tap on her arm. "Now run off to the restroom, so Lina and I can talk about what a mess you are." Tori to the rescue again: laughter through tears.

"You and Mack will be all right," Lina said. "Every marriage has highs and lows. And what do they say? The most stressful things on a marriage are finances, kids, and moving."

"They're right," Kat smirked.

"Absolutely," Tori said. "And Mack loves you."

Kat knew that. The fighting was rooted in feeling adrift. Neither of them wanted it. She needed to be his anchor. She needed him to be hers.

"You two are gonna be fine," Lina said.

"I hope so. But I need to go home."

The waiter brought the bill, and Tori threw down her card before Kat or Lina had the chance. "My treat, ladies." They both tried to stop her, but she put up her hand. "Zip it."

"Well, thanks, that's nice," Kat said. Lina agreed.

"Now, I hate to end this," Lina said, "but I've got to get home soon. My daughter said she'd call me at three for a catch-up. I don't want to miss it."

While the women waited for the server to process Tori's card, Kat turned the discussion to Lina's health. Lina said she'd been feeling better than ever, so perhaps the treatments were working. The women toasted to gathering again in another year, perhaps another lake house getaway, to celebrate Lina's complete recovery.

"Oh jeez," Tori interrupted, her focus now behind Kat, looking toward the bar.

"What?" both women said, following her gaze.

"Charlie," Tori said. "How will I ever look at that guy the same?"

He was sitting at the bar, watching a game on the big TV in the corner. "Well, no one says you have to," Lina pointed out. "He left Dee. She's our friend. Nothing wrong with taking sides."

The server brought Tori's receipt, and they left. Ryan was on the sidewalk, reaching for the door to the restaurant as they stepped outside.

"Oh, hi, Ryan," Kat said.

"Hey, Ryan," both Tori and Lina added, everyone taking turns to offer quick hugs.

"What are you up to?" Kat asked.

"Just gonna get a bite at the bar," Ryan said.

"You running out of home-cooked meals?" Tori asked.

"Hardly. Just needed a break from all the pasta. I'm craving a Reuben."

"Well, just a heads-up," Kat said. "Charlie's sitting in there at the bar."

"Oh," Ryan said, his tone suddenly somber. "Thanks, Kat. Perhaps this isn't the best idea. Maybe I'll get some sushi. Well, good to see you, ladies. And Kit Kat, will I see you again, or are you leaving today?"

"Soon, I'm afraid." She opened her arms, and he embraced her tightly.

"Thanks again for coming back for the memorial. We've missed you and Mack."

"Us, too. You take care, Ryan, and let's keep in touch," Kat said.

"Deal."

~ • ~

Tori and Kat dropped Lina at home and drove toward the center of town.

"This is it," Tori said, pulling up in front of Evelyn's building. "I've never been inside. Shea was thrilled to have sold one of those units."

They opened the oversize quartersawn oak entry door, finding a mosaic tile floor inside the vestibule, where all the old-style brass mail slots were housed. Tori scanned the names along the tops of the boxes and found Evelyn's name and her unit: *P*. The inner door was locked, and Tori pushed the intercom beside the letter *P*. A moment later someone replied, "Hello?" It was a man's voice.

"Hello?" Tori said. "We're looking for Evelyn Preston. Do we have the right place?"

"Sure," the man's voice said. "Come on up." The door buzzed, and Kat pulled it open before they could say more.

"Is she seeing someone?" Kat wondered aloud.

"No idea," Tori said. "Shea said she dates a lot. This could be interesting. Maybe she's got some boy toy stashed away in here."

Kat laughed. "You're ridiculous."

"Maybe," Tori smirked.

The inside foyer housed a few antiques and a large area rug over the old oak floors. The elevator bank was along the left side. When the doors to one of the elevators opened, the women were faced with an iron gate.

"Wow, this really is old. I'd hate to get stuck in here."

"Don't even joke," Tori replied as they stepped in to the small box, standing shoulder to shoulder.

"So it looks like *P* is for penthouse," Kat said. Every floor but one was numbered.

"Swanky," Tori said.

The elevator stopped, and Tori pulled the gate open. They stood in a large entry hall, facing the single apartment door.

Kat raised her hand to knock on the door, but it opened just before her hand touched the wood. A shirtless man, hair wet, a towel around his neck, stood there, barefoot, with sweatpants hanging loosely from his hips, his bare chest and flawless torso so surprising it was difficult not to stare.

"Hello," Tori said, attempting nonchalance. "We're so sorry to catch you at a bad time. We're friends of Evelyn's. Is she home?"

"I'm afraid not," the man said.

"And who are you?" Kat asked, compensating for the nosy inquiry with a smile.

"Oh, forgive me, ladies," the man said as he stretched out his hand. "I'm Evelyn's baby brother, Frederick Preston."

"Oh, hello," Kat said, shaking his hand. "I didn't realize she had a brother. I'm Katherine Burrows, Kat to my friends, and this is Victoria Youngren."

"Tori," she corrected. "Nice to meet you," she said, extending her hand.

"Hello there, Tori." He took Tori's outstretched hand and pulled it in for a kiss like Rhett Butler. It was laughable, really, and both women giggled. He was far too good-looking for them to be anything but flattered, and perhaps he was trying to be funny. Besides, it was difficult to focus while he stood there in his half-naked glory, an incredibly fit specimen for a guy who looked just a few years younger than themselves.

"Anyway," Tori said, "do you know when Evelyn will be back?"

"She's in Denver, setting up some computer network. I think she said she'd be back late tonight."

"Oh shoot. We assumed she'd be back by now. How long are you in town?" Kat asked.

"Actually, I'm heading out in another hour," he said. "Though, now that I've met you two, I'm sorry to leave. Evelyn's made some beautiful friends in this town."

Both women giggled, but Tori was bold. "Boy, you certainly are the flirt, aren't you?"

"Just honest. I met her friend Shea as well. Was she a friend of yours?"

"She was."

"Then I'm so sorry for your loss. What a tragedy."

"When did you meet her?" Kat asked.

"She came here, just before she died. I got to say hello before she and Ev left town. Anyway, it was a pleasure meeting you both. I'll tell Ev you stopped by."

A thin, black cat suddenly appeared between Frederick's legs, purring as she brushed against him. He bent over to pick her up.

"This one is always trying to escape," he said with a smile. "Say hello to the beautiful women," he said to the cat.

Tori reached to stroke her fur and said hello.

"Hi, kitty," Kat said. "Can't touch you, though—terribly allergic. Well, nice to meet you, Frederick."

After he shut the door, Kat and Tori stared at each other silently as they waited for the elevator. Once they were inside, Tori said, "Oh my. Me likey!"

But Kat had been breathlessly waiting to talk for an entirely different reason. "Didn't you hear that? Shea was with Evelyn just before she died. They left town together? Now I have to talk to her."

"Don't you need to leave?"

"I do. But maybe I can fly out late tonight after I see her. I need to check flights. Will you drop me at Lina's?"

CHAPTER 29

April 1
8:00 a.m.

SHEA ROSE EARLY, SHOWERED, AND was preparing omelets and bacon when Ryan came down to the kitchen.

"Wow, what's this?" Ryan asked.

"Payback," Shea said. "Coffee's made."

"Great." He headed to the cabinet for a mug.

"You made such a nice dinner yesterday. Sorry I ran out on you."

Ryan stepped over to the stove with his coffee and kissed her neck. "Nothing turns me on more than the smell of bacon."

"I know." She laughed. "Maybe I should look for some bacon perfume. Hey," she said, handing him a plate, "I completely forgot about Susie's play this weekend."

"What are you talking about?" He sat at the table to eat.

Shea turned back to the stove to prepare her eggs. "Susie's in a play. I told you about this."

"No, you didn't."

"Seriously?" she replied sarcastically. Of course, she hadn't told him, since there was no play, but for twenty years, they'd chided each other about forgetting plans the other had shared. And Ryan enjoyed children's theater about as much as dental visits. "I promised my sister

I'd come see her. Can you do without me for the weekend? I missed her last one."

Ryan took a few bites before replying. "Do you want me to go with you?"

"Thanks," she said, joining him at the table. "That's sweet, but I'd rather you stay home. I'm stressed that we're not going to be ready for the open house next week. There's still so much to do. Can you finish the basement this weekend without me?"

"Yes, boss."

~ • ~

Shea cleaned up the breakfast dishes and descended the stairs to the basement. Ryan was standing in the middle of twenty years of boxes, toys, a crate of Legos, two shoe boxes of Barbies, two garbage bags filled with costumes, games, ski gear, furniture they didn't use upstairs but she'd never wanted to give away, and computer equipment that was either broken or outdated. She climbed over the piles and gave him a hug and a kiss. "I'm off," she said.

"Maybe I should go to the play and you could do this," he joked.

"Yeah, right." She smirked, looking around. The tension had finally dissolved. They were a team again, handling life together. "What should we do with all this stuff?" she asked. "Should we keep the furniture? What if the kids want the toys for their own kids?"

Ryan chuckled. "No way. They're several years from any of that. Let them start fresh. I'm thinking this will be several trips to Goodwill."

There were so many toys and games. Years of their lives were bound by these walls, this town, all these things. It was hard to believe they were really going to say good-bye to all of it. She sat on the arm of the sofa, picked up one of Leigh's wigs from her dress-up phase, and put it on her head. "Can I keep some of these at least?"

Ryan looked over at the neon-green curls and laughed. "Hot. Okay, just the wigs."

Shea pulled it off, stood, and fixed her hair. "Costumes, too. I mean, some of those are adult size! You never know."

"Fine," he said with a grin.

"I love you, Ryan Walker."

"And I love you, Shea Walker. Call me later, okay?" he asked, heading toward the furnace room.

"Will do. I'll call you before I go to bed tonight."

"Sounds good."

~ • ~

Shea headed out, energized and relieved to have a friend for the trip. She'd considered asking Lina, but it seemed a lot to ask. She'd looked so thin at chemo a couple of weeks ago. She didn't need this kind of stress. Tori's weekends still involved high school sports, and she and Herman had a standing date night the first Saturday of every month. They never skipped it. Perhaps she and Ryan should try that.

Dee had never responded to Shea's text on Wednesday. Maybe only time and distance would repair that friendship. Or maybe she was just busy with her own life. She was ashamed to have so quickly assumed Dee would have betrayed her after all these years. When she'd returned home from Michigan in February and briefly panicked that Ryan had been with another woman, she'd almost expected to find Dee hiding in her closet. It was ridiculous and embarrassing now to admit that, even to herself. She'd let her imagination get away from her, suddenly looking back at every conversation between them, every offhand remark, distorting each exchange inside a new lens, simply because of that dinner party, because Dee was always up for anything, because Dee's husband was Charlie, the creep, and because Dee had often said that Ryan was one of the good ones.

Shea pulled up to Evelyn's building, jumped out, and rang the bell inside the door. "I'm here!" she hollered after Evelyn answered the buzzer. It had seemed like a long shot when she called Evelyn at ten thirty last night, asking if she was free for the weekend, saying only that she needed a wingman for a quick trip to Ohio. But Evelyn's response was immediate—she was happy to join her for an adventure. Shea was thrilled. She probably should have thought of Evelyn first. She certainly had the most freedom, without kids or a husband to contend with.

"I'll be right down," Evelyn replied.

"Can I come up?" Shea asked. Evelyn buzzed her in. In Shea's quest to get on the road quickly, she'd failed to hit the restroom. It would be a long drive.

A man answered the door and introduced himself as Evelyn's brother, Frederick, Red to his friends. "Really?" Shea asked, like he was pulling her leg. His hair was dark brown. Red smiled, exposing some great dimples. "I couldn't say Fred as a little kid. I said 'Red.' It stuck."

Shea realized that she'd never asked Evelyn much about her family. There was so much she didn't know about her. Evelyn came out of the bedroom, looking typically simple and elegant. Even in jeans, she had an air of formality. Much like that apartment. Always the pearls, her hair always perfectly neat and straight. Kind of chic, really. They said good-bye to Red and headed out.

"He's adorable," Shea said as they walked to the car.

Evelyn rolled her eyes. "He's not that cute."

"Tell me more. Why is he staying with you?"

"Just moving on again. He's pretty aimless. My father would say it's because of the money. I think he's just lazy."

"What does he do?"

"Honestly? Nothing. Dabbles in the stock market, lives off his trust, sleeps with lots of women. Your typical playboy."

"Were you ever tempted to not have the career?" With Evelyn having the name Preston, one of the oldest and largest brokerage firms in the country, Shea assumed money had never been an issue.

"No. I need to feel a purpose when I get up every day. I get that from my job."

"I used to get that from my kids," Shea said. "I'm determined to get that feeling again."

"So, what's the occasion?" Evelyn asked as Shea pulled onto the expressway. Shea had promised to tell her the purpose and destination of the trip in the car. "This feels very clandestine. I'm intrigued."

"Well, it is, kind of," Shea admitted. "I haven't even told Ryan where I'm going. He thinks I've gone to Grand Rapids for my niece's play."

"Really?" Evelyn said, drawing out the word playfully. "You are bad. Well, your secret's safe with me. What's in Ohio?"

"Can you keep a secret?"

"It's my specialty," Evelyn said.

"Remember that weekend in Put-in-Bay, last Thanksgiving?"

"Yes . . ."

"And remember how I got kind of drunk, and flirted with that guy . . ."

"I do," Evelyn said, removing her sunglasses, raising an eyebrow at Shea.

Shea told Evelyn exactly what happened in November, and that she'd recently learned that Blake died that night.

"That's terrifying. I'm so sorry, Shea. I take it you never told Ryan about that night?"

"God, no. We've been through enough. It's bad enough that I have to live with what I did, I didn't want him to have to visualize any of that. But Georgia's freaking out. And it's my fault. I put myself in a stupid situation."

Evelyn nodded, looking out the windshield. Her silence felt like judgment. She obviously thought it was Shea's fault, too. Evelyn would never get herself in such a position. Everything about her seemed controlled.

"I feel terrible," Shea continued, suddenly feeling desperate to have a friend on her side.

"A lot of people make stupid decisions," Evelyn said flatly, her eyes still on the road ahead. But then she turned, and Shea met her eyes. "It doesn't mean some psycho gets to rape you."

"Thanks," Shea said. "I think I needed to hear that."

"If you'd been walking through a dark alley, alone at night, that might be considered dumb. But it doesn't mean it's your fault if you get attacked. You changed your mind. He got violent. His violence isn't your fault."

Shea took a deep breath and smiled.

Evelyn's face had turned solemn, like something was weighing on her. Shea wondered if perhaps she'd had her own experience with a violent man. But she didn't dare ask. Evelyn was in some ways Shea's exact opposite. While Shea enjoyed sharing, and oversharing, and sometimes acting outrageously, just to make people laugh and relax, Evelyn was obviously less comfortable with opening up, or loosening those pearls.

"Anyway, I've got to find out what really happened to him," Shea said. "The memorial is at three o'clock this afternoon at the lighthouse. I booked a room at the Humphrey House B and B. It's a great old place I noticed once. You'll love it."

"Sounds perfect," Evelyn said.

Evelyn's tone suggested the opposite. Maybe she was already regretting this trip. "I can't thank you enough for coming with me. I know it's a bit of a downer to tease you with a weekend trip and spring this on you, but we can just get this done, and then relax." She fiddled with the radio. "That's what I'm counting on, anyway. Maybe we can even rent one of those golf carts and look around."

Evelyn smiled, sounding lighter. "Well, I'm glad to do it. It's been a long week, so I could use a little change of scenery. And it was such a nice place. It'll be fun to stay on the island and explore."

"I'll tell you another secret," Shea added.

"Okay . . ."

"I've been looking at real estate on the island. Ryan and I are thinking of a fresh start. With the kids off at college, we may be ready for a new chapter."

"Wow." Evelyn's voice was suddenly flat, like she'd heard tragic news. "You really are full of secrets, aren't you."

"Yeah, I haven't told anyone about moving, either. I hope you can keep that to yourself."

Evelyn didn't respond.

"Ev?"

"I promise," she said. But her voice cracked.

Shea looked over. Evelyn was wiping at her eyes. Was she crying? "You okay?"

"Sure," she said. "I just hate to see you go."

"Thanks. I do, too, in some ways. This town holds so many memories for us. But at this point, they're not all good. I think we may have lost Dee and Charlie altogether. Things have gone south in a way that we can't recover from."

Evelyn said nothing else, and the car fell quiet, despite the radio. Something felt different between them. Perhaps it would be tough on Evelyn when Shea and Ryan moved away. Perhaps she saw Shea as her only real friend in town. Hopefully Tori and the others would continue to include her in girls' nights and parties. It was great that she had such a big job, but everyone needed friends.

"So," Evelyn said, "you've forgiven Ryan for the whole cheating bit, I take it?"

"Actually, I was wrong about all that. That's what makes what I did with Blake even worse. It was all just a misunderstanding. Ryan has screwed up, but he wasn't cheating on me."

"You're sure?"

Shea didn't answer right away. Some things were no one's business. But then again, she'd already told the girls about her fears in November. And she suddenly felt like she needed Evelyn to understand, not to assume she was naive. "He did cheat once, a few years ago. That's probably why I was so quick to assume. But that's another story."

"I thought you found evidence. A bra or something, right?"

It was a quick, painful jab. A reminder that Shea never had found out where that came from. "It's . . . complicated," she said. "Marriage is always complicated, right?"

"For sure," Evelyn said, and Shea could feel her eyes on her. "It's just, I have my own issues about all this. Sometimes there's no going back."

"Is that what happened to you?" Shea asked.

"Yeah."

"I'm sorry, Ev. So, he didn't just walk out. There was someone else?"

Evelyn didn't answer, and Shea had nothing comforting to say.

"So, Ryan hasn't been cheating with Dee, then?"

The jab came more harshly this time. "Why would you say that?" Shea's fingers tightened around the wheel.

Evelyn didn't respond.

"What do you know about Ryan and Dee?"

"Nothing. I'm sorry," Evelyn said. She wouldn't look at Shea.

"No, you just said Dee's name. Why would you do that?"

"I guess I just assumed. In November, you said that he was cheating, and you just said you couldn't be friends with Dee anymore. You know Dee."

"What does that mean, 'You know Dee'?"

"I don't know. She can just be a little unpredictable, and she drinks too much. I assumed it meant she wasn't happy with Charlie. When I saw her and Ryan together after you'd told us all he'd been cheating, I guess I just assumed. But I shouldn't have. It's not my place. I shouldn't have said that."

Shea couldn't breathe. Her fingers were turning white. What had she seen? Shea stared at the road, her eyes fixed but unable to focus. Everything was twisting again.

"Stop," Evelyn said, putting her hand on Shea's knee. "I'm totally wrong, obviously. I must have jumped to conclusions. It's not like I saw them kissing or anything. I'm sure I misunderstood."

"What did you see?"

"I saw them getting in her car one night. I probably thought the worst because she's always been kind of a bitch to me. But she's your friend. Please, forget I said something. You and Ryan have worked it out. He wasn't cheating."

Shea couldn't let it go. "When was this? When did you see them together?"

"I don't know," Evelyn said. "I guess that was in February."

Shea could feel a heavy weight pushing her down, bringing her back to that moment she'd returned to the house in February after the weekend in Michigan. Ryan naked, the messy house. "You have to tell me exactly what you saw. And when."

Evelyn looked down at her phone. "Let's see . . ." She'd pulled up her calendar. "I guess that would have been February 18. It was a Saturday night."

A Tom Petty song came on the radio: "Free Fallin." That was what it felt like.

CHAPTER 30

April 14

KAT WAS LOOKING UP THE flight options. If she didn't get on the seven-thirty flight, there was nothing else open until three o'clock tomorrow. It was now four o'clock. The phone rang, and Kat looked over, hoping it wasn't Mack. She wanted to be able to tell him which flight she'd booked before they spoke again. She really didn't want to fight anymore.

The call was from an unlisted number. "Hello?" Kat said.

"Kat, hi, it's Evelyn."

"Well, that's a coincidence. I was just thinking about you."

"I just spoke with my brother. He said you and Tori came by looking for me?" Her voice rose then, like her day was brightened by the prospect of a visitor. Kat wondered if, with Shea gone, Evelyn was feeling lonely.

"That's right. Are you back in town?"

"Not yet. What's up?"

"I've just been thinking about Shea a lot, and it seemed like you might know more than the rest of us. I was hoping we could talk before I left."

Evelyn fell silent for a moment, and when she spoke, Kat thought she sounded even lonelier. She probably hoped it had just been a social call. "When are you going back to Texas?"

"I've got to get home by tomorrow."

"Oh, I won't be home by then. I get in late Saturday. Sorry."

"Do you have a minute now?"

"Sure."

"Evelyn, none of us knew about Shea taking pills. Even Ryan said they weren't an issue. But you seemed to know more. I thought maybe Shea confided in you about what might have been going on with her. And your brother said you two left town together just before she died? Where were you going?"

There was a long pause. Kat suddenly wondered if they'd been cut off. "Hello?"

"I'm still here," Evelyn said. "Kat, there was something strange going on between Ryan and Shea and Dee and Charlie."

"Yeah, I know all about that."

"Can I tell you something in confidence?"

"Absolutely," Kat said. She'd been oblivious to everyone's issues while she lived there, and suddenly, she was the keeper of all secrets.

"It's been eating away at me," Evelyn said.

Kat heard Evelyn sniffle and take a deep breath.

"I," Evelyn finally began, "I feel . . . responsible."

CHAPTER 31

April 1
11:30 a.m.

THE CAR FELT QUIET DESPITE the radio. Shea couldn't speak, and Evelyn seemed content to let her sort through the pain alone. Maybe she thought it was the best thing a friend could do.

Dee had been with Ryan on February 18. The night Shea was out of town, crying to her sister all night about their problems, after pleading with Charlie to leave her alone.

Ryan said he'd been drunk that night, sure that she'd run off with Charlie, and convinced their marriage was over. If Dee feared the same and they'd seen each other . . . could they . . . ? He'd sworn that he hadn't been with her.

But he lied. He'd lied about the affair three years ago. He lied about the job, the finances. Why did she trust him at all? She'd found that bra in his drawer right after their luau party last summer, and he'd never had an explanation. She'd feared cheating again but at the time had never in a million years considered one of her own friends.

She began replaying every moment she could remember from that party. She'd seen Dee heading upstairs. But lots of their friends went upstairs to use the bathroom. She'd never thought twice about it. She'd later seen Dee whispering to Ryan in the corner, seeming almost angry. But Dee was an animated storyteller. She could have been saying anything. It could have been the punch line to a joke.

But then she remembered Ryan's comment the night after those weird kisses with Dee and Charlie. "I've wanted to do that for a long time," he'd said. Was this always about Dee? He'd run off with her so fast that night, pulling her toward the basement like he finally had the green light to do what he'd always wanted.

And when Shea had returned from Michigan, he was naked. He'd changed the sheets.

She felt sick.

But Ryan had a tell. He had never looked her in the eyes when he lied. And he'd looked her in the eyes. She had always been able to trust him when he looked in her eyes. He was at home right now, sorting through their stuff, trying to fix their life. "I love you, Shea Walker," he'd said as she left him in the basement. He did. She knew it.

Maybe Dee had just found him drunk that night and driven him home. Maybe there was an innocent explanation. And she and Ryan had a plan. She believed in it. She wanted it. They were going to start over. She could not spiral down this road of assumptions again. She had to believe her husband. She had to stop listening to everyone else. Even Evelyn said she might just have been jumping to conclusions.

Shea looked over at Evelyn, who seemed as distraught as she was. "You okay?" Shea asked, turning down the radio.

Evelyn turned and gave a half smile. "Sure."

But she was not. "What are you thinking about?"

She shook her head. It was obvious she had no desire to open up. "It's just been a long week. Lots of work stress. I'm sorry. I haven't been sleeping. It makes me a little teary."

"I'm like that, too."

"I need to send off a few e-mails for work, okay? I'm sorry I'm such bad company."

"No, no. Do what you have to do."

~ • ~

It was after two o'clock when Shea pulled off the expressway toward the sign for Port Clinton. "Getting close now," Shea said.

Evelyn finally looked up, dropping her phone into her lap.

"You get it all done?"

"Yep. I tend to agonize about work problems. Like there's no way to fix them, but then it's like a lightbulb and I realize I've got a solution. I think everything will be okay now."

"I envy you," Shea said.

"Me? Why?"

"Just to have that. To be so needed. To have such a big job."

"Well, you have something, too. I envy that."

Ev was right. Shea had a husband who loved her, kids who made her life worth living. She needed to trust Ryan. They were a family.

Evelyn began squirming in her seat as they got closer. "I'm starting to feel a little desperate to use the bathroom."

"Oh, I'm sorry. You should have said something. We could have stopped."

"No, it's fine. I know we've got to get there by three."

"That's right," Shea said, checking the clock. "I always forget that we cross into Eastern time when we come here. We're going to be late, though I'm guessing these kinds of things last a few hours"

"How long is the ferry ride to the island?"

"About thirty minutes."

Ten minutes later, Shea pulled in to the parking lot of the ferry terminal. Evelyn put her hand on the door handle.

"You okay?" Shea asked.

Evelyn winced. "I just need to go."

"Oh, I'm sorry, Ev." She pulled up to the building. "Go on. I think there's one right inside. I'll park the car."

Evelyn said thanks and jumped out.

Shea parked the car, grabbed their bags, walked into the terminal, and checked the schedule. The next ferry was leaving in five minutes. Perfect timing. She went into the bathroom to check on Evelyn, still inside a stall.

"You okay?"

"I will be," Evelyn said. "I'm sorry, I know we're on a tight schedule."

"The ferry leaves in five minutes. I'll go get our tickets."

"Wait," Evelyn said. "I'm so sorry, Shea. I don't feel very good. I don't think I can go anywhere for a little while. Just get on the boat. I'll take the next one. I'll text so we can meet up."

Shea looked at her watch. The ferries only ran once an hour. The lighthouse was on the other side of the island, and it would take time to get there. "You sure?"

"Absolutely. Go. I'd feel terrible if I held you up. As soon as I feel better, I'll get a ticket and get on the next ferry. Can you just leave my bag here with me?"

"Oh, Ev, I don't want to leave you here."

The horn of the ferry blared. "Go," Evelyn said more firmly. "Really, I'll be fine. I'll get out of here as soon as I can."

"Okay," Shea said, sliding Evelyn's overnight bag under the door. "Remember, the B and B is called Humphrey House. It's not far from the main strip. It's on that side street right after you pass the chocolate shop. Blake's memorial is at the lighthouse, but if you don't feel good, just go to the room. I'll meet you there."

"Got it."

Shea left, grabbed a ticket, and rushed to the ferry just as the crew prepared to remove the gangway.

Standing at the bow, Shea held the railing, looking out at the water toward the islands. It was brisk, but the water shimmered under the bright sun. The view, so calm and inviting, was a strange contrast to her last trip here. The November trip had been plagued by rough waters, the pain of feeling like her marriage was collapsing, and her drunken determination to even the score. She didn't want to think about it, or Blake, or what she would say if she saw any of Blake's friends at the memorial. She wasn't even sure she'd remember them.

Instead, she focused on how beautiful it was out here, and how amazing it might be to start over with a little house, maybe a boat, kids and grandkids, a whole new life. She was not going to let Evelyn's comments ruin her plan. Nothing could ruin this plan. *Please let this be the end*, she thought to herself. *Please let this man's death have nothing to do with me or Georgia.*

Once the ferry had traveled a good distance from shore, it picked up speed, pushing against the choppy water. A few swells crashed against the boat, causing spray on the deck, and Shea went inside for a seat. The boat was only a quarter filled. She sat facing the stern and looked out at the ferry terminal still visible in the distance. She hoped Evelyn would make it to the memorial. She really didn't want to be there alone.

CHAPTER 32

April 14

KAT HUNG UP THE PHONE with Evelyn and rubbed her eyes. Everyone was holding secrets, each of them making Kat feel worse. Evelyn had broken down almost immediately as she told Kat what happened. Evelyn was certain that her comments about Dee and Ryan must have pushed Shea over the edge. She said the car had become silent after she'd shared what she knew. Evelyn felt like she'd let down the one friend who'd been so good to her in the last year. Shea needed a friend for that trip, and Evelyn had failed her. It sounded as if Evelyn believed it might have been suicide, after all.

It wasn't Evelyn's fault, getting so sick in the terminal, but Kat's reassurance hadn't eased her guilt. She said she'd felt sick for nearly forty-five minutes and couldn't stomach the idea of getting on the ferry. She also admitted to being a little heartbroken that Shea was planning to move away. She didn't much feel like browsing real estate. It wasn't rational, she said, but she'd eventually texted Shea an apology for getting sick, rented a car, and returned to Maple Park.

When Evelyn found out that Shea had died that night, she couldn't bear to tell anyone what she'd done. She didn't think anyone would forgive her for leaving, for not joining her like she'd promised, for sharing unproven allegations about Dee and Ryan. And Shea had told Evelyn at a Christmas party that in her drunken stupor on the island, she'd recalled Evelyn's suggestion that women with cheating husbands give them a taste of their own medicine. The very idea that Shea's flirtation with Blake had gone so wrong, and that she'd been the one to suggest it, even as a joke, left Evelyn beyond consolable.

Kat couldn't get her head around the idea that Dee had been with Ryan. Dee had sat with Kat in Lina's kitchen just two days earlier, talking about the whole swinging fiasco like that was all there was to it. Could she trust Dee? Had she said all that to Kat because she was afraid that Kat and others might suspect her after she'd seemed so hostile when they were in Catawba?

All of these revelations made Kat feel worse. Shea could have succumbed to a tragic impulse, she realized. She certainly had reasons. She might have caused Blake's death; she might have just learned that her husband and close friend had been lying. Even if it wasn't true, it could have devastated her.

~ • ~

Kat stood at Ryan's door. It was ridiculous that she was paying him a third visit, especially after they'd already said good-bye, but after speaking with Evelyn, she had no choice.

When Ryan opened the door, a cell phone to his ear, Kat didn't bother with the pleasantries. "I have to tell you something."

"I gotta go," he said, abruptly ending his phone call. "What's going on?"

"Evelyn went with Shea to Put-in-Bay on April first."

"What?" He stumbled back, as if her words had assaulted him. "How could she not say anything?"

"Can I come in?"

Ryan silently walked to the kitchen, and Kat followed. She sat at the kitchen table. Ryan went to the fridge and pulled out a beer. He raised one toward her, silently offering, but she waved it off.

"Evelyn didn't say anything because she feels responsible," Kat said. "She thinks she might have said something that upset Shea. Well, more than upset her, really."

Ryan said nothing. He was leaning against the island counter, his eyes glazed, burrowing a hole in the tabletop.

"Ryan, Evelyn told Shea that you'd had an affair. With Dee."

The name *Dee* seemed to pull him from the trance. "What? God dammit! I told you, Kat—"

Kat raised her hand. "Ryan, I know. Evelyn said she'd made an assumption. She felt terrible for putting that in Shea's mind. Apparently, Evelyn got sick in the terminal and never caught up to Shea on the island. She knows that if she had, this might never have happened."

He sipped his beer. He didn't say anything.

"It's all so crazy, Ryan. All of us—Georgia, Dee, Evelyn, me. Everyone is torturing themselves with the what-ifs and the guilt. We all feel like we failed her."

Ryan didn't look at Kat. His eyes remained fixed on the table in front of her as he spoke. "Why would you feel responsible? You weren't even here."

"Shea called me the night before she left. She wanted to talk. I ignored it." Kat started crying. "I'm so sorry, Ryan."

"You think you have the market cornered on guilt," he said, finally looking at her. "Don't be ridiculous."

"I'm going home, Ryan, but I couldn't leave without telling you everything. You have a right to know."

He swigged his beer. "Well, thanks for stopping by."

Kat didn't move. "There's more. We know why Shea went to the island two weeks ago. Last November, when the girls went to

Put-in-Bay, Shea was upset about you, and she left the bar with a man."

Ryan looked away like he didn't want to hear it.

"They went to his boat. Apparently, they kissed, and when Shea resisted taking it further, things got violent."

"What are you telling me?" He was staring at her, not blinking, holding her gaze. She could see his fear, the dread of where this was headed.

"We don't know everything, but either Shea or Georgia hit him over the head, and then they ran off."

He looked away and drank some more.

"Anyway," Kat continued, "a few weeks ago, Tori read about that man in an Ohio paper. He'd disappeared the night Shea was with him. He died. And it seems that Shea was concerned that she could have been responsible. His memorial was on Put-in-Bay. On April first. That's why she went. We assume she wanted answers. It doesn't even matter now. Obviously, Evelyn was the friend Shea referred to when she spoke to the innkeeper. And now, we know why she might have been so upset. I'm so sorry to be the one to tell you all this."

"Stop!" he yelled. "I can't listen to this anymore."

Kat stood slowly, taken aback by the outburst. She'd never seen him so angry.

"You should go," he said.

She walked to the door, suddenly afraid to speak, and stepped outside when he opened the door.

He closed it behind her, and she stood, stunned, unable to move. A moment later, she heard a glass shatter inside the house.

CHAPTER 33

April 1
3:55 p.m.

AFTER SHEA GOT TO THE island and checked in, she drove the inn's complimentary golf cart through the winding streets to the far side of the island.

Blake was right, she thought, pulling up toward the old redbrick lighthouse. It was different from any she had seen before. It looked like a stately, century-old home that just happened to have a lighthouse tower attached to it. A large expanse of green grass separated the house from the road, and it stood near the rocky edge of the island, the deep-blue lake surrounding all but one side of it. There were several cars and a few golf carts parked along the road leading to the lighthouse, and Shea watched a few mourners walking toward the building. The service was probably over, but she was obviously not the only one arriving late. *What now?* She suddenly panicked. Was she to eavesdrop on conversations? How would she introduce herself to these strangers? *And how did you know Blake?* someone might ask. *Oh, he tried to rape me the night he died. My friend hit him over the head and we ran.* Yeah, that would go over well.

She walked over to the large placard in the yard to read about the lighthouse. Anything to avoid walking inside. CONSTRUCTED AND

FIRST LIT IN 1897, it read, THE SOUTH BASS ISLAND LIGHTHOUSE
WAS IN CONTINUOUS OPERATION UNTIL 1962 . . . She couldn't read
anymore. She couldn't wait any longer, but she kept looking down
the street, hoping a taxi would round the bend and drop Evelyn. She
wanted a wingman. She sent her a text. Hope you're feeling better.
You catch a ferry yet? We have room #1 btw. See u soon.

"Hello," a woman said, coming up beside her.

Shea turned to the voice. "Hi."

"Are you here for the memorial?"

"I am," Shea said.

"Such a tragedy," the woman said. "But what a beautiful place,
right? And it's a perfect day. I think it's almost sixty degrees."

Shea smiled. "I was just thinking that, too. Well, I better go in."

"Me, too," the woman said. "I just want to read the history of the
building first."

Shea began walking toward the house. *That went fine*, she thought.
No third-degree questions. Nothing to fear. She was right to come.
This wasn't her fault. Or Georgia's. But a man had died and she had
known him, for better and worse. She was just paying respects. And
if anyone asked, she knew him from college. She was sure a guy like
that knew a lot of women.

The front door was on the far side, facing the water, but a large
mass of people was entering and exiting the building through the
glassed-in narrow porch that extended along the width of the back
of the building. Once inside, Shea followed the crowd through the
kitchen, which looked untouched since the sixties, and into the large
adjoining dining room, complete with ten-foot ceilings, a fireplace,
and an antique piano in the corner. The table, topped with white
cloth, presented a beautiful array of food for the forty or fifty people,
and along the fireplace mantel, pictures of Blake and his wife and
children sat perched, as if this was their family home.

Most of the visitors were standing in the adjoining living room to greet Blake's family. She would avoid that room. To see his wife, the mother of his kids, mourning a man whom Shea might have—well, not really, well, what? *I didn't kill him*, she screamed inside her head. Maybe his wife knew he was a pig. Maybe he was a serial cheater and she'd just been waiting for the right moment to leave him, waiting because of the young kids, the complications, the pain of breaking up a family. *Maybe he beat her*, she told herself. Maybe the woman in there was shedding tears of relief.

Get some food, Shea thought. *Look busy.*

With a plate full of appetizers, Shea meandered into the front hall. Several poster boards were filled with pictures of Blake and family and friends. Kids ran through the rooms, seemingly oblivious to the occasion or just incapable of being sad when there was cake and other kids, a lighthouse tower to climb, and an enormous expanse of green grass outside.

Shea stood in front of one of the poster boards, looking at the pictures, examining the life of this man she barely knew. It was a seemingly idyllic family. But to her, he was a stranger. These pictures were no more revealing than the thousands of Facebook posts she'd seen and shared over the years. They were the best shots, the thin shots, the good smiles, the better sides—just like the fiction of reality TV—edited and shaped and framed in the way people wanted to be seen.

A couple of women stood behind her, pointing toward photographs, while speaking to each other. They referenced the kids in the photos by name. "I don't know," one woman said to the other, as Shea began to eavesdrop, "I just told Jerry that I had no interest in getting a boat. He had a hard time arguing, since we had this on the calendar."

"Yeah," the other woman said, "but Blake was drinking. Everyone knows you can't drink and drive. Boat or car. It's not like we refuse to buy cars, right?"

Shea stood frozen, listening. That was all anyone thought. And why wouldn't they? He got drunk with his friends, his boat turned up on an island, and he obviously disappeared into the lake. None of this had anything to do with her. Her guilt, and Georgia's panic, was silly. Blake had died almost five months ago, a tragic boating accident, and it was just a coincidence that she'd been with him that night. Nothing more. The weight lifted from her shoulders, and she took a breath as the women behind her walked away.

Shea popped one more appetizer in her mouth and tossed the plate into the garbage can. Those women had been like angels with a message. Suddenly, she felt like a funeral crasher, here for free food and strange voyeurism, and she turned toward the front door. There was no need to stay. A little boy ran past her, yelling back that he was heading for the tower. Shea stopped. Blake had said the view from the tower was beautiful.

Shea followed the little boy out the front door, onto the other glass porch, to a spectacular view of the lake. How fantastic it must have been for the lightkeepers who lived here over the years to have had that view every day, watching waves crash onto the boulders along the shore, watching the boats, sitting along those rocks and casting a line. Even during the cold winters, she envisioned an amazing view. Tori had once remarked that Lake Erie sometimes froze over entirely. It was the shallowest of the Great Lakes. Tori said she'd even read a blog posted by some guy who had walked across the lake to Canada a few decades earlier. That was a little more adventure than Shea needed, but Tori's pictures of the lake in winter looked like the moon or some other cosmic frozen tundra.

The entrance to the light tower was right here, inside the glassed-in front porch. The little boy she'd followed out had already climbed up and down and run off before she stepped inside. She marveled at the curved redbrick walls, partially covered in plaster, as she started her ascent up the sixty-foot gray metal circular stair. But hearing the pounding of feet on metal, she looked up. It seemed impossible to pass someone on such a narrow stair, so she waited for the people coming down to reach the bottom. "How's the view?" she asked one of the men as he arrived on the ground.

"Incredible," the man said. "It's such a clear day."

Shea made it to the top and stood inside the old light, fully encased in glass and protected from the elements. There was a small platform with a railing that encircled the giant light. A few others were standing outside, though there was little room to maneuver. She went to the railing and looked out. Blake had been right. Why was it that the sight of water made everything in the world seem okay? She wanted to look at water every day. Suddenly, she could hardly wait to jump in a golf cart with Evelyn and see the homes she'd viewed online.

"Hey."

The voice came from behind her. She turned.

"You're the woman," he said. "You were with Blake at Rudolph's."

CHAPTER 34

April 14

KAT LEFT RYAN, RETURNED TO Lina's, and called Mack. It was five thirty.

"I'm sorry," she said. "I know this has taken too long. I'm coming home. I've stayed too long and I miss you. There's a flight in a couple of hours. I'm going to try to get on it."

"I don't think you should do that just yet," Mack said.

"What do you mean?"

"I just bought a plane ticket. I'll be in Maple Park by noon tomorrow. I'm going to pay my respects and take my wife out for a night on the town in one of our favorite cities. I happen to know someone who has an in with a luxury hotel downtown. I think I can get us a room."

Kat chuckled.

"Then we're going to invite some old friends to join us for brunch in Maple Park before we head home. Together."

Kat smiled and took another cleansing breath. At least she and Mack were going to be okay. They were a team again. "That sounds amazing, and I can't wait to see you. But . . . I may have made it difficult for you to see all our old friends."

"What do you mean?"

"Ryan just threw me out of his house."

"Why?"

"I'm not sure, really. I learned some things about what was going on with Shea and I thought he had a right to know. I thought it might help. But he freaked out."

"Don't worry about it too much. I'm sure he's not thinking straight these days. I'd be a mess if you suddenly died."

Kat hoped Mack was right, but something about that whole exchange with Ryan gave her a sick feeling. Like his anger came from hearing that Kat knew something. He hadn't looked surprised by the information she shared. He hadn't even reacted to the information that Shea went to the island for Blake's memorial. He'd just looked angry. She didn't know what to make of it. Could any of what Evelyn said been true? Was he suddenly horrified that Evelyn knew about him and Dee? Kat could hardly believe she was even entertaining the idea.

"Mack, I know I've opened a can of worms here and it's none of my business, but can we talk about that conversation you had with Ryan at the luau again? Can you please just try to remember every-thing Ryan said to you that night?"

"It wasn't a long conversation, Kat. I told you, I really didn't want to know. Sometimes it's just better not to know certain things about your friends."

"I know, but please. Was anything else said?"

"Just something like 'Be careful' and 'No one is safe.' I asked if he meant he'd fallen in love with someone else. He said no way. That it was just a thing. He wasn't going to screw up life with Shea. I got the sense it had happened a long time ago, though."

"Why?"

"I don't remember, exactly. Just something about how you think something's behind you, but it could haunt you forever. I don't know. I'm paraphrasing. I just got the sense that he'd cheated, it was a while back, but it was still messing with their life."

Was that about Dee? Why would he think she would be safe? She was one of Shea's closest friends. And Kat had thought that whatever Shea feared was based on things happening last fall, not years earlier. She remembered seeing Dee and Ryan together the night of the luau, talking in the corner—their faces close, but he was a close talker. The music was loud. Kat hadn't given it any thought.

But something told her that her blind trust in Ryan might have been misplaced. He swore there'd been no affair. He blew up at the mention of Dee's name. And if he'd done something like that, she didn't know what else he might have done.

After hanging up with Mack, she called Martin at the hotel offices. "Hey, I need a favor and I need you to drop everything and handle this, okay?"

Martin agreed.

"Remember the reservation info you sent me via e-mail this morning? Go to the security office for the hotel. Get a copy of the video feed from the elevator bank on the forty-fourth floor for the day of that reservation."

"The entire day?"

"From the time of Ryan Walker's check-in until midnight."

"Got it."

If Ryan was with someone other than Shea that night, Kat would know soon. And if he was, she couldn't trust him, let alone look at him. If it was Dee in that hotel . . . she didn't even know what she'd do.

But someone had been on that island with Shea. Charlie wasn't the guest, she reminded herself. Though that didn't mean he hadn't been there. She'd sat at the bar with someone. Mary hadn't locked the front door of the inn until twenty minutes after Shea went to her room. And if Dee was in Michigan waiting for Charlie's return on April 1, Kat suddenly realized, there would be no one who could verify where she was, either. What if Dee had known about Shea's trip to the island? She could have driven there in a frenzy and found Shea at the bar with Charlie. She could have . . . Kat didn't know. Her conspiracy theories swirled about. She felt like a lunatic. But the depth of lies she'd discovered made her trust nothing. It felt like the entire neighborhood knew more than they'd shared. Any one of them could have been with Shea that night.

CHAPTER 35

April 1
4:20 p.m.

"Hi," Shea said. There were six of them, all men. They had all come out onto the platform, some from the left, the others from the right. She was surrounded with almost no room to move, and she stood with her back against the small metal railing. She recognized one of them now. The big one. He'd been the loudest of the bunch when they met last November.

"Dave," he said, putting his hand to his chest. He sounded annoyed, as if she should have remembered him.

"I'm Shea," she said, offering her hand.

He didn't take it. "I remember you, but we didn't have your real name. Weren't your friends calling you Chardonnay that night?"

That silly nickname. She smiled, embarrassed. "Right," she said, pulling her hand back.

But Dave didn't see the humor. He folded his arms across his chest. "What are you doing here?"

"I just wanted to pay my respects. I'm so sorry for your loss," she said carefully, trying to defuse the tension. She raised her arms to rest them on the rail. If felt as forced as any bad pose.

"Jesus," Dave said, turning to his friends. "She wanted to pay respects. We've been wondering for months the real name of the woman Blake ran out of the bar with, what happened to him, why she came back to the bar that night and he never did, whether she was with him, what she knew, and she's standing right here."

Shea felt her cheeks turn hot. "I'm sorry, I didn't know about any of this until recently."

"But what happened that night?" another of the men asked, stepping closer. "You were with him. Did he take you down to his boat? Did you go out on the water?"

"No," Shea said, vehemently shaking her head. "I was with my friends."

"Shea, huh?" Dave said. "Shea what?"

"Johnson," she blurted out. Anything but the truth.

Dave turned to his friends. "Let's remember that. Isn't it weird that she and her girlfriends were using fake names at the bar? So when Blake disappeared, we didn't even know how to find them."

"Why would you use fake names?" one of the guys asked, stepping closer, the accusation obvious.

Shea glanced behind her, at the sixty-foot drop to the ground. "It was just a game," she said softly.

"Where are your friends?" Dave looked toward the spiral stairs. "Are they here, too?"

"Just one. I'm sorry," she said again. "I'm really sorry for your loss. I don't know anything about what happened that night. We'd only just met."

"So why are you here?" another one asked.

"My friend read about it in the local paper, and I felt terrible. I wondered how it happened." She could feel the energy of these men coming at her even though their feet hadn't moved. Despite the wind, her armpits felt wet with sweat.

"Us, too," Dave said.

Shea stepped toward the men, faking confidence, and maneuvered herself to put her back against the light, anything to get some distance between herself and that railing. It would only take a slip, a push, a toss—a quick and painful death. "So, you didn't see him that night after we were all together? I assumed he met back up with you."

"Nope," Dave said.

"I told him I needed to get back to my friends." She moved her eyes from one face to the next, avoiding any real contact, any chance that someone might see through her. "He said he was going to pop into another bar. That's it."

"What bar?"

"I don't remember the name."

"Where was it? Where were you when you had this conversation?"

Shea swallowed before answering. "I'm sorry, I just don't remember. We all drank a little too much that night. If you'll excuse me, I need to use the restroom."

Dave's face softened then as he stepped forward. "Yeah, sure. But find us again, okay? I'd really like to talk more about this."

"Of course," Shea lied again, already moving toward the steps.

She rushed down the spiral staircase. The pounding of her feet on the metal steps echoed through the tower. She went back into the main house, through the crowd, and found the restroom under the hall stairs. She locked the door and braced the sink. She could practically hear her heart beating outside her chest. What if someone from the police department was here? What if those guys asked her to talk to the police? She looked at her reflection in the mirror. "I didn't do anything." Georgia was right. This was just asking for trouble, coming here. Anything she could tell those men would only cause problems for Georgia, cause Blake's wife to know what he had done, cause nothing but pain. None of them deserved to have their lives thrown upside down because of what Shea or Blake had done.

She turned on the faucet, splashed some water on her face, and patted herself dry. She had to get out of there. She went to the commode and sat, searching her purse for a pill. She'd promised Ryan she would stop, and she knew she could, but today was not the day.

She found the bottle; only two remained. She took them both, swallowing them dry, dropped the purse on the ground, and braced her head with both hands, rocking back and forth, willing herself to breathe, to let the pills work their magic.

Finally, she calmed down enough to stand. She grabbed her purse and pulled out her phone. Evelyn hadn't called or texted, so she sent her a text, asking her to meet up at Rudolph's. She needed a drink.

She quickly left the bathroom, walked through the crowd of well-wishers back into the kitchen, looking out for Blake's friends, and ducked out the back door to her golf cart.

As she drove the few miles to the north end of the island, she noticed a few real estate signs in the front lawns of houses along the road. Suddenly, everything had less appeal. Georgia was right. She never should have come. The idea of starting over, here of all places, suddenly seemed beyond absurd.

She drove back to the inn, parked the cart, and stopped in her room. It was empty, no sign of Evelyn's bag. Mary was nowhere to be found on the main floor, so she walked over to Rudolph's.

CHAPTER 36

April 15

KAT WOKE UP ON SATURDAY morning and checked the phone. It was before eight o'clock. Mack would be there soon. She couldn't wait to wrap her arms around him.

But he'd already sent a text: Flight delayed. Should be there by two.

Kat rolled onto her back and opened her e-mails. Martin had gotten back to her.

Here's the security footage. Hope it helps.

She couldn't open the compressed file from her phone, so she jumped up and grabbed her laptop and waited impatiently for the computer to turn on.

When she opened the mail again and clicked the attachment, she held her breath, waiting. Finally, her screen expanded into video, and she stared at an empty elevator bank. She fast-forwarded the footage, stopping each time the elevator doors opened—six times, strangers coming and going on the forty-fourth floor.

When the door opened again, Kat's breath caught in her throat.

Feeling nauseated, almost light-headed from the evidence in front of her, she fast-forwarded past two more door openings until, finally, she saw Ryan. She grabbed her phone, hands shaking.

Get over here. 911, she wrote.

Kat threw on some clothes, still trying to sort it all out. Within ten minutes, she heard the front door open as Tori asked Lina where to find Kat. Kat came out of the bedroom and looked at her friends. Lina was still in her robe and slippers, with coffee in hand.

"Ryan is having an affair."

"With who?" Lina asked.

"Evelyn."

"What?" they both nearly shouted.

"I saw them. On the tape, she got out of the elevator on the forty-fourth floor. Within an hour, Ryan did, too. And she was there."

"Wait, back up. What are you talking about? What tape? She was where?"

Kat collapsed onto the sofa and explained what she'd seen on the security tape, why she'd looked at the footage, and what Evelyn had said during their phone call last night.

"Evelyn drove Shea to the island," she continued, speaking slower now, trying to absorb it all. "Evelyn said she never got on that ferry, that she'd been sick at the terminal, and after what happened, she was afraid to tell anyone because she thought we'd all hate her for leaving Shea."

The women sat in stunned silence, each trying to process what it could all mean.

"If she was having an affair with Ryan, and she knew where Shea went, so did he," Tori said flatly.

"Did they want to get rid of Shea?" Kat asked, her words aimed at the emptiness in front of her. "Was it all a lie? Was Ryan the man at the bar?"

"Did you ever hear back from the bartender at Rudolph's?" Lina asked.

"No."

"So that man could have been Charlie or Ryan," Tori said.

"I'm going to be sick," Lina said, collapsing into a nearby kitchen chair.

"Where is Evelyn now?" Tori asked.

"She said she gets back later today. Do we call the police?"

"Hold on," Lina said. "Back up a second. Okay, Ryan and Evelyn were having an affair. That's horrifying."

"And maybe she told Shea about it," Kat said. "Maybe she drove her to . . ." She shook her head, unable to utter the words.

"Even if that's true," Lina said, "that makes Evelyn a terrible person. Ryan, too. But it doesn't make them murderers. Right? But if you tell the police all of this, they could end up on trial for murder. This isn't just about ruining their lives. Those kids . . ."

Kat was nodding, Lina was right. "We need to get in there," Kat said.

"Where?" Tori asked.

"Evelyn's apartment. Maybe there's some proof that she was on the island. She said she never got on that ferry, that she took a rental car and returned home. If she was on the island . . ."

"Well, that's easy enough for the police to investigate. Maybe we just tell them everything," Tori said.

Kat stood up, suddenly struck at the thought of precious time slipping by. "What if she called me last night because she knew her brother had just told us about her leaving town with Shea? If she suddenly thinks people are looking . . . what if there's something in there that proves she was there or even proves what happened? What if we do nothing and she comes home and destroys the evidence before the police have the chance to look into it?"

"But how?" Lina asked.

"Georgia," Kat said as she walked to her bedroom.

"What do you mean?" Tori asked, following her.

Kat was back with her purse in hand. "Georgia has a key. She took care of Evelyn's plants in the summer and fall. She has keys to Evelyn's. She told me on Thursday."

Lina left the mug and went to her friends. "Now you want to break in there?"

"It's not breaking in," Tori said. "We're friends. With keys."

"We can't involve Georgia in any of this," Kat said, walking to the door.

Tori followed.

"I don't feel good about this," Lina said.

"We'll be back within the hour," Kat said. They were out the door before Lina could protest.

"What are you thinking?" Kat asked as they climbed into Tori's car.

"Georgia's got my spare keys, too, for emergencies. It's Saturday," she said, looking at her phone. "She's at yoga." She turned on the ignition. "Hold on." She quickly dialed a number. "Hey, Bob. It's Tori. I need to pop over and get my house key from Georgia."

Kat couldn't hear his response.

"Sure, okay. Thanks, will do." She ended the call and tossed the phone at Kat.

"What did he say?"

"He was walking out the door with Tessa for her gymnastics. He'll leave the back door open. I even know where she keeps the keys."

"How will you know which keys are Evelyn's?"

"Have you ever seen the way Georgia organizes that house? She's like an obsessive-compulsive labeler. Her canned goods are alphabetized."

Within minutes, Tori had pulled up in front of Georgia's house. "Wait here," she said, jumping out of the car.

Kat watched Tori walk around to the back of the house. She could hardly believe they were essentially about to break in to Evelyn's home. The woman who'd promised to be a good friend to Shea during that girls' night out just a little more than three months earlier. It was the going-away party Shea had organized in Kat's honor. Of course, Shea had invited Evelyn, her new, dear friend, despite the fact that Kat didn't know her well. As they shared sushi rolls and wine, Tori, Dee, Lina, and Georgia had all made toasts involving fun memories and promises to visit. Shea's toast had included her impression of Kat the first day they met. She'd said she found Kat orchestrating her moving men like she did everything else in life, with kindness and patience. She said she'd been struck by Kat's beauty, inside and out, and that she knew instantly she'd made a friend for life. It was such a generous, distorted depiction of that afternoon on the sidewalk, and Kat had been unable to hold back the tears. "See," Shea had exclaimed with tears in her own eyes, "just like the day we met! I told you I loved to cry, too!"

After they had hugged and taken their seats, Evelyn had stood and said something about not knowing Kat well, but she could tell that Shea would miss her terribly, and that she'd do her best to be there for Shea. It was the wrong thing to say. Kat didn't want to be replaced.

And what a friend Evelyn turned out to be, Kat thought, anger building. She was a liar. Ryan was lying, too. She had lost faith in everything they'd said to her.

She looked at her phone. It was still early. Evelyn had said she was coming home late today. They'd get in there, look around, and decide what to do. She didn't even know what she might find, but if she didn't look, it was going to eat away at her. She sat back, crossed her arms, and took another deep breath.

Shea had saved Kat's life in a thousand different ways. She'd been with her through those darkest postpartum days, she'd taken care of Kat's son when he was sick and Kat had to get to the office, she'd gotten Kat out of the house when her father died and she began eating through the pain. She couldn't stop the tears from falling as she thought of all those moments. And the moment she'd tossed the phone aside when she saw Shea's text, simply because she didn't want to hear about life in Maple Park, because she was thinking only of herself, of missing her friends and not wanting to make it harder on herself. It had never occurred to her that Shea, who she'd thought was always coasting on the top of every wave and enjoying the ride, was going through something or needed to talk. She'd failed Shea when she ignored that call, but she would not ignore the mounting evidence that someone might be responsible for her death.

A moment later, Tori appeared and quickly returned to the car. "Got it."

CHAPTER 37

April 1
5:30 p.m.

"ANOTHER CAPE COD?" THE BARTENDER asked.

"Yes, please." The first one had gone down too fast. Shea turned to check the front door behind her again. Still no sign of Evelyn. When she turned back toward the bar, a man was standing to her left. She looked into the mirror behind the liquor bottles and watched the man looking at her before he addressed the bartender. "I'll have what she's having."

Shea turned.

"Hello, beautiful," he said.

"Hi," she responded, turning away from his gaze.

"May I?" he asked, nodding toward the open seat between them.

She looked around the room at the bar, only a quarter filled with patrons. There were plenty of other empty seats to be had.

"Actually, I'm meeting a friend," she said.

The man nodded but didn't move. "Maybe I'll just save her seat?"

Shea didn't want to be unkind, and there were open seats on both sides of her. "Sure."

"I'm Ted," he said, extending his hand.

Shea shook his hand and introduced herself.

"That's an interesting name," he said.

"Yeah, my dad was a big Mets fan. Shea Stadium. It opened just a few weeks before I was born."

"Well, if you wouldn't be too annoyed, I've had a pretty crappy day. I saw you sitting here, and I thought maybe a friendly chat with a beautiful woman would turn my day around."

"Thanks," she said, taking in the kind words, offering a reluctant smile. "But I'm probably not great company, either. Sounds like we've had the same kind of day."

"Well, maybe we can cheer each other up."

The man was ridiculously attractive. *If Evelyn would just get in here*, she thought, *maybe this could be a good match*. That would make Shea feel a little better about this whole fiasco. She'd dragged her all the way out here, only to find out Georgia had been right to worry. She was stupid to come and to drag along Ev, who, as far as she knew, had spent most of her time since arriving sick. She looked over at the door again. Where was she? Even if she'd missed the four o'clock ferry, she should have been here by now.

"You look familiar," Ted said. "Do I look familiar to you?"

"I don't think so. Have we met?"

"I don't know. Have you been here before?"

"Many times. Usually with lots of girlfriends."

"Me, too. Well, not with girlfriends. Men. Boyfriends? I guess that might give you the wrong impression."

Shea chuckled. "No, I get it."

"Anyway, it's just me today."

Neither said a word for a moment, both sipping their drinks in silence.

"I don't suppose you knew my friend Blake?" he asked.

Shea stared at the ice melting in her glass, determined to control every muscle of her face, to give no hint of recognizing that name. Had Ted been at the memorial? Had he been here all those months ago? Suddenly, she wondered if he could be a police officer. What if he'd been at the memorial and Blake's friends had pointed her out? What if he'd followed her here? She couldn't look at him, terrified of what she might see in his eyes, what he might say.

"No," she said. "I didn't."

"Oh, I was just wondering. I came here for a memorial."

Shea nodded.

"But I missed it. He was an old family friend. I felt bad."

She wanted to exhale the air she'd been holding since hearing Blake's name. But it would be too obvious. Instead, she took a sip and nodded, like there was nothing to say. She felt the liquid warm her throat as it went down.

"Do you know what today is?" he asked.

"What?"

"April Fools' Day."

How perfect. She felt like a fool. "Planning to pull a prank, are you?"

"Not at all. I just have had some bad luck today. Losing my wallet, then missing the service. I thought I'd have heard from my friends, but so far, nothing."

Shea nodded and finished her drink.

Ted signaled the bartender and ordered them two more.

Shea had nowhere to go. She licked her lips, finally feeling those pills kicking in. That yoga without the yoga. The memory of Blake's friends cornering her at the lighthouse was beginning to feel more distant, even unreal, like a scary movie. Maybe she'd just been paranoid.

After two rounds of drinks and polite conversation about weather, news, and fishing, Ted signaled the bartender for another round.

Shea hesitated. "Not for me," she said. "I think I've hit my limit." She was feeling too loopy. She looked at her phone. The numbers were blurry. She closed one eye to focus. It was now six thirty.

"Just one more?" he asked. "You've really turned my day around."

Shea smiled. At least Ted was nice. A nice man. Not like Blake. Not like Charlie. "You, too." She heard it. The words had blended together.

"So why are you sitting all alone, anyway?"

"My friend was supposed to meet me here." She looked at the door again. When she turned back, two fresh drinks had arrived. "I don't know what's happened to her."

"You worried?"

"Well, she was sick at the terminal, so she didn't get on the ferry with me. But she said she'd get the next one. That was like . . ." She looked at her phone again, unable to remember the time. "Three hours ago. I thought she might be in our room lying down, but she's not there, either."

"Maybe she was too sick to come. That ferry ride can be tough if you've got a weak stomach. Perhaps she went home."

Shea shook her head. "No. It's a five-hour drive. And we took my car. She would have called."

"Friends. Not always reliable, right?"

Shea wasn't sure how to respond. Was she reliable? Had she been a good friend to Evelyn, leaving her at the ferry? To Georgia, refusing to call the police all those months ago? To Dee, never telling her what had happened with Charlie? To Kat? She'd never even called Kat since the move. Not until last night when *she* needed to talk. No wonder Kat never picked up or replied to the text. She hadn't called Kat in three months. Because if they'd talked and laughed and traded stories, it only would have reminded her of how much she missed her, how home had felt a little emptier since they'd moved away, like every memory she had in that house had been connected to Kat and Mack and their kids. Christmas mornings always involved the kids running back and forth in pajamas, sharing their excitement and gifts. The toddler years were just a blur of tantrums, comparing notes, and communal Sunday dinners. Summer block parties and barbecues were never planned without Shea knowing that Kat and her family were available. Even when the kids got older and realized they were forging different paths, with different friends, Kat and Shea never went more than a week without a walk, or a glass of wine, just to catch up.

"Hey," Ted said. "You look a million miles away. Any chance you'd let me take you to dinner?"

"I'm sorry," she said. "I can't." Her phone pinged then, and she looked down at the screen. It was a text from Evelyn.

"Oh, excuse me a second. My friend," she said, raising her phone. The man nodded, and Shea read the text. "Well, so much for that," she said, dropping the phone on the bar.

"What's the matter?"

"She's not coming." She couldn't believe Evelyn had been that sick. That she'd rented a car? That she'd drive ten hours in one day? She shook her head, struggling to focus now.

"Hey," Ted said. "Let me take you to dinner. It'll be fun."

Shea smiled. As she blinked, she noticed her lids closed and opened slowly. "I can't . . . I hope you don't take offense, but I'm married. I don't think it would be . . . *appropriate* to have dinner with a handsome stranger I met in a bar." She stumbled on that word, *appropriate*, tongue-tied. She'd definitely had too much. How many had it been? She counted back. *Just a couple*, she thought. But . . . wait. One before this guy. More together. The pills. One, two? She couldn't remember now.

Ted smirked. "I'm flattered. And I get it. In fact, I'm married, too. But this has been harmless enough, right?"

"Right," she said.

"I'll just grab a slice of pizza and head back to the Humphrey House."

Shea grinned again.

"What?"

"I'm staying there, too."

"You're lying," he said.

"I'm not!"

"The innkeeper said there was one other guest. I can't believe that of all the people on this island, I walked up to the most beautiful woman at this bar, and you are the one she was referring to. Don't tell me, room three?"

She shook her head. "One."

"I'm in four. I was going to say, if Mary had put us right next to each other, I'd have been convinced that some force was trying to bring us together."

Shea laughed. "I don't think so."

He looked at her square in the face, as if examining her, or hoping to know what she was thinking.

She sat back, furrowing her brow. "What?" That was how Blake had looked at her that night.

"May I ask you something? If you won't be too offended—"

"Okay," she slowly replied.

Ted leaned toward her and lowered his voice. "Do you ever wonder what you might do with a total stranger if there was no chance of it blowing up your life? I mean, I have a lovely wife, beautiful kids, a home, a job, and no chance I'd ever want that to end. But here I sit, alone, away from my reality, having a drink with this spectacular beauty who is from somewhere else, with a life of her own, and no chance that our worlds will ever intersect again."

Shea could hardly believe what she was hearing. This gorgeous man was suggesting some anonymous night of . . . She shook her head and giggled.

Ted continued. "I know I shouldn't say this, Shea, but I can't help but wonder how spectacular it would be to take you back to my room.

I mean, just thinking about kissing you is killing me right now." He stopped to take a breath and a sip.

Shea took a sip of her drink as well. She couldn't stop smiling. It was so outrageous.

"Think about it. I've been fixed, so I can't get you pregnant."

She laughed out loud. At fifty-two, children were the last thing sex brought to mind.

"I've been only with my wife for the last twenty years . . . so there's no chance of disease."

"I appreciate that," she said, throwing a little sarcasm in there.

"I think it's a safe bet that we could walk back to that inn, have an incredibly passionate night, and simply go forward, always remembering each other without anyone ever knowing. I'd be nothing but a *really* pleasant memory."

Shea took a deep breath. She said nothing for almost thirty seconds. This was a first.

"It would be amazing," he said, like he'd come to the end of the big pitch. He sat back, sipping his drink, like he was waiting for her to realize her good fortune.

But Shea didn't hesitate. "I'm really flattered, and you're a handsome man . . . and you're doing wonders for my ego here, but I really can't do that."

"You sure?"

"I'm sure. In fact, I should probably go."

"Oh, don't do that. I didn't mean to scare you off. You're right. Of course, you're right." He took another sip. "I hope I didn't offend you, and I'm sure that in the morning I'll thank you for saving me from my own urges. Let's just enjoy these last drinks together and I'll go take a cold shower."

"You're on," she said. "I just need to use the restroom for a minute."

"Sure, I'll save your seat."

CHAPTER 38

April 15

KAT AND TORI STOOD IN the vast living room of Evelyn's penthouse. It seemed to have more living space than Kat's entire house. The vintage details were everywhere, the high ceilings, ornate moldings, and beautiful wood floors, but someone had obviously renovated and modernized it years ago with a more open concept, because the kitchen, which had to have been a tiny portion of the space a hundred years ago, was fully visible, filled with custom cabinets, stone counters, and top-of-the-line appliances. Every piece of furniture, every lamp, every vase, every painting was carefully placed, and there was not a single extraneous item to be found. No stacks of mail, no wastebasket, no tray of odd items by the door, nothing. It was a perfectly manicured, magazine-ready spread of two-hundred-year-old antiques.

"Where do we start?" Kat asked.

"Bedroom," Tori said. "Everything personal is in a bedroom."

The entry had brought them into the main living, dining, and kitchen area, but two hallways were visible, each on opposite sides of the large open space. They headed down the hallway on the left, past a long console table below a portrait of an old man. Sitting on the table, nearly a foot high, was a black onyx cat, perched like some majestic guardian. Kat brushed her hands over the smooth stone as she passed. It was the only kind of cat she dared touch.

The first door they encountered brought them into an office and makeshift gym. A desk was against one wall. Its surface was bare—no laptop or desktop, no papers or bills—just a spotless writing surface with a cup of pens off to the side. An antique armoire, nearly nine feet high, stood against the opposite wall, and a rowing machine, the only evidence that someone actually used the room, was angled toward the door.

Kat pulled the desk's pencil drawer, but it was locked shut. Within a few moments of standing in the room, she began to feel a tickle in her throat. Her eyes began to itch.

They moved farther down the hall, past a bathroom, and opened the last bedroom door. The room was empty of personal belongings, but the bed hadn't been made. This must be where Evelyn's brother had stayed.

"Her bedroom must be at the other end," Kat said.

They were headed back toward the living room when Tori's phone pinged. "Oh shit!" she yelled, looking at the screen. "Oh shit, shit, shit!"

"What?"

"The SATs! My daughter is freaking out. I'm her ride. Shit!"

"Go," Kat said.

"But—"

"It's fine. I won't stay longer than fifteen minutes. Text me after you drop her, and I'll have you pick me up. I can always walk back to Lina's. It's like seven blocks."

"You sure?"

"Tori, go."

Tori ran out of the apartment, and Kat slowly opened every door she encountered in the second hall. She passed a guest room and a bathroom and, finally, came to the last door. It had to be the master. The door was closed. Kat instinctively knocked. "Hello?" she called out, as if she could come up with some perfect excuse for breaking in, should she find someone inside. But with no answer, Kat opened the door and found a large four-poster bed in a spotless room the size of one of her hotel's most luxurious suites. Silver picture frames were lined up atop the dresser. There were a few childhood photos, and that same photograph from Shea's luau-themed party that Kat had, too, the one used in the memorial program. It was one of those rare photos in which everyone looked good. She couldn't believe that Evelyn had stood there, her arm linked in Shea's, like a dear friend, and then betrayed her.

Kat wandered to the closet. The clothes were color coordinated from left to right. White tops, then pale yellows and pinks, a few blues, and finally black. Evelyn was seriously organized. In the bathroom, perfume bottles sat atop a silver tray, each one turned at the exact same angle. Every towel hung perfectly folded on the towel bars.

Kat went to the bedside table. She always kept random but personal items in her own bedside table—things she looked at right before sleeping or things she wouldn't want someone to find, as if putting something in those drawers had a magical do-not-disturb effect.

She found some cell phone chargers, a few receipts and loose change, batteries, a lighter . . . She picked up the receipts. Local gas station, drugstore, movie house. Each receipt dated several weeks back. This was useless.

What did she hope to find, anyway? The stub from her ferry ticket? A diary entry admitting what they'd done? Life was never that easy. Kat sat on the bed and looked around.

Something touched her ankle, and Kat jumped, pulling her legs up, like a kid terrified of a monster under the bed. A black cat ran out from below her. "Oh jeez!" She took a deep breath. That explained the itchy eyes and closing throat. She needed to get out of there before it got much worse.

Kat looked around the room again, exasperated, annoyed at her childish fantasy of catching a criminal.

CHAPTER 39

April 1
6:40 p.m.

SHEA DROPPED HER PURSE AND drink on the vanity, washed her hands, and laughed out loud. She ran her damp fingers through her hair, smiling at her reflection, still shaking her head in disbelief. "Crazy," she said.

She and the girls had literally joked about this kind of scenario last November when they were here, about whether anyone would ever be tempted to have a tryst with some beautiful stranger if there was no chance of it affecting their lives.

"Don't you miss that feeling?" Tori had asked, sipping her wine.

Dec chimed in, "You mean when your body lights up like a pinball machine?"

Everyone laughed and agreed that only someone new could probably bring on that feeling, admitting that despite loving their husbands, the inevitable habits and rituals of being with the same person for twenty years left them all nostalgic for that "quiver." It was Evelyn's word, and they all chuckled and nodded. Of course they missed it. But everyone had joked about all the necessary requirements of any potential man who could turn their head, most of which were so outrageous and unrealistic—like Tori's requirement that he actually be George Clooney—that it was clear none of them were the straying type.

She pulled out her phone and began typing Georgia's name, then Tori's and Dee's, but stopped, quickly deleting what she'd started. Georgia didn't want to hear from her, Dee, either. There was too much to explain, anyway. So much had happened. It felt like her friendships were in ruins.

But her marriage was not a sham. She didn't care what Evelyn said. Evelyn didn't know Dee like Shea did. She didn't know Ryan. She was just bitter. Her own marriage had fallen apart, so maybe she wanted Shea's to fall apart, too. "Wow," she said, looking into the mirror again. Was that true? Was Evelyn one of those people? She had to have heard the hope and excitement in Shea's voice as she shared their plan for a fresh start somewhere new. And her response was to put more doubt in her head? To make her think her best friend and her husband were together? *Who does that?* It was as if she wanted them to break up.

Shea leaned against the counter. It was getting hard to balance. She shook the crazy thoughts from her head. She was being ridiculous. Evelyn had just been trying to be a good friend. She probably didn't want to see her get hurt the way she had been hurt. She sent her a text: E—hope you're feeling better. I can't believe you actually went home! So sorry for dragging you all the way here. Let's talk in the morning.

She leaned toward the mirror, refreshing her lipstick, fluffing her hair. She could barely keep her eyes open, but she winked at her reflection. "You still got it, baby," she grinned. That man, who Tori might even say met her Clooney requirement, wanted her.

But he had no idea that he'd suggested an anonymous one-night affair with the woman least likely. Not after everything she and Ryan had done to each other, everything they'd been through. She was done with the lies and secrets. She took another sip of her drink, grabbed her purse, and froze as she reached for the door handle.

She was still lying and keeping secrets, hundreds of miles from where she told Ryan she was going, on some clandestine, misguided mission to rid Georgia and herself of their guilt over Blake's death.

How could she and Ryan start their next chapter like this? She let go of the door and fell back against the wall, wobbling. She pulled out her phone and hit the speed dial for home. It rang twice before she cut the call. She couldn't do this now. Not here, in this bathroom. But she'd call him tonight.

CHAPTER 40

April 15

KAT WENT TO THE OTHER side of Evelyn's bed. When she opened the drawer, her heart nearly stopped.

She couldn't take her eyes off the granite-colored steel, the shiny grip, sitting there on top of a tablet and several papers like a life-ending paperweight. Kat hated guns—even the sight of a gun made her feel a little sick. There was nothing illegal about owning one and nothing out of the ordinary in finding a gun in someone's bedside table. Even Shea and Ryan owned a gun. But Kat had made Shea show her where it was kept, safely locked away, high on a shelf, before she could relax about their boys playing together in Shea's house. Shea had thought Kat was being irrational, but some people feared spiders, others bats or snakes. Kat feared guns, as if they were just as alive and unpredictable. She had heard too many stories of children and accidental deaths, sudden violence.

But Evelyn was a single woman. There were no children in this home. She was obviously incredibly wealthy. Perhaps she saw herself as a target. Kat focused on the tablet. Maybe that was as close as she'd get to a modern-day diary. She slowly reached down and lifted the gun, terrified by the weight of it in her hand, and placed it onto the soft bedspread. It felt like a grenade.

She turned on the tablet, and the screen lit up, revealing an array of app icons. Movies, news, social media, calendars—nothing that seemed extraordinary. She clicked the calendar and scanned the dates. March 25, that was the date she'd been at the hotel with Ryan. The calendar entry for that date: *Rendezvous with RW.* Ryan Walker. Kat felt sick. Even after seeing them on that hotel surveillance tape, she could not get her head around Ryan betraying Shea with Evelyn. Though, why was that so hard to believe? He'd admitted cheating to Mack, warning him, "It's never safe." What did that even mean? Had he been referring to Evelyn? At the luau party? When had it begun?

She closed the calendar and noticed a Facebook app. She clicked, unsure what she was looking for, other than a general realization that she didn't know this woman at all. Tori had said Evelyn wasn't even on Facebook—at least she hadn't found her. But when the app opened, it automatically logged in to Evelyn's account—Evelyn Alison. No last name. That explained it. Kat quickly scanned Evelyn's list of friends but didn't see any of the women from the neighborhood. There were not that many friends, actually. She found Ryan's name.

The photos were categorized into those Evelyn had posted and those that had tagged her. She clicked Evelyn's photos. Nothing caught her eye. She clicked the tagged photos, scanned the faces, and stopped on a group shot. A group in a conference room, a wall of floor-to-ceiling windows behind them, city buildings beyond. Everyone in suits. Evelyn sat in the middle of five men. And there was Ryan, sitting to her right. Just when Kat thought she'd wrapped her head around Ryan's betrayal, she was hit with something worse. Evelyn's hair was several inches shorter. This was an old picture. They'd known each other for years.

Kat fell to a seat on the bed, sick to her stomach. This woman had come to Maple Park a year ago. She had to have known Shea was Ryan's wife. Ryan's Facebook profile made it easy enough. Evelyn had sought Shea out.

She closed out the photos and clicked the messenger bar on top, scanning Evelyn's private conversations until she found what she feared: messages between them. The first notes were three years old.

Kat sat, entranced, reading their private conversations. She could feel her eyes swelling, her throat tightening, but she couldn't leave.

The front door suddenly opened and slammed shut.

Kat jumped, searching the room, unsure what to do. Was it Tori? She threw the tablet down on the bed and knocked into the open drawer as she stood. The remaining contents of the drawer shifted from the force. She glanced down, just for a second, her eye moving to the neon-green case.

Shea's phone.

CHAPTER 41

April 15

KAT STOOD FROZEN INSIDE THE closet, waiting, listening. She looked down at her feet. That stupid cat, curled into a ball, relaxed in the little bed tucked into the corner. She had to get out of here.

Keys dropped onto the glass table by the front door. Shoes with a small heel clacked against the wood floor. Wheels rolled beside them. She was coming this way.

Suddenly the clacking stopped. She was in the room. On the carpet. Kat was shaking, fighting against the urge to cough. She needed air.

The closet door swung open as Evelyn hit the light switch by the door frame. The light poured down on Kat, on the gun in her hands. Kat's eyes filled with tears.

Evelyn screamed and stepped back. "Kat! What are you doing? Did you break in?" She was acting indignant, as if she had the right.

Kat stepped forward, her hands shaking, pointing the gun at Evelyn. "What did you do?"

Evelyn was backing up, her hands up. She backed into the bed and fell to sitting. "Kat, please put that gun down. Don't be crazy. You don't understand."

"She was nothing but nice to you!" Kat took a few steps forward, trying to scare her into a full confession, but she couldn't keep it together. The tears clouded her vision. She frantically wiped, removing one hand from the gun for just a second. Her face was itchy, hot.

"I didn't do anything, I told you. I never got on that ferry. I was sick. I'm sorry. I swear."

"You're a liar. I know all about you and Ryan. You were there."

"You don't understand, Kat. It's not that simple."

"Don't lie to me!" Kat said, stepping closer.

Finally, Evelyn began to break. "He loves me, Kat," she said softly, like it was a secret, but then her face became hard, her voice raised. "He didn't want to hurt her, but Shea didn't deserve him. You don't know what she's done."

"I'm calling the police." She knew it needed to happen, but she could barely see straight. She didn't know where her purse was, where the phone was, what to do.

"You don't understand. I went with Shea. I told you the truth about that. I know you don't believe me, but I got sick at the terminal. Kat, don't you see? We were there because of her stupidity. She caused all of this."

"Stop! You're lying. You moved here to break them up? Is that what this is about? Who does that?"

"You don't understand." Evelyn was shaking her head. "Ryan loves me. And it's not like Shea's some innocent. You've seen the way she behaves."

"You got on the ferry. You were on the island. I saw the proof," she said, waving the gun toward the bed. "So don't even—"

"Okay, stop. Kat. Yes. I went to the island. I was upset. She was ruining everything for me and Ryan. He wouldn't leave her. I knew if Ryan knew what she'd done with Blake, if he realized her recklessness caused some man's death, it would finally be over between them. So I pulled myself together and got on the ferry. You know what I found?

Shea, sitting at Rudolph's, flirting with some man! Can you believe that? After all that she'd done, after dragging me to Ohio because of Blake, she was sitting in a bar, drinking with some guy!"

Kat stepped back, leaning against the wall, the gun dropping just slightly. "What did you do?" She barely got out the words. She didn't want to hear it, but she needed to hear it.

"She was going to betray Ryan. Again! And after he'd said it was over between us, that he couldn't hurt Shea, that he'd put her through too much. I couldn't stand it. Kat, please."

Kat looked around for her purse. She had to get out of here. She'd take what she'd found and go to the police. Evelyn stood and began moving toward her.

"Stop!" Kat yelled. "Don't move. I swear to God . . ."

"Listen to me. Kat, listen. It's not what you think. I left," Evelyn pleaded. "Kat, I left! I was never in that room. I couldn't tell anyone. How could I say I was with her on the island? I couldn't tell anyone why I was upset. Why I left. No one would understand. But I left! I swear, Kat, I left!"

The front door slammed shut again.

CHAPTER 42

April 1
6:55 p.m.

SHEA RETURNED TO THE BAR and plopped back onto the seat beside Ted. She suddenly felt like she weighed a thousand pounds. "I should go. You're very cute and nice and sweet, but it doesn't matter."

"To harmless flirtation," he said, raising his glass. "The kind that never leads to trouble, but can provide fond memories and will certainly help me sleep tonight."

Shea laughed and took a final swig of her vodka.

Ted put his elbow on the bar and rested his face in his hand, smiling sheepishly at her. "Since we're being good, why don't we talk about whether we've ever been bad. I'll go first. Yes, I have, but you would have been different. I'm sure of it."

"Mmm-hmm . . . thought you said you'd never cheated on your wife?"

He smirked, like a kid who'd been caught stealing candy, a petty offense. "I lied."

"Of course."

"What about you? Have you ever cheated?"

Shea considered it. She didn't think so, but did Blake count? Did it matter what she believed at the time? "I guess it depends on how you define 'cheating.' I've learned that none of this is black and white."

"So true," he said, sitting up taller.

She watched him brush his hair from his forehead, mesmerized. "You have great hair," she slurred. It was a struggle to keep her eyes fully open.

"Thanks," he replied with a shoulder lift, head turn, and sudden feminine lisp. "It's just such a mess sometimes."

She nearly spit out her drink, cracking up, and threw her hand to her mouth to stop the explosion.

He grinned. A million-dollar smile.

"Okay, okay," she said, swatting the air like he wasn't going to tempt her with that smile or hair or humor. "I gotta go."

"Me, too," Ted said, standing. He threw some twenties on the bar. "Well, lovely Shea, I'm starving. I need to find some food, and I must leave you now because it's just too difficult to remain casually seated next to such exquisite and forbidden fruit." He took her hand to his lips and gave it a soft kiss.

Shea chuckled and said good-bye. "I need to get going, too." She heard the slur in her words and closed her eyes. "Sorry," she said. She stood, stumbled, and Ted caught her.

"Okay," he said. "Maybe I should walk you back to the inn."

"No, I'm fine," she insisted. It was embarrassing. She heard the bartender ask if she was okay. Oh, God, she looked like a drunk. But Ted told him not to worry and held the door for her. "Thanks," she said, linking her arm in his. "You're a nice man."

CHAPTER 43

April 15

KAT'S FOCUS SHIFTED TO THE door for a moment. Maybe it was Tori.

Evelyn moved closer.

"Sit!" she yelled, pointing the gun at her face.

"Evelyn!" It was Ryan. He sounded angry.

"In here," Evelyn yelled, backing away from Kat, returning to the bed, her expression shifting, like help had arrived.

Kat didn't know what to do. She heard him coming toward the room.

Ryan walked in, and Kat waved the gun at him.

"Kat, what are you doing?" he said, staring at her, the gun, Evelyn. He hadn't shaved. He was wearing sweatpants. He looked like he hadn't slept since she saw him the day before. "What's happening here?"

Kat couldn't stop crying. It was getting hard to breathe. "Don't, Ryan. Please don't lie to me anymore. I don't know what the hell happened on that island, but I blame you both!"

"Kit Kat," he said, his hands up. "Stop. Please, put the gun down. You don't know what you're saying."

"You lied to me! My best friend is dead, and you two have been lying and sleeping together . . . and planning who knows what."

"No . . . Kat. You're wrong," Ryan said. "You've got it all wrong. I'm not sleeping with Evelyn."

"Why, Ryan? If you weren't happy, get a goddamn divorce!"

"Kat, stop," he yelled and stepped closer. "You're wrong," he shouted.

"Don't come any closer," she said. She could feel her eyes swelling. It was hard to keep them open.

"Kat." His voice softened. "Yes, I had an affair with Evelyn. It was a mistake. We met through work. I swear to God. I never wanted to lose Shea."

"You told me you loved me!" Evelyn yelled. "And I lost my husband over that affair, so please don't—"

"Stop!" he yelled at Evelyn. "I told you, I love my wife." He turned to face Kat. "Listen. It was a fling, three years ago! It was never supposed to be any more than that."

Evelyn began falling apart. "You're a liar."

Ryan ignored Evelyn. "She showed up in town—she befriended my wife. I didn't know what to do. She said it was a coincidence, that she'd never say anything to Shea, that she liked her. But when she came to our party last summer, I begged her to leave, to make different friends and stay away from Shea. The whole mess terrified me."

Kat was shaking, both arms locked, the gun swerving back and forth between Evelyn on the bed and Ryan still near the door. She didn't know what to do, how to call for help. She couldn't shoot a gun. She couldn't put it down. She could hardly see. Her eyes, itching and raw, flooded with tears.

"Please," Ryan continued. "Kat, I swear to God, I loved my wife!"

"You're lying!" Kat yelled. "I know you were together before Shea left town."

Ryan's hands were up, but he stepped closer. "Kat. You don't understand. Shea took off to Michigan. I thought she was sleeping with Charlie. I thought I'd lost her. I got drunk, and Evelyn found me at a bar and drove me home. I slipped—one time, but only because I thought my marriage was over. As soon as Shea got back, I realized what a mess I'd made. I swear, we were working things out."

Evelyn was shaking her head, her hands to her mouth. "It's not true," she mumbled.

Ryan kept his hands up, his focus on Kat. "I didn't know Evelyn went with Shea to the island, not until you told me last night. I'm not sleeping with Evelyn."

Kat looked over at Evelyn, whose head had dropped, like she couldn't listen to what he was saying. "I don't believe you. I saw you on tape. With her," she said, waving the gun between them. "You used Shea's vouchers. I saw you!"

"You don't get it," Ryan pleaded. "Evelyn took the vouchers from our house. She called me after checking in under my name and threatened to tell Shea if I didn't meet her. I went there. But only to tell her that it was over. That I'd been wrong about Shea and Charlie. I told her that whatever had happened between us was over. I never wanted to leave my wife."

Evelyn was shaking her head. "You don't understand, Kat. Ryan acted like she was some victim, like he couldn't do it to her, and then she drags me to Ohio and I see her. She got drunk in that bar with a man, and they left together. I watched. They went into the inn together. Ryan, she wasn't good enough for you. And you were oblivious. You were going to move away with her."

Ryan focused on Evelyn. "What are you saying? What did you do?" His voice cracked.

"Stop! Don't put this all on her. It was you, too!" Kat shouted. "You knew where Shea was that day. I saw. Evelyn sent you a message on April first. She told you where Shea was. You could have gone there. You could have done this."

"Kat," Ryan pleaded, stepping closer, "Evelyn wanted to break us up. Please believe me. She'd been screwing with me since summer. She put a fucking bra in my drawer. She was trying to end my marriage. I didn't listen to her. We did not kill Shea. I swear to God. Please." He stepped closer.

CHAPTER 44

April 1
7:20 p.m.

SHEA WAS LYING ON THE bed with her eyes closed. The room was spinning. Mary's voice was still in her head. *You'll feel better tomorrow.* What a joke. She felt nauseous and sat up, each arm locked, hands against the mattress. The room was moving, the floor sloping at an angle as she tried to stand. How many drinks had she had? She felt like she'd been drugged. *The pills*, she thought. She'd done this to herself. She had to stop. She and Ryan were making a fresh start. She stumbled into the bathroom for some water.

She stared at the mirror, examining her reflection. It wasn't pretty. "Get yourself together," she said. Her focus shifted to her shoulder, to a beautiful old claw-foot tub behind her, a pristine antique on display atop the black-and-white mosaic tile. She remembered her last bath. With Ryan. The bubbles and candles, the wine. There was still something really good between them. Still, after all these years, and everything that had gone wrong. She didn't care what Evelyn had said in the car about Dee. It wasn't true. *He loves me. I know he does.* And Dee wouldn't do that. She needed to call her.

She shuffled back into the bedroom and looked around. Where was her phone? She scanned the room. It made her dizzy. She stumbled back to the bed and sat, leaning forward, bracing her head in her hands. She couldn't talk to anyone right now, she realized. She was a mess.

She should have told Ryan about Blake. Too many lies. Too many secrets. They'd almost lost everything. She sat up, locked her arms against the mattress again, bracing for stability, determined to get out of this state. Her head felt heavy. She rested her chin on her chest, her eyes closed. But the spinning resumed. She fought to open them, one lid at a time, and looked around. There would be no fresh starts on this island. Too much had happened.

She thought again of Blake, his fingers digging into her arms when she tried to pull away. His hand pressed hard against her face after she'd screamed. And Georgia. She hated to think what might have happened if Georgia had not come running. Georgia had yelled at him, "Get off her!" and pulled hard at his arm.

It was almost funny now, thinking of cute, soft-spoken Georgia. That southern belle had been such a badass. Her hero. He'd stumbled back and called Georgia a bitch. But he'd released his grip on Shea and she tried to wedge past him.

"You're next," he'd said to Georgia before grabbing Shea from behind, a full bear hug, and throwing her back. She fell to the floor. He would not stop. Drunken, violent madness. But just as Shea got to her feet, she heard the whack and turned back, seeing the oar in Georgia's arms. Blake's hand rose to his face, stunned, as blood began to trickle down his forehead. He'd spewed more hatred and anger, but when he reached out, he'd stumbled, fallen to his knees.

They ran, never stopping to cry or think or even scream until they'd hit the park bench and collapsed in shock. And now Georgia was losing sleep, fearing the loss of everything she loved, all because Shea had refused to find police or help, or to tell a soul. All because of her shame. Georgia deserved better.

She fell back onto the bed, turned on her side, moved one foot to the floor to keep the room still. She would fix this. Maybe she could find a lawyer and tell her what happened and see if there was anything to fear. Maybe she could come forward with the truth without hurting anyone else.

She felt nauseated. She pushed herself up again and stumbled back to the bathroom. Spotting a white terry cloth robe hanging on the back of the door, she stripped off her clothes, leaving them in a pile, and put on the robe. She drank more water and looked at the tub again. Maybe a bath would help.

She sat on the edge of the tub, but just before she turned on the faucet, she heard a knock at the door. Shea looked up, startled.

CHAPTER 45

April 15

KAT DIDN'T KNOW WHAT TO believe or what to do. She'd gripped the gun so hard for so long, she was losing feeling in her arms. She felt dizzy, like she might collapse. "Why didn't you tell me the truth?" she begged him.

Ryan dropped his hands. He began to cry. "Because Shea died. I didn't want everyone thinking the worst, making assumptions, gossip swirling about some stranger's death, wondering if she'd committed suicide over it. I didn't want that for Shea or the kids."

Kat didn't know what to believe.

"After Shea died, Evelyn came to me. She told me why Shea went to Put-in-Bay. But she lied to me, Kat. She told me that Shea had asked her to go with her, but that she'd refused."

They both looked over at Evelyn, who was sitting, frozen, her posture erect, her eyes glazed, staring at the wall, like she was in a trance.

"Evelyn was in the room that night, Ryan," Kat said. "Shea's phone is in that drawer." She pointed toward the bedside table.

He looked at Evelyn and spoke, but almost no sound came out. "Is that true?"

She started crying. She finally looked at him, her eyes pleading. "You don't understand. I knew what everyone would think. I saw her go in the inn with that guy. I knew what she was doing. But you've got it all wrong. I went to Rudolph's for a drink. Her phone was on the bar. She'd left it. Ryan, no. I wasn't in the room. I swear. I was going to return it. But then . . . she died. I couldn't do anything. I couldn't tell anyone. I left. I swear, I left."

CHAPTER 46

April 1
7:30 p.m.

SHEA STUMBLED TOWARD THE DOOR. "Hello?" She wasn't going to open the door for Ted. She'd learned enough about putting herself in vulnerable positions.

"It's me," she heard. "Open up."

Shea unbolted the lock and opened the door. Evelyn walked past her into the room, dropping her bag. "What are you doing here? I thought you left."

"Sorry, am I interrupting something?"

Shea could hear the anger in her voice. "What are you talking about? No. I don't understand. You said—"

"Yeah, I felt bad about leaving you, so I came back." She walked through the room and into the bathroom, looking around. "But then I saw you with that guy at Rudolph's. I didn't want to interrupt."

Shea sat on the bed. "Don't be crazy. We were just passing the time."

"I saw you walking in here together, though."

"He's staying here. What's wrong with you?"

Evelyn opened the closet door and looked inside. "So you're alone?" She sounded like she didn't believe it.

She scoffed. "Are you crazy? Of course I am. In fact," she said, falling back toward the mattress again, "I'm glad you're here. I feel sick, Ev."

"How much did you drink?"

"I didn't think it was that much." She could hear her words coming out in a puddle. She couldn't separate each sound. "I took some pills at the memorial. It was awful. His friends looked at me like I killed Blake, Ev. I thought . . . I've made such a mess. And I can't even close my eyes. I get so dizzy."

"What kind of pills?"

"Vicodin," she said. "Ev. I thought they'd help. I been sooooo stu-pid."

Evelyn didn't say anything.

Shea looked up. Evelyn was scanning the room. She looked like she'd been crying. "You okay?"

"Fine," Evelyn said briskly.

"Because you seemed upset in the car. And then you left me all day . . ."

"No, no, I've just got my own stuff going on. You're not the only one with problems."

Shea could hear the bite in those words. She was a bad friend. "You can talk to me, you know."

Evelyn stood and went into the bathroom again, her heels clacking on the tile floor. The faucet came on. Shea let her lids close again. She was so tired.

The mattress moved. Evelyn was sitting beside her. "I'm sorry, Shea. I haven't been a good friend today. I'm running you a bath. It'll make you feel better."

Shea leaned on Evelyn's shoulder and smiled. "Thanks, Ev. I was just thinking I'd do that."

A few minutes later, Evelyn helped Shea stand, and together they walked into the bathroom.

Shea got into the tub and leaned back against the slick porcelain. Evelyn folded a towel and put it behind her head. "Will you stay with me?"

"Sure," Evelyn said. She went over and sat on the toilet.

Shea closed her eyes, relaxing, the world finally steady. "You know, I was afraid that you were the man from the bar . . . he propositioned . . ." It was a tough word to get out. "Ev . . . it was crazy." She chuckled.

"Really?"

Shea didn't have the strength to open her eyes anymore, but she smiled. "This feels so good. You better be sure I don't fall asleep in here."

Evelyn didn't respond.

"Ev?" Her eyes were still closed.

"I'm here." Evelyn's voice sounded funny, as if she was trying to sound interested but was a million miles away.

"It was crazy, Ev. I mean, any woman would have been tempted by this guy. He was *really* good-looking and I am . . . not . . . in my right mind. You can see." It was getting harder to get out each word. "There's just one problem." Shea opened her eyes and lifted her head. It took all the strength she had.

Evelyn was leaning forward, elbows propped on her thighs, her head in her hands. "What's that?"

"I . . . love my husband. A lot. And he loves me, and that's . . . just . . . the way it is."

Evelyn said nothing, and Shea's gaze returned to the water. She focused on her knees protruding like two little islands. "I'm a mess." She closed her eyes and relaxed her head against the towel. She was so sleepy. "I've got some things to fix . . . when I get . . . home." She took a deep, cleansing breath. "But it's going to be okay. I think it'll all be okay now."

She heard Evelyn's shoes clacking against the tile. "Can I use your phone? Mine is dead."

"I don't know where it is. Check . . . my purse," she mumbled.

She heard Evelyn's feet on the carpet. A moment later, she heard the feet return. "Find it?"

"Yeah, thanks," Evelyn said, her voice coming closer.

"You're a good friend," Shea mumbled. She listened to her own breath, in and out, in and out. Her body began feeling heavy.

You'll feel better tomorrow. It was Mary's voice in her head . . . nice woman.

Her thoughts turned to Blake again . . . that night. The wind, the cold air. His fingers . . . she could still feel them squeezing her flesh . . .

She felt hands on her shoulders. "Shh." Evelyn's voice was just a whisper in her ear. "I'm sorry."

For what?

Her muddled brain envisioned a hot spring, its floor like quicksand . . . It was like that middle ground between reality and dreams . . . nothing made sense . . . But something was pushing her down . . . first to the shoulders, then the chin, cheeks, eyes, hair. Her whole body submerged. She hesitated, something inside wanted to hold on, but . . . her feet pushed against the slick tub. They slipped; there was no way up. She tried . . . she couldn't. She . . . tried. She opened her eyes; she didn't understand why . . .

CHAPTER 47

April 15

KAT WAS EXHAUSTED, THE ENERGY draining from every inch of her body. It was difficult to breathe. She was getting light-headed. Ryan's arms had collapsed, too. His head was down. Kat's arms began to fall, her knees buckled.

Suddenly Evelyn was lunging, then Ryan. They were coming toward Kat. It was a blur of movement. Hands in her field of vision. Hands on hers, fighting the gun loose. She lost her grip. Someone had it. "No!" she cried. It was a scream inside her head, but the sound barely escaped her constricted windpipe. Her eyes closed. She could hear them wrestling for the gun.

"Baby, no, please," she heard Evelyn say. "I love you. I just wanted it to be you and me."

The blast shot through the room, so loud, so close to Kat's head, it felt like she might never hear another sound. She felt a body collapse beside her.

Kat struggled to open her eyes. Ryan was in front of her. On his knees, his head on the carpet. She could hear him moaning. She moved her gaze, searching for his hands. Where was the gun? Evelyn was crumpled on the carpet, dead.

Ryan was weeping, a pained, guttural cry, like a wounded animal. "What have I done? What did I do?" he sobbed.

It was hard to focus on his words, to stay conscious. She could hear her own short breaths, fighting to get through her now tiny airway.

"I didn't love Evelyn, Kat. I swear. I loved my wife. I thought we could start over. I never thought . . . I didn't know . . ."

The front door slammed again.

CHAPTER 48

KAT SAT IN A COMFY CHAIR by the open window in Evelyn's living room, sipping water, her eyes fixed on the dark grain of one oak plank on the floor in front of her. Tori had wrapped a blanket around her shoulders, and the white sheers blew in the breeze beside her. Her throat had relaxed and her eyelids felt lighter. She could open them fully. Paramedics were walking around. Police, too. Tori was sitting beside her, stroking her hand. Kat finally looked at her.

"Better?"

Kat nodded.

"Goddamn SATs," Tori said. "Look what I missed."

Kat smiled. "That cat." She looked around the room, a little disoriented. She barely remembered Tori's arrival. Just a vague recollection of Tori and Ryan getting her to the window, of Tori's voice on the phone.

There was an officer seated on Kat's other side. "You doing okay?"

Kat nodded.

"Mr. Walker has given a statement, but I'd like to hear from you, too."

"Evelyn came at me. I heard them wrestle for the gun." Kat looked at Ryan on the sofa, his eyes red, his body still, as if he could hardly believe what had happened. An officer was sitting beside him.

Ryan looked at her, his face weary. "After you told me Evelyn had gone with Shea, I thought she'd told her about us." He began to break down again. "I thought Shea ended her own life, taking a handful of pills because of my betrayal, because of whatever Evelyn might have said to her. I came here to get answers, Kat."

Kat didn't know exactly what had happened in those final moments as her body began to fail. But Kat could think only of Leigh and Stephen. They'd already lost their mother and spent nearly two weeks believing that she might have killed herself. Torturing themselves for being oblivious about whatever was going on, probably guilt ridden, just as they'd all been. And now they would learn of their father's betrayal. They'd learn of his lies, his secrets. And the woman who'd set about to destroy their parents' life together. How that family would ever recover was hard to imagine, but at least they could know their dad's pain and remorse.

Kat had heard Ryan's cries after the blast. She believed his pain. He'd made terrible mistakes, but she believed in his love for Shea. He was not a murderer. He was heartbroken. Kat didn't want any more lives destroyed. "He saved me," she said.

The officer let Tori take Kat home, saying they'd be in touch.

"Kat," Ryan said, extending his arm toward her as she walked by. She stopped. He stood and hugged her. She felt too weak to do anything but stand there. "I never meant to hurt Shea." He began to cry.

She patted his back. "I know." She pulled away.

Kat and Tori walked out together, neither saying a word as they descended the old elevator. They stepped outside into the bright sunshine. The parking lot was filled with squad cars and an ambulance. A crowd had gathered in the park across the street, trying to determine what had happened.

"My heart breaks for Leigh and Stephen," Tori said as she pulled out of the lot and headed north to Lina's. "First they lost their mom. Now this."

Kat wiped the tears from her eyes. "I just wanted to find the truth. I didn't want everyone to believe she'd killed herself. I didn't want to ruin those kids' lives."

Tori patted her knee. "You didn't ruin their lives, Kat. You found the truth. It's always better to know the truth."

"I hope so."

~ • ~

When Tori pulled into Lina's driveway, the front door flew open and Lina, Dee, and Georgia stepped out of the house. The troops had circled, ready to comfort the wounded again. They went inside and collapsed onto the couch together. After Kat gave them the five-second recap, Dee had some secrets to share as well. She'd had no idea Evelyn had been with Shea on the island, and never suspected anything as terrible as the truth, but there was a reason she'd been so rude to Evelyn. She'd seen something at the luau party. It wasn't enough to share with Shea, but it was enough to make her wary of Evelyn. She'd been on her way up to the master bathroom when she saw Ryan coming out the bathroom door. He'd looked flustered; he was wiping his neck. When Dee got up there, Evelyn had been standing at the mirror, putting on lipstick. Dee hadn't seen anything between them, but she had a sinking feeling. And she'd said as much to Ryan that night, warning him that he'd better not hurt Shea. She didn't think it was her place to say something to Shea, to meddle in their marriage and cause trouble when she had no proof.

The women agreed that they would not have said anything, either.

"I still don't believe Shea was with Charlie," Kat said. "And Ryan swore that it wasn't true, either. He knew about Charlie's feelings but said she didn't share them."

"I know," Dee said. "I was so certain. When I went to Michigan to talk to Charlie the weekend she died, I found proof that she'd been at our place. But I finally talked to my soon-to-be ex, the shithead, last night. I told him what I'd found, and he told me the truth, that she'd gone there to protect my feelings, and to reject him. If only I'd talked to her . . ."

Georgia admitted that she'd been the one who'd hit Blake that night and refused to go with Shea to the memorial because of her own fear, just as Tori had suspected. In one way or another, they all knew that if only . . . Shea would still be alive.

Kat pulled both Dee and Georgia in for a hug. She felt Tori's arms around her back, and Lina's, too, a giant huddle. There was comfort in the fact that the guilt and second-guessing had been universal among them and that they'd finally learned the truth. "Let's keep the blame on the woman who actually killed her," Kat said. "None of us are perfect friends, but . . ."

"We're human," Lina chimed in.

"And humans aren't perfect," Tori said. "Well, except a few of us."

Everyone chuckled.

The doorbell rang, and Tori was the first up to answer the door.

When Mack stepped inside, Kat sprang from her seat and ran to him. They held on tight, and she fell apart all over again. This time, with tears of relief. She finally felt like she was home.

EPILOGUE

One year later

KAT AND MACK SAT IN the back of a taxi, holding hands. With legs crossed, she nervously tapped her heel against the floor. She checked her watch several times while the driver maneuvered through traffic. Even though she traveled nearly every week for work, flying into Chicago was never quick or painless.

Mack finally put his hand on her knee and squeezed. "Breathe."

"We're late," she said.

"No one will mind. We'll just sit in the back."

She smiled, sighed, and put her hand on his.

She removed her dark glasses as the driver turned off the expressway and began driving through the streets of Maple Park. Despite the sight of budding trees, blooming magnolias, and children playing T-ball in the park, everything about this journey was different from last time, except for the fact that Saint Andrew's was, again, filled to capacity.

They quietly found seats in the back pew as the minister began the service.

When it ended, Mack squeezed her hand. "You okay?"

"Yep." She wiped her eyes and blew her nose before they followed the crowd outside. Tori and Herman came out after them.

"Tori!" Kat yelled, waving at her from across the crowded sidewalk.

Tori's face was priceless as she and Herman rushed over. "You said you couldn't come!"

"We figured it out," Kat replied, looking at Mack.

Kat and Tori embraced while the men did their half hug and handshake move, followed by quick hugs between the couples.

"That was a beautiful service," Kat said to them both.

"It was. Oh, Lina would appreciate this so much."

"I had to be here," Kat said. "I mean, it's weird, but I think I felt closer to her in the last year than I did in all the time we lived here."

"She told me that you two would FaceTime when you were traveling."

"Yeah, we kept each other company. We played a lot of Words With Friends." They had also begun a name-that-face game in which Kat would take pictures of random people she'd see at airports or on the street while traveling around the world, and Lina was given three guesses to determine what celebrity the person most resembled. Some were impossible to guess, which made them both laugh, but on two different occasions, Kat actually captured genuine celebrities walking by. One aging rock star—far kinder than his reputation would have suggested, and someone Kat knew Lina admired—even agreed to record a video greeting that she sent her. Lina told her she'd watched it at least a dozen times.

"She always put on a brave face when we talked," Kat said. "How was she, really, at the end?"

"You know Lina. She was so strong. But she was ready. She was sick of the pain. It was a long year."

Kat nodded. Unlike Shea's death, which felt so sudden and impossible to grasp, Kat had seen Lina's thinning face and the wincing with each move in the final months. She'd wished for an easy, painless passing for her friend. It was the only comfort left.

"Her kids were here," Tori continued, "by her side, holding her hand at the end. I know it gave her a lot of peace that they both seem to be doing well. And she talked about getting to be with Bill again. I think in some ways that makes it a little easier for the kids, too."

Kat dabbed her eyes with a tissue and wrapped her arm around Mack's back. It would be a great comfort to know they'd see each other on the other side.

"Georgia, Dee, and I were at the hospital a lot in the last several days," Tori continued. "We all knew it was coming. And amazingly, she had good humor, even at the end. I was sitting at her bedside, feeling a little overwhelmed, tearing up, and she squeezed my hand and whispered that I needed to come closer. So I leaned in, very near her face. And she said, 'Now don't forget, if you go to my bedside table before the kids find it, there's some pretty sweet Mary Jane in there. You ladies go have some laughs. My treat!'"

Kat, Mack, and Herman all laughed. "Did you get it?" Kat asked, giggling through tears.

"Absolutely!" Tori replied.

Dee came out the church doors, and they all took turns embracing.

"Oh, I miss these faces," Kat said to Tori and Dee.

"Hey," Tori said. "Guess where we're going this weekend?"

"Lemme guess," Kat said. "The lake house."

"Yes! This time the men are coming, too," she said, poking Herman with her elbow. "So we'll behave," she added with a laugh.

"My presence has never curbed any of you women," Herman chided.

"True," Tori said. "The guys are going to take the boat out and fish. Georgia and Bob are coming . . ."

"And I'm bringing a date!" Dee added.

"What?"

"Oh yeah. This is my new young beau's coming-out party."

"How young?" Mack asked with a smirk.

"Don't you worry," Dee joked. "Nothing too scandalous, but just a lot of fun."

"Well, you deserve it," Kat said. "What's the occasion?"

"As it turns out," Herman said, "all our kids are on spring break . . ."

"And none of them are coming home!" Tori finished his sentence. "Mexico and Florida are far more appealing. So we're going to cheer each other up."

"Georgia still has kids at home," Kat said.

"Yeah, but she didn't want to miss out. They've arranged for some sleepovers and grandparent time, just for the weekend."

Kat was glad to hear Georgia was going along. Blake's death and the uncertainty of her own culpability had haunted her, but a couple of months after Kat went back to Texas, they learned that Blake's body had finally been found. It had been a gruesome discovery by a couple of fisherman who were casting lines along the boulders by the lighthouse. The official conclusion was that Blake must have tried to tie up his boat, slipped on one of the large wet boulders offshore, and fallen in the deep water. His body had been found wedged between two boulders, entirely submerged under the surface.

It meant he'd been coherent enough to unmoor his boat and drive all the way there. That was enough for Georgia to let it go. She'd hurt him, but she hadn't killed him.

"You two should come with us!" Tori added.

Kat and Mack looked at each other and smiled.

"We're bringing Lina's stash," Tori added with a laugh. "Come on. It will be just like old times!"

"Actually, we rearranged our flight to stop in Chicago, but we're on our way to Europe!"

"No way!" Dee said.

Mack put his arm around Kat. "Yep. This sugar mama is taking me on a spectacular two-week vacation to one of her hotels on the French Riviera."

"Finally putting all those frequent-flyer miles to use," Kat added.

"Well, it sounds amazing," Tori said. "But better than Ohio?"

Everyone laughed.

"Okay, then, when will we see each other again?" Tori asked.

"I'm sure we'll be back," Kat said. "Perhaps right here even, as your kids start getting married."

"Bite your tongue," Tori joked.

"Well, how about a girls' trip to Texas? You could see our house. We could do a road trip to Austin or Galveston. It would be great."

"I'm in!" Dee said.

"Me, too," Tori mimicked, wrapping her arms around Kat. "No boys allowed," she added over her shoulder.

ACKNOWLEDGMENTS

To my beautiful, spirited, hilarious, complicated, and generous girl-friends, thanks for your friendship, support, love, and inspiration. And a special shout-out to Heather Pflederer—thanks for introducing me, all those years ago, to Lake Erie's treasured islands and for the years of girls' getaways that inspired the what-if for this story.

As always, a big thanks to all the Cains and Diskins for your love and support (and, in particular, to Jim, Jimmy, and Caroline, because you're the ones who had to live with me during that intense month of edits last winter). Thanks to my early readers, Maury Cain, Cynthia Quam, Martha Whitehead, Julia Buckley, Maury Byrne, Tanya Cain, and my dear Jim Diskin. As usual, your feedback was enormously helpful. Thanks to Craig Genheimer at Ohio State University for your help and insights regarding the South Bass Light Station on South Bass Island, Ohio. And, of course, thanks to everyone at Inkwell, with special thanks to Liz Parker and David Hale Smith, and the whole team at Thomas & Mercer, with special thanks to Jessica Tribble and Caitlin Alexander for your expertise and insights.

To all the librarians, book clubs, booksellers, and writers who have become supporters and friends, thank you. And finally, thanks to my readers. Whether you've read all three or this is your first (hopefully not your last!), I'm eternally grateful for your interest and your time.

ABOUT THE AUTHOR

Photo © 2017 Sandy Sameshima

E. C. Diskin is the author of the bestselling novels *The Green Line* and *Broken Grace*. She lives outside Chicago with her family. Find out more about E. C. and her work at www.ecdiskin.com.

31901060873652